TWIN FLAMES

TWIN FLAMES

Olivia Abtahi

TU BOOKS
An imprint of LEE & LOW BOOKS INC.
New York

TU BOOKS, *an imprint of* LEE & LOW BOOKS INC.
95 Madison Avenue, New York, NY 10016
leeandlow.com

Edited by Stacy Whitman
Book design by Sheila Smallwood
Typesetting by ElfElm Publishing
Book production by The Kids at Our House
The text is set in Minion Pro

Manufactured in the United States of America
Printed on paper from responsible sources

SUSTAINABLE FORESTRY INITIATIVE   Certified Sourcing
www.forests.org
SFI-00854

The text paper is SFI certified.

10 9 8 7 6 5 4 3 2 1
First Edition

Library of Congress Cataloging-in-Publication Data
Names: Abtahi, Olivia, author.
Title: Twin flames / Olivia Abtahi.
Description: First edition. | New York : Tu Books, an imprint of Lee & Low Books Inc., 2024.
    | Audience: Ages 12–18. | Summary: "On estranged twins Leila and Bianca's eighteenth
    birthday, Leila suddenly gains a djinn's superpowers, and the twins realize that their
    town can only survive the djinns' secret plans if they learn to work together as sisters"
    —Provided by publisher.
Identifiers: LCCN 2024008493 | ISBN 9781643790435 (hardback) | ISBN 9781643790442 (ebk)
Subjects: CYAC: Twins—Fiction. | Sisters—Fiction. | Ability—Fiction. | Genies—Fiction. |
    Multiracial people—Fiction. | Fantasy. | LCGFT: Fantasy fiction. | Novels.
Classification: LCC PZ7.1.A186 Tw 2024 | DDC [Fic]—dc23
LC record available at https://lccn.loc.gov/2024008493

For my daughters

Part 1

Solomon said (to his own men): "Ye chiefs! Which of you can
bring me her throne before they come to me in submission?"
Said an ifrit, of the djinns: "I will bring it to thee
before thou rise from thy council: indeed I have full
strength for the purpose, and may be trusted."
Said one who had knowledge of the Book: "I will
bring it to thee within the twinkling of an eye!" Then
when [Solomon] saw it placed firmly before him,
he said: "This is by the Grace of my Lord!"

—Quran, Surah An-Naml 27:38–40

BIANCA

Her eighteenth birthday. This year it lined up with Shab-e Yalda, the longest night of the year. She looked over at her twin, Leila, as they each hovered over their homemade cakes, the candles flickering in their drafty farmhouse living room.

Despite having identical DNA, her twin carried herself completely differently from Bianca. Bianca was all sharp curves and black nail polish, blunt-edged bangs and ripped jeans. But Leila was soft gingham and lace and low ponytails tied with homemade bows instead of the black barrettes Bianca preferred. Bianca held herself tall, while Leila preferred not to take up space. How the Mazanderani sisters had shared a womb, Bianca would never understand.

Their mother and father sat across from them and sang "Happy Birthday," once in Spanish and once in Persian, as was tradition. Bianca sang along, the muscle memory of each language taking over. She prided herself on her knowledge of Spanish and Persian. Talking in a different language was like a puzzle to solve, her tongue growing fatter for English and lighter for Spanish and Persian, ducking and dodging irregular verbs and relishing the way Persian had none.

Leila, however, refused to speak in Persian or Spanish at all, for fear of making people feel "uncomfortable." Anything that was too "exotic" always seemed to drift past Leila's threshold, including her own heritage. And thanks to their Argentinian mother's fair features, the twins' blend of Persian was light enough to be considered vague—never something as aggressive as Iranian American.

Bianca sang loudly as her best friend, June McCullough, struggled to follow along. June had been Bianca's best friend since elementary school, from a family that had too many kids and not enough money between them all. Bianca's parents were still making their way in this new country, while June's had deep roots here with their six kids.

Despite their wildly different backgrounds, June and Bianca were bonded, and Bianca loved how her friend gamely butchered "Happy Birthday" in Spanish every year, just for her.

Leila had invited a friend too. Shivani Shah was one of the most popular girls at school, with long glossy hair and a dozen gold bangles on each arm. Bianca tried not to choke on her designer perfume.

The fact that Shivani had even deigned to be here was unusual. In a surprising move, Shivani sang the Persian version of "Happy Birthday" flawlessly.

"What?" she demanded, as everyone stared at her after

they'd finished singing, her hair bouncing from its latest blowout. "Gujarati and Farsi are super similar!"

Bianca stared.

"Nandani isn't the only one who can speak Gujarati, you know," Shivani huffed. Shivani's older sister, Nandani, was legendary at Ayers, the kind of once-in-a-lifetime student to go to Harvard as she followed in their doctor parents' footsteps. The Shahs had specifically requested Ayers, Virginia, during residency, knowing that a rural posting would be all but guaranteed as they started their family. They practically ran the local college's hospital at this point and couldn't wait for Nandani to join them.

"That makes sense," the twins' father said excitedly. "Persian originally comes from Sanskrit. Did you know that Persian was the language of Sanskrit foot soldiers? Actually, Gujaratis have a lot of Parsis, or Zoroastrians—"

"Leila, blow out your candles first!" Mamá interrupted. The candles were melting onto their homemade cakes. Leila was technically older than Bianca by two minutes, meaning she got first-wish dibs. "Dalé!"

Bianca watched as her twin closed her eyes and extinguished her cake in one go. *I wonder what she wished for*, Bianca thought. And then: *Whoever thought twins could mind-read was full of crap.* Leila daintily licked a single candle, then wiped it down afterward with a napkin. Bianca tried not to roll her eyes.

Finally, it was Bianca's turn. She knew the power birthday

wishes could have, and she didn't want to waste hers. She sat there, lungs full of air, savoring the feeling.

"Are you wishing up a whole grocery list? Hustle up, Bianca!" June cried, her eyes glued to the pair of cakes.

Next to the cakes sat a platter of pomegranates, persimmons, and sliced watermelon: all the bright foods Iranians used to keep away dark spirits who waited until the longest night of the year to unleash havoc. At least, according to Bianca's dad. June's stomach rumbled loudly.

Bianca leaned over her cake. *I wish I could get the hell out of this tiny town*, she silently prayed. *Please, please get me out.* Then she blew out every single candle with one obnoxious gust. She finished with an exaggerated bow.

"Finally," June sighed. Her eyes looked as big as dinner plates, her thin blond hair peeking out of her trademark uniform of a drawstring hoodie with an Ayers sports team logo.

"Is this gluten free?" Shivani asked as the twins' dad cut slices and handed her one. Funfetti for Leila, dulce de leche for Bianca, same as every year.

He frowned. "Gluten free? No. Are you gluten intolerant?" Their father wore a floral apron that Leila had helped sew for him, his domestic getup at odds with the burly, thickset Persian man in front of them.

"No," Shivani sighed. "Just trying to cut down on my carbs." Then she flicked her glossy hair again, perfuming the whole room with scent.

"That's not how being gluten free works," Bianca pointed out.

Shivani said nothing, eyes narrowing as she took a bite of the slice in front of her—Bianca's cake. Bianca watched in satisfaction as Shivani's eyes went wide. Gluten, delicious gluten.

Their father had slathered dulce de leche between each layer of cake, making it taste like a delicious burnt-caramel sponge. There was no way they could buy something this Argentinian in their small college town nestled in the foothills of the Appalachian Mountains. He'd had to make the dulce de leche from scratch, coaxing the condensed milk into the caramel-style sauce their mamá grew up with.

The girls watched solemnly as Mamá poured an inch of wine into everyone's glass. In Argentina the drinking age was eighteen, and Alma Hernandez took her wine very seriously. "Don't tell your parents," she warned June and Shivani, who shrugged.

Bianca knew for a fact that Shivani partied every weekend with way more than an inch of wine. Why she was even at this boring birthday for her so-called best friend was a mystery. Surely there were more exciting places for her than a silly homemade birthday. And where was Leila's boyfriend, Foster? Probably listening to some red-pill podcast with all his other mudding friends.

"Bokhor, Behnaz jan," her baba said, using her Persian name. He handed her a slice, and all thoughts of her sister's unreliable boyfriend went out the window.

The room was silent as the small group inhaled their cake. June unabashedly licked her plate clean. She then took dainty sips of the malbec wine while peeking at her phone to get sports updates. Shivani downed her cup of wine in one swallow.

A glimmer of light sparkled in the corner of Bianca's eye, and she looked down at the new jewelry on her hand. Earlier, the twins had each received a beautiful iron ring. The box's label said the ring was crafted with ore mined from the Atlas Mountains, and it had inscriptions in Arabic. Bianca couldn't wait to look up what the words meant, saving the research as a treat instead of cheating and asking her dad directly. The Atlases weren't in Iran, but they held a significance to her father that Bianca was sure she'd be able to figure out.

Bianca had loved her ring and instantly put it on, admiring the hammered metal, but Leila had simply smiled and kept hers in the box. It sat on the table, like an unspoken conversation.

While Bianca embraced her heritage, Leila seemed to think of it as an inconvenience. She wouldn't even drink tea in a glass cup, Persian style. She always insisted on it being poured into a coffee mug. This ring, it seemed, was too Other to be worn.

Their parents didn't press Leila, though. They knew how hard it was to assimilate to a new country. It infuriated Bianca, how whitewashed her twin tried to be. It didn't matter how much Leila tamed her hair or waxed her eyebrows or dressed full cottagecore—she would always be an outsider. Why she tried to be anything else baffled Bianca.

Before she could stew in these dark, uncharitable thoughts that always surfaced whenever she had to spend time with her sister, their dad turned on some music. Iranian music typically had 6/8 time, with fast drums and a singer who could wail through octaves like a hot knife through butter. The music made everything feel like a grand event, even a birthday party with a paltry six people. Bianca's mood lifted.

Their mother pushed the dining room table aside, leaving nothing but the Shirazi rug their father had somehow managed to cart all the way from Iran. Her parents danced together, their shoulders and arms moving in unison, Alma letting loose in the severe pantsuit she'd worn to campus that day. Shivani began clapping and hollering, imitating their moves perfectly as she got up to join them.

Bianca hated to admit that Shivani was starting to grow on her.

"Come on, Leila!" Shivani cried, but Leila just smiled politely and looked away.

June got up hesitantly, and that simple gesture made Bianca feel guilty for wishing herself away from this town and her best friend. What would she do without June?

"Here, move your arms like this," their father instructed June.

June watched as he rolled his wrists and shimmied his shoulders, motioning for her to copy. Their father's bushy black hair and eyebrows could not have looked more different from June's pale skin and blond eyelashes, but she obliged and rotated her wrists like she was doing stretching exercises.

"Dance, monkey, dance!" Bianca cried, jumping into the circle. It was time to shake off this glum mood. She took another bite of cake and shimmied her shoulders, the sugar perking her up.

"Leila, come *on!*" Shivani grabbed her friend's arm and suddenly all four of them, Bianca, Leila, Shivani, and June, stood on the rug.

One big happy family. How Leila could even stand to be at a party with her less-popular twin was beyond Bianca, but they all gamely watched as Shivani taught them some Bollywood dance moves that involved screwing a lightbulb with your hands. Even their father got into it, but then again, Khosrow Mazanderani loved to dance.

Shivani, Bianca decided, wasn't *all* bad.

Just then the landline rang, a sound so foreign Bianca had almost forgotten they even had one.

Their mother picked it up, her face instantly shifting from happy to horrified. "No me digas. Really? Yes, yes, of course we'll help, Buddy. We'll be right there."

"What's wrong?" their father asked. But she didn't hear him. It must have been bad for her to accidentally burst into Spanish.

Mamá abruptly turned off the music, swapping songs for loud, wailing sirens. She ran to the window.

"Ay Dios," she said, crossing herself. "There goes the Elmhursts' barn."

Bianca joined her, staring out the bay window of their sitting room and into the next field over, where an inferno now burned in their neighbors' barn. The bright red and white paint had been swapped for a raging fire, the whole scene looking like something out of a horror movie.

"Oh, my word," June breathed from behind them. Bianca's heart plummeted. Where there had once been a picturesque view a couple of acres over, there was now an inferno. They were lucky the creek divided them, or they'd be evacuating instead of celebrating right now.

"What do you think happened?" Bianca wondered out loud, heart hammering. Leila, too, seemed unnerved for once. Her annoyingly calm twin looked shaken, the fire reflecting in her wide eyes.

"We should go over there and help them," Leila said quietly. "They're probably terrified."

"Sorry, nenas, the party's over," their mother said. "Shivani, can you give June a ride home?"

Shivani nodded, and June had the grace not to roll her eyes at the thought of hitching a lift from one of Ayers High's most pampered princesses. In fact, she looked just as shocked and pale as the twins' mom did.

"Get home as quick as you can, okay? Drive the long way, away from the fire trucks," Mamá added.

"See you at school tomorrow," Shivani said to Leila but not Bianca. *Never mind.*

"I'll text you," June muttered to Bianca.

They watched as Shivani backed out of the gravel driveway in her white Lexus like a bat out of hell, June grimacing from the passenger seat.

Bianca turned back to the living room, and that's when she noticed their father standing in the back corner, his body shivering. He twisted his wedding band anxiously, the thick ring comically inconvenient for someone who worked on cars all day. It was made from the same material as their birthday presents, and it shone in the fiery light coming from the window. Their mother had once gotten their father a silicone stand-in so he wouldn't have to wear the big, clunky ring, but their dad had looked so horrified at the thought of wearing it that she never brought it up again.

"Baba?" Bianca asked, concerned. He was usually the one who was best in a crisis. It was incredible he wasn't already packing bottled water and space blankets. He was older than most of the other dads at school, and in this moment, he looked it. His face was ashen, his skin crumpled. He just stood there, frozen in terror. *What is going on?*

"Dad?" Leila asked, gently touching his shoulder.

He looked up, startled, as if he'd forgotten he'd been in the room with them.

"Alma, you go see if the neighbors need anything, okay? I'm gonna grab some supplies," he said, suddenly snapping to attention.

Mamá nodded, her husband's awkward moment gone.

"I'll help you, Dad," Leila said, throwing on her barn jacket. "We can bring over that lasagna you froze," she added.

"Good idea, baba jan," he said, kissing Leila's forehead.

Bianca tried not to look annoyed. Their father had a special connection with Leila, who loved pickling and preserving and homemaking just as much as he did. Bianca, however, identified more with their mother, a career-minded woman who was pursuing her PhD at Ayers College, the town's beating heart.

"Bianca, you come with me, okay?" her mamá said.

Bianca nodded, grabbing her trench coat and lacing up her boots. "I hope they're okay."

Her mom bit her lip. "Nobody's hurt, but they said something was wrong with the electrical wiring. We'd better hurry."

"Thanks for the party," Leila said to her mom.

"Yeah, thanks," Bianca added quickly, not wanting to be shown up. Other seniors in Ayers hosted keggers in empty houses or had bonfires in the middle of the woods, but Bianca preferred this kind of celebration.

Their mom kissed Leila on the cheek, her dark blond hair brushing against Leila's face. "What did you wish for, mí amor?"

Bianca watched her sister carefully. She had absolutely no clue what Leila, with her perfect life and handsome boyfriend and popular friends, could possibly ask for. Leila felt completely alien to her.

Leila smiled back sweetly. "If I tell you, it won't come true."

"And you?" Mamá turned to Bianca. "What demonic thing did you wish for?"

Bianca shrugged, not wanting to waste the power of her birthday wish by saying it out loud, either. "I wished that the entire football team got chlamydia."

Baba guffawed. Mamá pursed her lips. The football team included Leila's boyfriend, Foster.

"I'm not even going to respond to that," Mamá sighed. "See you all soon." She opened the door and let in the frigid winter air.

"Eighteen years old," their dad lamented as Bianca walked out. "My bachehah are eighteen years old!" He headed to the root cellar to grab some supplies with Leila, leaving Bianca alone.

Suddenly, Bianca felt the prickle of someone's gaze on her skin. She turned back to the now-empty dining room.

Somehow, even though she had blown out all the candles on her cake, a single bluish-green flame flickered back at her. It twinkled on the icing, standing atop the last slice.

Bianca shrugged. She blew it out and stomped into the cold night.

LEILA

W*hen Leila closed her eyes* and blew out her candles, she wished for the most impossible thing she could think of.

I wish that nothing changes, she prayed. *I wish things would stay like this forever.*

She couldn't help it. She loved Ayers. She loved the blue sky and green forests and the acres of fields she could walk whenever she wanted. She loved looking through seed catalogs with her mother, loved making homemade yogurt with her father. She loved going to school and seeing Shivani and Foster and sitting in the same place at lunch and laughing at the same recycled jokes.

These familiar patterns comforted Leila, and she hoped that she'd get to enjoy them as long as she could, even as everyone around her began getting acceptance letters that she would never recieve from far-off schools.

The truth was, it was easier to ignore the changes she felt inside when everything else stayed the same. It was easier to push down the alarming, niggling feeling that something was off if everyone around her acted like all was right with the world.

She had a plan: graduate, go to Ayers College, marry Foster, and start a family. It soothed her, this steady rhythm of prophecy. She would get a degree in agricultural sciences and learn how to run her own homestead. She would live ten minutes from her parents on a farm of her own.

Leila could practically feel the weight of a baby in her arms, feel the bracing air of doing chores at six A.M. every day. In a small town like this, it wasn't unheard of to get married young.

Sure, her mother was a high-powered career woman, but look how miserable that had made her. Mom came home most nights exhausted and left before Leila and Bianca were even awake. Her degrees in Argentina hadn't transferred to the US properly, and now she was stuck redoing the same courses she'd already taken in Spanish, just to prove a point. What kind of life was that?

Her dad seemed a bit less miserable, running their household while fixing cars on the side. But still, her parents' life seemed so thin and flat compared to the other parents of Ayers, who had all married much younger than hers and started sprawling families. All of them seemed to know one another from church, or work, or their old days at Ayers High. Leila felt left out of this comfortable, warm feeling of belonging that her classmates at Ayers all took for granted. She was excited to one day put down roots of her own here.

But what if Foster isn't The One?

An image of Nandani, Shivani's older sister, rose unbidden in her mind. How her laughter sounded the way seltzer water fizzed; how she had always asked Leila how she was doing even though she had been a lowly ninth grader and Nandani was headed for Harvard. Her bright smile and warm eyes were enough to make Leila stumble over her own feet.

She hated how her heart would race every time she came to pick up Shivani from her house, hated how her mouth went dry whenever Nandani so much as looked at her.

I don't feel the same way about my own boyfriend, Leila realized. She shoved this uncomfortable thought down and quickly buttoned her barn jacket. *It's time to help our neighbors, Leila*, she reminded herself. She repeated her birthday wish: *please let everything stay the same.*

She wedged her feet into her muck boots, heading into the root cellar where the chest freezer was.

There, in neat, tidy rows, were frozen foods and meals that she and her father had put up over the summers from their garden. They'd traded bushels of produce for meat from their neighbors who raised livestock, their generosity spilling over on processing day, and the result was practically an entire store's worth of food with a long shelf life.

She rummaged around until she came upon a frozen lasagna (made with tomatoes and basil from the garden) and a frozen pie (made with wineberries from the creek and butter she'd mixed herself). Her father was already there, looking around for the extra flashlights and space blankets they'd stored in their emergency kit.

"Got 'em," Leila said, placing the frozen trays into an old basmati rice sack.

"Great, give me a sec," her dad said, loading up his own bag full of supplies. Leila could smell the fire in the air now, the sirens giving the night a weird, nightmarish soundtrack. She looked at her phone and scrolled back to the text Foster had sent her earlier that day:

Can't make it tonight, babe.

It was wrong, how relieved one text could make her feel. Foster was her boyfriend. She loved him, didn't she? But she couldn't ignore this feeling of emptiness. Every time he kissed her, or they fooled around in the back of his car, she just felt painfully alone. He loved her, but what did love even mean? She felt great affection for Foster. She cared for him. That, she knew for certain. But all-consuming love felt far from their relationship lately.

Foster would make the perfect husband, the best kind of dad, and perhaps that's why Leila cared so deeply for him. He was the key that could give Leila that future she wanted, one he expected for himself too. But something was missing, and she wasn't prepared to think about what that could be and disrupt the perfect bubble she'd built around her life.

"Okay, I think I got it all," her father said, hefting a giant sack onto his shoulder. But his hands were trembling, and Leila didn't think she'd ever seen his face so gray before.

"Dad, are you okay?" she asked, her heart racing. Seeing her father look so fragile unnerved her.

Instead of answering, he set the bag down and reached up to his neck. Clasped around it was an old evil eye necklace that he never took off. "I know you don't like to wear these kinds of things, but could you wear my necklace? Even if you won't wear the ring?"

Leila froze. Bianca always wore the same evil eye necklace they'd both been given at birth, saying that it elevated her eldritch outfits. Leila hadn't ever outright refused to wear it, but she had an unspoken rule that Iranian stuff was at odds with her prairie-chic aesthetic. A necklace like that garnered questions in a way the gold crosses at her school never did. Having her dad bring it up for the first time right now felt beyond strange.

But here he was, practically begging her to put his own talisman on, and that's when Leila realized: her father was *terrified*.

"Sure, Dad," Leila said carefully. Her dad visibly exhaled, his shoulders retreating from his ears.

"Thank you," he whispered, and placed the gold chain around her neck. The blue, white, and black circles clashed with the pale green scarf she wore (hand-knitted, of course), but Leila didn't say anything. The necklace sat uncomfortably on her neck, practically screaming *we're not from here!* the same way gold jewelry and thick eyeliner did with her complexion too. She shoved it under her shirt.

They stomped up the stairs and into the backyard, where light snow dusted the hard-packed dirt. She followed her dad toward the bright lights of the fire and emergency vehicles in the distance, the fields too wet and frozen to carry a fire across and risk their own home.

It was jarring to see the dark horizon lit up with blue and green flames. The barn was more of a skeleton now, the bones of it smoldering as the blaze ran out of things to consume. Leila covered her face with her scarf in case of smoke, but she couldn't smell any.

They crunched their way over their property and hopped the three stones that served as a makeshift bridge over the narrow creek that separated their fields. Some folks in Ayers still referred to this part of town as Elmhurst Holler, an old name for the lush valley and stream that was tucked into the rolling hills. The Elmhursts had been here since the 1800s, and their homestead was just as old. Decades ago, Leila's house had been part of their property before it was parceled off.

She walked faster now, her chest aching with cold and the thought of her neighbors, who were always kind to them, losing so much.

Suddenly she stepped on something squiggly that let out a squeak. "Gah!" She lowered her cellphone light to the ground and saw dozens of field mice fleeing the fire.

"Must have been living in the barn," her dad said, frowning as he held his LED lantern to the dirt. Leila tried not to squirm. She didn't hate mice, but this many was disturbing. It looked like the ground was moving.

They walked past the mice while Leila's mind buzzed. How could there be an electrical fire in a building she was pretty sure had zero electricity? The Elmhursts hadn't housed livestock there in years, using the barn more for storage. Plus, the weather had been so cold and damp, it was hard to imagine anything in there being dry enough to be used as kindling. Something didn't add up.

They could see the outline of the fire engines and cop cars now. Leila spied her neighbors huddled on their front porch, their actual house saved by the twenty yards of distance between them and the barn. Everyone who lived there—just the older couple these days—was accounted for and appeared to be uninjured.

She walked up the stairs, giving the couple a sympathetic look as she held up the food. "Hi, Mr. and Mrs. Elmhurst. We brought some dinner. Want me to preheat the oven?" she asked them. "I'm sure you haven't had a chance to eat yet."

"Oh, Leila," Mrs. Elmhurst said, dabbing at her already wet eyes. "Thank you, sweetheart." Her hands were knotted and weathered from decades of backbreaking farming, and Leila admired the older woman, who had provided for her family with their own land. They'd had goats, a dairy cow, chickens, and pigs, but had since sold them off once they became too much to handle. Now the barn stood empty. The better for burning.

"We're so relieved you're all right," her father said, putting space blankets over her and her husband's legs as they watched everything, stunned. In front of the house, firefighters and police officers buzzed, the noise of their walkie-talkies echoing in the darkness. It felt like a movie playing out in front of them as officials tried to figure out what to do next.

Just then her mom and sister exited the front door onto the porch, carrying a tray of mugs.

"Here," her mother said, handing Mr. Elmhurst a cup. Bianca gave one to Mrs. Elmhurst, and the two neighbors thanked them, neither of them taking a sip, just clutching the warm mugs in their hands.

"So, do they know what happened?" Bianca asked, breaking the sad silence.

"Nope," Mr. Elmhurst said with a gravelly voice. He didn't speak much in general, and tonight was no different.

"What they don't understand is how the flames got so hot," Mrs. Elmhurst added. "Those flames are blue and green, which isn't normal. The firewood in the barn hadn't even cured yet, but there's no smoke from the wet wood. There's a whole cord in there. They're still scratching their heads."

Leila looked at the stumped firefighters, who were now standing in front of the smoldering barn. The flames had died out for the most part, yet there wasn't as much smoke as one would expect from the giant inferno that had blazed fifteen minutes ago. It had run out of fuel, and all that was left was this small fire with strange-colored flames.

Her dad took a long look at the building and twisted his wedding ring.

"Huh," Bianca said in response to Mrs. Elmhurst. "Weird."

Nobody said anything, just clutched their tea as they waited for Mr. and Mrs. Elmhurst's son to arrive from Richmond. Buddy Elmhurst always checked in with the Mazanderani household on how his folks were doing, and he'd been the one to call during the birthday party.

Leila found she couldn't look away from the dying embers, the fire hypnotizing her. The roof and beams had been eaten away, leaving burnt walls with the same blue-green tongues licking the leftovers.

And then she saw it: a small flash of something in the fire. Two eyes burned like hot coals, and a gash of a mouth sneered. It was a face, staring back at her through the knee-high flames.

Leila gasped.

"Leila?" her mother asked. Leila turned her head to Mom. "Que te pasa?"

But when Leila looked back at the barn, the flames were completely extinguished, the face gone.

Her father said nothing, just twisted his ring grimly.

That night, after Buddy had arrived at his parents' burnt property and Leila and Bianca had gone home and cleared away
the birthday cake, Leila curled up in bed. She wrapped herself in the first quilt she'd ever made, and she loved the feel of
the fabric on her cheek. Each square was a scrap saved from
another sewing project, and the mishmash of pastel colors
and neutrals always helped calm her. She was wired from all
the night's excitement, but the last two days of school before
winter break began tomorrow, and she needed her sleep.

Gingerly, she took off the necklace her dad had insisted
she wear and placed it on her nightstand. Then she rolled
over, glad she had chosen warm flannel pajamas tonight. She
inhaled deeply into her pillow, smelling the lavender sachets
she'd stuck there. Finally, her heartbeat slowed.

The adrenaline from the fire rushed out of her like a sugar
crash, and she fell into a deep sleep. In her dream, images of
the roaring blaze surrounded her, the blue and green flames
licking her legs. It was pleasant, almost, feeling the inferno
tickle her body. In her dream state she looked around the
charred barn, unfazed.

Then the face she thought she'd seen within the confla-
gration stepped out of the burning barn and walked up to
her. The being was at least seven feet tall, towering over her
dream form. It smiled wickedly, its figure shifting with flames
that made up its body.

The thing crept closer and closer, its twisted face grinning. Leila was frozen. She couldn't scream. Still, she knew it was just a night terror, and so she tried to wake up.

Leila opened her eyes, safe and sound in her bedroom, but realized she still couldn't move.

Wake up! she wanted to scream. *Wake up!* She'd heard of sleep paralysis before, but the claustrophobic, leaden feeling of not being able to move was worse than she'd anticipated. It felt like a crushing weight pressing down on her, preventing her from budging even an inch under her covers.

She tried to shift her gaze and was relieved to find her eyes could move. Her clock said 3:00, and she swiveled her eyes upward.

There, on her chest, separated only by her precious quilt, sat a monster.

She was fully awake now, the dream trespassing into her reality. It was the monster from the barn, the monster from her nightmare. And it was here in her room, its body smoldering with flames.

"AHHHH!" she screamed, her arms finally moving. Like a blown-out match, the burning figure disappeared. She felt its weight on her chest evaporate. *It was right there!* she wanted to shout. *The thing was in my bed!*

Footsteps pounded outside her room. "Leila?" Bianca asked, cracking the door open. "Are you okay?" The two so rarely went into each other's rooms that Bianca looked uncomfortable just standing in the doorway. Her parents' bedroom was downstairs, which meant they'd probably slept through Leila's squeal.

Leila gasped for breath, realizing she'd flung her body out of the bed and onto the floor. She stood up next to her side table and turned on the light, hands still shaking. It had all felt so real, the feel of the thing's pressure on her blanket, the way the smokeless flame had crackled on top of her. But now, in the light of her bedroom, she knew it couldn't have been. The line between her dreams and reality must have simply blurred, the night's excitement and exhaustion catching up to her.

"I'm okay," Leila lied, breathing heavily. "Just a nightmare."

Did I imagine it, though? She couldn't tell what was a dream and what was real anymore. But Leila could still feel the oppressive paralysis, could still reach into her subconscious and call upon that feeling of dread.

Instead of asking any more questions, Bianca just nodded. "Goodnight." She gently closed the bedroom door.

Leila took a deep breath, drank some water, and tried to clear her head.

Her heartbeat slowly went back to normal, and with it, her conviction that it had ever been real. Clearly, this had all been a hallucination. There was no other explanation for it. She was just overtired, that's all. She probably shouldn't have had that cup of tea on the Elmhursts' porch before bed.

Still, she looked at the evil eye on her side table, the one she'd taken off before falling asleep.

Just a bad dream, she reminded herself.
She didn't put it back on.

BIANCA

Bianca swore as she skidded into the parking lot of Ayers High, her tires too bald to handle the December ice. Just a couple more days of school until winter break and she could curl up in bed as long as she wanted and read all the manga she'd downloaded onto her tablet. *Yes*, she thought, *that is my kind of holiday.*

Leila had stopped riding to school with Bianca the second she'd started dating Foster Hutchins last year. The two had become inseparable, with Foster always picking Leila up from their home and never asking if Bianca wanted a lift.

Whatever. Bianca didn't care. She slammed the door of her truck and walked carefully on the salted parking lot in her Doc Martens, grimacing at the biting wind that howled through her thin black sweater. She was too cool and rebellious to wear weather-appropriate clothing, obviously.

"Bianca!" a voice called out. June sidled up in her older brother's varsity football jacket, the thing practically engulfing her. As the youngest, June had a wardrobe that mostly consisted of her siblings' hand-me-downs. Her love of sports had turned it into a fashion statement more than a budget choice, though. She had shirts from just about every sport Ayers offered thanks to her family's athletic legacy. "So, what happened with the Elmhurst fire? Everyone's talking about it."

Bianca shoved open the double doors of the school, stepping in from the cold sidewalk and onto the brown slush that stuck to the linoleum entryway. "Their barn just completely disintegrated," Bianca replied, still in shock that it had happened at all. "This morning when I woke up, I could barely see any of it still standing."

June gave a low whistle. "Did they find out why it happened, though?"

Bianca shook her head. That had been why the fire trucks had stayed at the Elmhursts' so long. They were trying to find the root cause and couldn't. "No accelerant. No electrical wires. No wind, no likely cause. It's spooky."

June turned with Bianca into the senior hallway. "There was a fire down at the old rail yard too," she said.

Bianca stopped walking. "*Another* fire?"

"They said it was lucky it didn't reach the coal pile left over from the mine."

"Dang," Bianca breathed, leaning against her locker. Like a lot of towns in Appalachia, Ayers had been founded on coal, though the mine had been closed for almost seventy years. If it had hit that coal seam, the fire might have lasted forever.

Two fires during the coldest season of the year had happened the same night. *How could that be possible?*

June spun the combination on her locker a couple down from Bianca's and grabbed her books. "May saw the station fire. She says she saw *someone's face in the flames.*" She whispered the last part.

May was June's eldest sister and worked as an engineer for the town's commercial rail yard, specifically the line that chugged over the mountains and into West Virginia or down to the Chesapeake.

Bianca gasped. "Someone got caught in the fire?"

June shook her head, then checked around to confirm no one was near. "No, that's the weird part. May said no one else was working that night. She swore up and down she saw a face in the flames, and—get this—it was *laughing* at her."

Bianca shivered. Their town had its share of ghost stories and creepy lore, but never something like this. A face in the flames, a disembodied cackling. *It sounds like one of the storylines in my manga*, she thought absently.

"Don't tell anyone, though," June added. "Mom about tore May's head off for mentioning anything satanic."

"I won't," Bianca said solemnly. June's family was incredibly religious, and just saying the words *Happy Holidays* was enough to make Mrs. McCullough apoplectic. She was not thrilled her daughter had a "foreign" friend, despite Bianca having been born in the US.

The warning bell rang. "Shoot, I still have to ask Liam

about the swim team," June said. Winter was her slow season, the time of year when people could only bet on swim, basketball, or volleyball at school. The big moneymakers were football, lacrosse, and soccer, but June still took it upon herself to research Ayers's winter teams for her sports-betting customers. That was how June secretly made most of the money she was squirreling away for college.

Bianca admired June's resourcefulness. The McCulloughs had made it clear for all their kids that there was no free ride for tuition, so June did a good job of becoming the school's secret bookie. She'd taken years of watching her older siblings compete in sports and turned herself into an eagle-eyed spectator.

Still, Bianca shuddered at what would happen if June's mom found out about her daughter's illegal side hustle. Nobody at Ayers besides Bianca and Liam Fitzpatrick knew the identity of the town's online sports bettor, and Bianca prayed it would stay that way.

"I'll see you at lunch?" Bianca asked. June nodded and set off, while Bianca headed to AP Spanish.

AP Spanish was probably her least favorite class at Ayers. Not because she hated the subject, but because the teacher, Señora Thompson, always gave Bianca grief for her Argentine accent. She turned into the language hallway, heaving a massive sigh.

Alas, her path was blocked.

"*I* heard it was a demon." Foster's loud, brash voice rang

out. "That's why the firefighters couldn't find anything." He said this to a half circle of his cronies, who all blocked the hallway, a group that unfortunately included Leila.

Bianca exhaled slowly through her nose, trying to find a way past. God, she hated Foster so much. He wasn't just an asshole; he was an asshole who thought he was a nice guy, and that made it so much worse.

Foster continued, "*I'm* going to go check out the barn tonight and see for myself."

Bianca looked at her twin, who watched Foster with a pleasant smile on her face. What could she possibly see in him? Foster's thick blond hair and ice-blue eyes were the talk of the school, but to Bianca he just looked plain and predictable, the kind of handsome she found boring.

She hated hearing girls giggle in the bathroom over Foster's winning smile and broad shoulders, or how he was one of the best quarterbacks the school had ever seen. He was like a Beach Boys song, only with crappier lyrics. No, Bianca would never like Foster Hutchins, and that fact made her like her own twin even less.

She pushed past the crowd, but something she overheard made her stop in her tracks.

"I bet it's a monster who's starting all these fires. James swore he heard someone cackling near the rail yard last night, and it didn't sound human."

Bianca froze, straining to hear more without obviously eavesdropping, but then someone shouted, "You're just messing with us!" and the conversation changed to who was having the best pre–winter break party.

Bianca clenched her jaw and walked on. For once, something interesting was happening in Ayers, and she was determined to get to the bottom of it.

"Ahora vamos a empezar con el subjuntivo," Señora Thompson called out. *The subjunctive*, Bianca groaned inwardly. *Why does this tense even exist!*

"Subjunction junction, what's your function?" Shepherd Neely sang out unhelpfully from the back row. How he made it to AP Spanish, Bianca would never understand.

"Subjunction isn't a word," Bianca snapped.

"Señorita Mazanderani? Estás terminado?" Señora Thompson's simpering voice cut through the bustle of the classroom. *Are you finished?* Bianca hated the way she pronounced her last name, steamrolling the *a*'s even though Bianca had corrected her many, many times. The way that Señora Thompson smirked every time she pronounced Bianca's last name made her think she did it on purpose.

"Lo siento, Señora Thompson. Solo quisiera explicar que *subjunction* no es una palabra." *I was just explaining how* subjunction *isn't a real word*, Bianca shot back. Yes, she had used the subjunctive in that sentence.

Señora Thompson frowned. Sometimes, Bianca enjoyed

speaking quickly with an Argentine accent to make things difficult, as payback for the way Señora Thompson pronounced
her last name. Bianca's Argentinian *ll*'s and *y*'s sounded more
like *shhh*'s than anything else, making her Spanish sound
vaguely Italian. Virginia's Latino population was mostly
Mexican and Salvadoran, and Bianca's accent stuck out like
a sore thumb. Argentinian was completely useless unless you
were watching a fútbol game on Telemundo.

Spanish, French, Portuguese, Italian—Bianca knew she
could school Señora in just about any romance language
thanks to all the language apps she obsessively used. But
Bianca had the feeling her teacher didn't care, that her experience as a native speaker wasn't valid. Señora Thompson had
never even been to a Spanish-speaking country. The Make
America Great Again bumper sticker on her car made Bianca
wonder if she ever would.

She couldn't wait to get out of this small town with its
even smaller people.

"*In good Spanish, please,*" Señora Thompson snapped back
with a warning, unable to say anything else. There it was. She
was ragging on her accent again.

"*I wish I could say the same,*" Bianca spat, with lightning-
fast fluency.

Whoops. Did I say that out loud?

"That's enough, young lady." Bianca knew the fact that
her teacher couldn't even respond in Spanish said something
about her fluency. When you learned a language, you couldn't

just translate it from English in your head. You had to *think* it. You had to feel it. "Principal's office," her teacher barked.

Bianca recoiled. It was the week before winter break, and she was getting sent to the principal's office for what? Raising their AP exam curve? "En serio?" Bianca cried.

"What'd she say?" Shepherd asked behind her. "I heard *principal*."

"Ahora." Señora Thompson looked murderous, her ugly red Christmas sweater the same color as her face.

Bianca gave a loud sigh and noisily scraped her desk chair back. Understanding other languages was easy. It was the people in Ayers that left her confused.

LEILA

"*I heard it's a ghost* from the old mine," said Shepherd. It was finally lunchtime, yet no one had changed the subject about the fires. It was all anyone at school seemed to want to talk about. "Over a thousand people died getting coal from the seam under the rail yard. You can still see the souls screaming in the flames."

Leila frowned and stabbed at her salad. She made her lunches for the week in batches, throwing lettuce, tomatoes, roast chicken, and croutons into mason jars with homemade vinaigrette at the bottom so as not to get everything at the top of the jar soggy.

This level of domesticity horrified her mother, who had left Argentina in search of a life free of patriarchy and gender norms. Bianca was even more incredulous, insisting that buying lunch at school was just easier. But their father had always supported Leila's interest in homemaking, and the crust of sourdough bread she'd made from scratch helped settle the queasy feeling she'd had in her stomach since hearing about this face in the flames.

The ghost Shepherd described sounded exactly like the demon—no, *dream*—she'd experienced last night. The one that had felt like a real person sitting on her chest, keeping her from moving.

"No way," Shivani said loudly next to her, buoying Leila. "You guys are full of crap."

"Seriously!" Shepherd said, his face solemn. "Ask Delilah Meade—her house is right next to the rail yard, and she said the laughing kept her up all night!"

Shivani whipped her head around to Delilah's table, where the girl known for taking the gymnastics team to state was deep in conversation with eight other girls, their faces wide-eyed and rapt. "Okay, well, clearly she's on board with this whole conspiracy too," Shivani relented.

Leila could see Shivani's face recalculating, not sure what to think anymore. Shivani was always the most suspicious person in the room. Leila would have asked more questions too, if she hadn't been so shaken by the fact that she seemed to be the one with the most experience with this so-called demon.

"Happy belated birthday, babe," Foster said, sliding into the seat on her other side. He squeezed a warm, muscular arm around her, and Leila remembered to smile. She looked up at Foster, at his strong chin and adorable dimple, and nuzzled him back. "Sorry I couldn't make it yesterday," he said quietly to her. "But we can celebrate after school today, okay?"

"Okay." Leila nodded, giving him a small smile.

"Meet me in the parking lot," he added. He gave her a kiss, his lips soft and familiar, just before the bell for next period rang. "Love you."

"Love you too," Leila replied automatically.

Leila spent her free period after lunch looking at YouTube videos, like she usually did once she finished her schoolwork. They soothed her, and she always bookmarked her favorites for later. She even found a video on how Nordic women did laundry before electricity was invented and made a note to buy something called borax. *I was born in the wrong century*, Leila thought glumly. It wasn't the first time she'd had that bitter realization.

"Oh my god," Shivani sighed, rolling her eyes from the desk next to Leila's. "You've gone full cottagecore."

Leila quickly closed her laptop. "It's not cottagecore; it's slow TV. There's a difference!"

"I burned toast over the weekend," Shivani confessed. "I have no idea how you do all that homemaking stuff." She tossed her hair, her expensive perfume overtaking the natural rosemary spray Leila put in her own.

Leila laughed. Shivani always poked fun at Leila's hobbies, but never like Bianca, in a way that made Leila feel defensive. If anything, Shivani admired Leila's resourcefulness. Frugality was not one of Shivani's strong suits.

"Nandani is coming back for winter break," Shivani sighed.

Leila's heart hiccupped. Shivani's older sister, Nandani, was always a tricky subject.

Leila knew she liked boys; she liked how they smelled and felt, but Nandani had always been this shining, bright light that made Leila weak in the knees. The way she felt for Foster and Nandani was just so, so different. Foster was all sharp angles and heft. She liked the feel of his weight on top of her, but she also longed to feel the soft skin of Nandani. What did that mean? If Shivani ever found out about Leila's pathetic crush on her sister, Shivani would probably feel even worse about living in Nandani's shadow. How many times had Leila peeked through Nandani's door at Shivani's house, watching her curtain of black hair cascade over her schoolbooks?

Leila pushed the thought away. *It's not even a crush*, Leila convinced herself. *More like admiration.*

"Shiv, you know you're just as smart, right?" Leila said, hoping it would help her brain stop obsessing over Nandani's smooth skin and kind eyes and—

Shivani snorted. "My goal is to get into a school with a good fashion-marketing program. Hers is to cure cancer. I think it's safe to say I am not as smart as her."

Leila shook her head. "Okay, maybe not book smart. But who else could organize prom with two weeks' notice when the senior class president got mono? Or get the entire school to pronounce my name correctly instead of as 'Leela'? Or, or . . . set me up with Foster!"

"I'm still not sure I did you a favor setting you up with Foster," Shivani said quietly, interrupting Leila's deep, secret ache. "I don't like the way you are around him. You seem . . . like . . . like Leila at thirty percent or something."

Leila's heart twitched. Was it that noticeable? Lately it felt like she had just been going through the motions with Foster, worrying that whatever spark had been between them was now gone. She hadn't counted on her best friend noticing, though.

"Am I wrong?" Shivani asked, cutting through the silence of Leila's whirring thoughts.

"I . . . ," Leila began. How to explain to someone like Shivani, who had already applied early to Fashion Institute of Technology, about her dream of staying in Ayers and starting a family? How she needed Foster for that? It didn't matter how Leila felt if the end goal was so clear.

"I know," Leila murmured, trying not to draw the attention of their free-period teacher, Mr. Lasseter. "Things have just been . . . weird lately."

Shivani nodded. "I can tell. You seem even quieter than usual. Who's gonna back me up at lunch when Shepherd starts spouting off nonsense?"

Leila's serious face cracked a tiny bit, the smile peeking through. "He still thinks corn is a fruit."

"It's a grain! God, if he mentions one more conspiracy theory about the barn fire I'm gonna throw a corndog at him."

What little smile Leila had begun to show clamped shut. *Barn fire.* She shivered, something in her body recoiling at the memory of that night. "You can hang at my house if you need space when Nandani is here," she said quietly.

"Thanks," Shivani said. "Do you think your dad will make that crunchy rice thing for me?"

Leila frowned. "You mean tahdig?"

"Yeah!" Shivani shouted.

"Shhh," Mr. Lasseter called from the front of the room.

"Oops," Shivani whispered. "Yeah, that. I want to eat that. But not just as a side dish. For like, the whole meal."

Leila tried not to laugh. Shivani was one of the few friends Leila brought home to eat their family's more "interesting" food. Then again, crunchy carbs covered in fat was delicious no matter what the culture.

"I'll ask, but no promises," Leila said.

"Thank youuuuu," Shivani sang, already perking up. The bell rang. "All right, time to prepare for two weeks with my overachieving sister," Shivani said grimly.

"Tahdig," Leila reminded her. "Crunchy rice. My place. Whenever you want."

Shivani gave her a hug. "Thanks, bestie."

"See you soon."

The two parted ways for the rest of the school day. When the final bell rang, Leila met Foster at his parking spot, the one reserved for his prized Jeep Wrangler. She exhaled, cueing up the daydream that always calmed her whenever she was having a rough day: her and Foster raising their cute kids in Ayers, the two of them getting a fixer-upper on the other side of town, Leila with her kitchen garden and Foster, wedding band on his finger, gripping a plump child. Her heartbeat went back to normal; the cold air began to soothe instead of sting.

Foster would get a job at his dad's construction company, and she'd stay home and raise the kids, pickle vegetables, and mend whatever was in the basket they'd put next to the fireplace for shirts with holes in them. It was a fantasy to Leila, a secret, shiny thing that kept her steady. There was no way she'd voice this desire out loud, no way she'd admit to her friends that her dream was to become a mom and a wife.

She could already smell the sweet, milky scent of a baby's head. She smiled at Foster and could see how his blue eyes would play out in their first kid. Surely, that had to be love.

"Hi." She smiled, stepping up and over onto the passenger side.

"Hi, babe," Foster said, grabbing her hand over the gear shift, planting a warm, familiar kiss on her temple. "I was thinking we could go to The Grove today."

Leila's hands went clammy. The Grove. The Grove was an empty clearing on her side of town where a lot of teens in Ayers went to "neck," as they jokingly called it. Leila didn't *mind* doing that stuff with Foster, but she didn't exactly enjoy it, either.

But that's how babies are made, Leila, she reminded

herself. *One day you'll go off birth control and that'll be how you start a family.*

She couldn't help her lack of enthusiasm, though. For Leila, sex with Foster was like looking at rice in the pantry. She had no feelings about it, good or bad. As if reading her hesitation, Foster quickly added, "I just wanted to give you your birthday present there."

Leila nodded tightly. "Yeah, that sounds great."

Foster smiled and they sped off, the weak winter sun making it feel like evening despite it being barely four o'clock. They arrived at The Grove ten minutes later, their conversation consisting mostly of Foster talking about their friends at school, what sports everyone was doing in the off-season, and how he couldn't wait to play football for Ayers College. In short: all the things they usually talked about.

Leila rested her head against the cool glass window, glad that she had this familiar drive to clear her thoughts after the disturbing fire-related news from lunch. Her head swam, wondering what had been real last night and what had to have been a hallucination. The weight of the demon on her chest had felt so *real.* Then again, every vivid dream did.

Too soon, Foster put his Jeep in park by the old ring of oak and hickory trees. The sun was setting thanks to midwinter, and they were the only ones parked there. Her house was a half mile away, through the thicker part of the creek bed that marked the border of their property.

"Happy birthday, Leila," Foster said, holding out a small

box. Leila flinched. It looked like the jewelry box her parents had gotten her, the one with the iron ring.

She opened it tentatively.

This was a ring as well, but it was an Irish promise ring, the kind with a heart nestled into a woven metal band. She'd seen other girls at school wear them, the heart pointed a certain way to denote a promise kept or a girl waiting to promise someone else. Instinctively, she knew this ring was more acceptable than the thick iron band she'd been gifted yesterday. She slipped it on her finger.

"Thank you," she said. "It's perfect."

Foster smiled. "Glad you like it, babe." Then, he went in for the kiss.

Leila knew a gesture like this would lead to a long, drawn-out make-out session ending with Leila murmuring, "No, not now," and Foster sighing, saying something like, "But I just love you so much."

They'd done it before, but the thought of doing it in his cramped back seat was too uncomfortable to bear today. This time though, Foster was the one to pull away first.

"So, I was hoping you could show me that barn. Now that we're nearby."

Leila froze. "What?"

"You know," Foster said, walking his fingers innocently up her arm in what he probably thought was a cute gesture. "Since you live so close to it, and all. I just wanted to check it out. See what happened."

Leila bit her lip. There weren't any firefighters left, but there still was caution tape saying DO NOT ENTER. What would the Elmhursts think, with someone prowling their property?

"Pleeeeeeease?" Foster wheedled. "I wanna see this face, or whatever. See if it was at this fire too."

This face. The face that had haunted her dreams last night. The face that had sneered at her in her bedroom. Leila cringed at the thought of going back to the barn, conflating last night's fire with the demon from her dreams.

"How about we go to my house, and you walk from there? I have to talk to my dad, anyway," she said, hoping Foster would believe her lie. Her parents weren't going to be back until dinnertime, but he didn't have to know that. She just didn't want to see that barn again, and her body felt clammy at the thought of being near that burnt-out shell, her body paralyzed, her eyes barely able to move, her limbs like lead—

"Yesss, I knew I could count on you, babe!" Foster said, squeezing her arm.

He turned the ignition and launched the Jeep through the old logging road that cut into Leila's family's back field. He parked in her driveway and hopped out, running to open Leila's door like he always did, no matter where they were, or how long she'd gotten used to driving with him. *Can't it be okay to want this?* she wondered.

"You go on ahead," Leila said, unable to even look at the next field over. "Just meet me back here when you're done."

Foster smiled at her and kissed her forehead, and Leila watched him stride through the dirt to the other side of the dim expanse. He was so sure of himself, so determined. Would she ever feel that way about herself?

She turned to go back to the house but caught a glimpse of the barn by accident. In the waning light, it looked even more menacing. She inhaled and walked inside, scrubbing the dream from her mind, once and for all.

And then she heard a scream.

BIANCA

Bianca had been in her room when she heard it: the sound of a male voice yelling in surprise. At that moment, the new iron ring on her finger burned her hand. She jerked her head up from her AP Spanish and AP French books.

She had always figured that her aptitude for languages was her ticket out of Ayers—a translation job, a job in another school's languages program, even becoming a linguist for the army. Anything to get out of a boring town.

But now, as she looked out her window, she saw the most interesting thing to have ever happened. There, by the Elmhursts' barn, was a guy next to what looked like a human engulfed in flames.

She heard a door slam downstairs and watched, stunned, as Leila sprinted toward the figure. Bianca's brain finally caught up to her surprise and she threw her books down, following Leila out the front door.

Someone is on fire! Someone is on fire! her brain kept

screaming inside her skull. Then: *But I thought the barn fire went out? How did they catch on fire?*

She ran over the cold dirt, the bitter wind biting through her clothes. She couldn't remember the last time she'd ever run so fast. She jumped over the creek, ignoring the bridge, and practically sailed onto the other side of the bank. Up ahead she could see Leila's silhouette against a burst of blue and green flames that towered over her, its limbs surprisingly calm for someone who was probably burning in agony. Next to her was Foster, now lying in a crumpled heap.

"LEILA!" Bianca screamed. Her twin turned around, face pale. And that's when Bianca finally saw it, past Leila: the face in the flames that everyone had been talking about.

What had been a fire full of lashing tongues suddenly turned into a body with arms and legs, and a face that twisted and sneered as Leila dropped to the ground by Foster's side. It wasn't a person on fire—it was *made* of fire.

Bianca joined her sister, registering how cold she still felt next to the strange fiery thing, the flames not providing any warmth. The ring on her hand, however, remained hot, and she could feel a searing lump coming from the evil eye necklace she always wore under her shirt. *It must be because the ring is metal*, a small part of her thought as the rest of her brain struggled to make sense of the sight in front of her.

"Leila!" Bianca shouted again.

Leila sucked her gaze away from Foster's unconscious form to the blazing figure that slowly approached. Ten feet away, nine feet away—it didn't walk so much as ooze forward, setting the earth in front of it aflame before shifting its weight closer and closer.

"Help!" Leila screamed, trying in vain to move Foster's bulk away from the fiery being. Bianca looked down, shocked to see him completely knocked out, his face ghostly white. Leila reached under his armpits to carry him back to the Elmhursts' house, but it was no use. He was too heavy.

Bianca hurried to help, still unable to process how a demon made of fire was stalking toward them. Where were the Elmhursts? Could nobody hear their cries for help? Bianca lifted with all her might, trying to shift Foster's heavy legs, but he wouldn't budge. The light from the flickering fire-thing came closer and closer, and Bianca's heart hammered in her throat, her muscles straining to move Foster as she straddled his ankles. The physique that had been the talk of the school was now his downfall.

Bianca frantically scanned her neighbor's house, but the cars in the driveway were gone. Her own parents weren't home. They were the only ones out here for miles.

Then she heard it.

"We were promisssssed," the flames hissed. "Our payment is due."

Bianca and Leila froze, Foster comically strung up between them. It had said the words in English, but Bianca heard echoes of other languages underneath it, like a polyphonic chorus of translation. Bits of Farsi, Spanish, Arabic, and something older, something powerful, resonated deep beneath. Slowly, Bianca turned to face the monster head-on, her eyes not wanting to believe what she was seeing.

It was a horrible, twisted thing, its mouth a gash of yellow and its eyes two black holes. Its limbs were too long, its arms hanging far below its torso, while its legs were so tall they had to bend at a strange angle for him to look down at her. Like a rabbit in headlights, Bianca couldn't look away.

"We were promissssed," the thing repeated, its many voices blending.

Bianca wasn't imagining it anymore—her ring was scorching her hand, the pain deep enough to snap her out of her trance. This was no normal metallic reaction to heat. She tried to pry it off, but to her horror, it wouldn't budge.

"*What were you promised?*" she finally asked, her voice breaking. She hadn't known why she'd spoken in Persian. It was just the first language that came to her in that moment.

"Bianca!" Leila gasped behind her, as if scolding her twin for engaging with this beast. Even now, Bianca couldn't help but feel like she was an embarrassment to her sister. But the thing didn't mind. It looked at Bianca, head tilting, its coal-black eyes considering hers.

"*Flesh,*" it said simply, letting the word hang there. Bianca's top was starting to smoke now, her evil eye necklace searing her cheap polyester sweater and making it smell like burning plastic. *This can't be real*, she thought dimly. *This can't be happening.*

"I don't understand!" Bianca shouted in English, gritting

her teeth. *Flesh? Had it really said* flesh? Her whole body shook from nerves, and the effort of not dropping Foster made her hands ache.

"Flesh!" the thing cackled in English, pointing a fiery finger at her.

Bianca didn't know what to do or how to respond. It stood there as if waiting for a reaction. Bianca looked at Leila. Leila looked back at her, their expressions identical for the first time in years.

Then the thing exploded, sending flames in every direction.

Bianca screamed, the fire almost engulfing her. Her ring cut into her hand, and the necklace heated up so much she felt the excruciating pain of its burn on her chest.

"AHHH!" the demon shrieked the second its flames touched Bianca. But instead of burning her, its flames poured *around* her. Like water around a rock in a stream, the flames avoided Bianca and headed to Leila instead.

"NO!" Leila shouted, then Bianca heard a distant *thunk* as Leila dropped Foster's shoulders, and his head hit the cold dirt. Bianca's hands were still clenched around him, unable to let go as the pain of her jewelry burned brightly against her. She couldn't see her sister anymore; all she could see were the blue-green fires that had swallowed them both.

And then, just as quickly as it had started, it stopped. The jewelry on Bianca's body went ice-cold, soothing her skin. She blinked at the scene before her.

Foster was still unconscious, his legs held in Bianca's hands. But Leila, instead of being upright, had collapsed next to him.

"Leila!" Bianca screamed. She went to her twin, dropping Foster's legs with a cold smack. Leila had passed out, her brown gingham dress splayed over her muck boots, her barn jacket askew.

"Wake up wake up wake up!" Bianca pleaded, patting her sister's face. It was pale, the cheeks drained of color, her long eyelashes resting against them.

"HELP!" Bianca screamed one more time, but it was no use—they were still alone. She plunged her hand into her pocket for her phone, then moaned as she realized she'd left it inside.

"Bianca?" a thin voice croaked. Leila blinked her eyes open.

Bianca looked at her sister. Her jaw dropped.

It was Leila, but it *wasn't*. Instead of soft brown eyes, her sister's eyes blazed. The life that had been gone from her complexion suddenly was back in full force, her skin almost glowing. Her mousy brown hair was now glossy and thick, her black eyelashes even longer and more pronounced. She looked like a completely different Leila, one who glittered and gleamed instead of the muted sister Bianca had always known.

"Leila?" Bianca asked, cradling the back of her twin's head. "Are you okay?"

Bianca didn't realize she had been crying. She pushed stinging tears away with her sleeves, registering that there was now a singed hole of fabric on her chest.

"I feel weird . . . ," Leila said, her voice cracking.

"Does it hurt anywhere?"

Leila shook her head, slowly putting her elbows underneath her as she tried to sit up.

"Take it easy," Bianca said. "You passed out."

With a start, Bianca realized this was the most she'd talked to her twin in years. She watched as Leila gingerly put her hands behind her, sitting up in the frigid field.

"I don't feel so good," Leila groaned, suddenly losing her balance. Bianca grabbed her elbow as Leila threatened to tip over. She looked like she was going to vomit.

But then, Leila shot up, her back ramrod straight. Bianca scrambled to stand with her.

"Leila?"

"I—I—" Leila began, panicking.

Bianca stared at her twin, and she knew she wasn't imagining it this time. Leila *was* glowing. She looked into Leila's eyes and almost screamed: they had gone completely gold.

"I can't . . . I can't . . . I can't stay . . . ," Leila was now muttering. But even though she was staring at Bianca, she could tell that Leila was looking past her, dazed, into something that Bianca couldn't see. Flames began to lick Leila's body. Where had the fire spread from? How could little flames dance along the hem of her dress now? Whatever relief Bianca had felt at Leila's recovery evaporated in an instant. Bianca yelped, trying to pat the fire down with her holey sweater. It was no use—these flames wouldn't die, and what was worse, Bianca realized they didn't actually burn the way flames should.

Leila didn't seem fazed by it, though. She looked at Bianca, her gaze empty, her golden eyes hollow. Her lights were on, but no one was home.

"Leila?" Bianca asked, hysterical. "Leila! What are you—"

And then, in a burst of flame, Leila's body disappeared with a *whoosh*.

"LEILA?" Bianca screamed. "LEILA!"

But Leila was gone.

Bianca dropped to her knees in the dirt, next to the quarterback's useless body.

This was not the kind of excitement she had hoped for.

LEILA

Leila reappeared in front of a mountain.

She screamed.

It was unlike any mountain she'd seen. Instead of the gentle rounded peaks of the Blue Ridge, this was a tall, jagged crag, its tip covered in clouds. Sand dunes whirled and shifted around her, the geography completely alien. She tried to catch her breath, but her brain refused to compute how she had been in front of her neighbor's burnt barn and was now here—in front of what looked like one of Bianca's fantastical desktop wallpapers.

"Young Mazanderani, of the salt marsh sea, of the river of silver," a husky voice said from behind her. Leila whipped her head around. There stood a boy, over six feet tall, with raven-black hair and bright red eyes. His cheekbones stood out sharply from his face, and his long nose had the trademark crick of many Iranians. He was handsome in a harsh, brutal way. His round, full lips looked like they were trying hard not to sneer at her.

Leila stared in shock. Yet the more she looked, the more he seemed familiar. Sure enough, his body seemed to shimmer and shift like a mirage. It was the fire demon! The same creature that had rushed them in the Elmhursts' field was now a human, staring back at her.

Instead of flames, he wore a regal-looking outfit, with a fur-lined cape and an obsidian uniform with shining gold buttons. He bowed low, almost mocking her. "Your debt must be paid."

Leila finally found her voice. It sounded thin against the whipping wind of the dunes. "What debt? Where am I?"

"The promise of your ancestors is your burden to bear," the boy's low voice growled, not really answering her. "Even if you are innocent, a debt is a debt. Now you are of age to pay it."

Of age, the words repeated in her head. She had just turned eighteen. Is this the age he was talking about? And what did someone gamble away to make her in debt to this . . . this . . . *thing*?

Leila sank to her knees, her skirt puddling into the warm sand. She didn't understand. Where was she? Why her? And what did this demon have to do with it? *Maybe I'm just dreaming again . . .*

"But . . . who would bargain me away?" she finally asked.

The boy laughed. It was that same cruel, cold laugh she had heard in her dreams, the voice cackling over and over in her head. *He was the demon from my dreams too*, Leila realized, the horror setting in.

Then: *I'm not dreaming now, either.*

Leila stared helplessly at the mountain. At first glance it looked like a pillar rising to the sky, but the closer she looked, the more she realized it wasn't *just* a mountain: it was a city.

Nestled into each crack of the mountain were homes, stores, and mansions. At the very top was a palace, so big she could see it from here at the mountain base as it kissed the sky. There were terraces and balconies spilling over every square inch of mountainside, each home carved into the rock face. Flickers of flame dotted each curve and crag, the whole peak blinking like a million fireflies.

Emeralds and rubies, diamonds and sapphires, all twinkled from the summit, giving the mountain a kaleidoscopic effect. The whole thing looked like it was fit to burst, and that a stray gust of wind could topple the overburdened mountain any second. Everything felt surreal and hazy, the rules of reality shifting. Her brain simply couldn't believe that she was somewhere different from Ayers.

"It's not all bad," the boy chuckled, interrupting her stares. "Should you want to prosper, this could all be yours." He gestured to the twinkling city with a lazy wave. "The djinn plane needs a princess, after all."

"What?"

Here the boy dropped his pompous act. He crouched, meeting Leila's eyes from where she stood on tiptoe to look into his.

"Help us grow our numbers," he said, his voice suddenly

desperate. "Help us swell our ranks. All we need is one bridge, one aide, and we could expand our empire."

Leila was tired of asking questions, tired of being completely out of her depth, but still, she couldn't help herself. Her body shook. Her throat was dry as sand. "What?" she asked again. "How?"

"My father, the king, thinks we should just move." The boy shook his head in disgust. "It's the coward's way. This mountain has been our home for millennia. It has been our home since humans were shaped from clay! But if we took over the human plane, we wouldn't need to leave. We could live in both worlds, prosper on both sides."

Leila's heart raced, trying to keep up with everything he was saying. *The human plane? Clay? What is he?*

"Help us," he said, holding out his hand. "You could be my bride. Together we could rule both planes, you and I." His hand glittered with jewels, each ring as big as a knuckle.

Leila recoiled. "I don't understand," she said firmly, stepping away from him. "What debt?" she demanded. "What *are* you?"

The boy snatched his hand back, sneering again at her. "I never thought a dirty human would ever turn down a djinn." He tucked his hand back into his fur cloak, the offer clearly gone.

A *djinn*. He'd said the word *djinn*.

"Never mind," he said, more to himself. "We'll just do this the hard way."

Leila struggled to remember where she'd heard the word *djinn* before. There were genies in American pop culture, but *djinn* felt like something from her father's side. Images of his Quran swam in front of her, his tasbih—black prayer beads—resting on top. Djinn had something to do with Islam, she was pretty sure.

She looked back at the boy, ready to demand even more answers, but it was clear the conversation was over. He snapped his fingers, using the two-handed snap her father insisted on, and flames grew around his body, swirling out to reach her.

Leila felt her own body grow warm like before, and flames tickled her toes. Before she knew it, the fire he'd made engulfed her, her view of the mountain blocked.

"Wait!" she cried. And then, the boy rushed at her, his body turning to flames as they poured directly into Leila.

She screamed.

She reappeared next to Bianca in the field, the sunshine of the mountain burning an afterimage into the wintry Ayers air. The sneering boy was gone. She was back.

Silence. Bianca stared at Leila like she'd seen a ghost.

Then Bianca screamed. "WHAT! THE! HELL!"

Leila stood still, completely thunderstruck. *This is really happening*, she repeated to herself. *I'm not dreaming anymore.*

"You were just there"—Bianca gestured with both hands

like a football referee—"and then you were not there. And now my brain is broken."

Leila tried to verbalize what she had witnessed, but it was no use. "I went to a mountain. . . . It was like nothing I've ever seen. Who was that guy? There was something about a bridge . . ." She was babbling now, but she didn't care. How to explain what she'd witnessed? How did she communicate the wildest, most jaw-dropping thing she'd ever seen to her estranged sister?

Bianca's body stilled. "What?"

She doesn't understand, a small voice inside Leila said. *She'll never understand.*

"Slow down," Bianca finally said. "A mountain?"

Leila took a deep breath, pushing her reaction inside. "It was this mountain covered in gold and jewels and it was full of houses, and then this guy said . . ." She trailed off, realizing how ridiculous she sounded.

Bianca frowned. "If you hadn't just disappeared, I would think you hit your head pretty badly."

Leila toed her boots in the ground, embarrassed. "Never mind. This is stupid."

"No! That's not what I said! I meant—" Bianca cried.

"Why are you yelling at me?" Leila demanded.

Once again, Bianca seemed to be punishing Leila for reasons she didn't understand. Her sister's brusque, direct manner was scolding her even now, after a supernatural run-in. Bianca's hysterics left little room for Leila's own.

Foster's limp body lay between them, completely forgotten.

"I'M NOT YELLING!" Bianca replied, practically hyperventilating now. "This makes no sense." She began to pace. "There was a fire next door and at the train station, and some demon thing tried to eat us, and you somehow disappeared?"

Now Leila felt like she had to be the calm one despite the major bomb that had just dropped on her life, this huge fever dream she needed to dissect immediately once she was on her own. Bianca's emotions always sucked the air out of a room, and today was no different. "We need to get Foster home. Mom and Dad will be here soon," Leila said evenly, shoving the last ten minutes out of her head.

Bianca opened her mouth, closed it, then opened it again. "That's it? That's all you have to say? You just . . . well, you, I mean—"

Leila said nothing, even as her own thoughts raced. *Where did that boy go? What did he mean by "helping" them? What's this debt, and how can I pay it?* "Foster. We gotta move him," Leila repeated.

Bianca searched her sister's face, as if looking for something, then exhaled. She turned to Foster. "Hey, asshole, wake up." She nudged Foster's shoulder, but he didn't budge.

"Bianca!" Leila said, horrified.

Bianca sighed, blowing a strand of hair out of her face. Leila noted how ragged Bianca looked then, her sweater coming apart at the chest, her mascara running down her cold cheeks. Had she been crying? She couldn't remember the last time she'd seen her sister shed a single tear.

"Fine," Bianca said. She bent over Foster's body and rummaged in his pockets, pulling out his keychain, the one with the Tennessee Titans bottle opener on it. "Be right back."

"Where are you—" But Bianca was already off, jogging toward Foster's car. Leila bent down next to him. "Foster? Babe?"

She put a hand in front of his mouth and confirmed that he was still breathing. His forehead felt cold, her palm much warmer by comparison. He had no visible bruises, no cuts or scrapes. She wondered if the demon had hurt him, or whether Foster had just passed out from fear.

She looked at the back of her hand, suddenly so much tanner against Foster's pale skin. The olive undertones of her coloring stood out now, giving her complexion a full, healthy glow. But before she could think about what that meant, the sound of Foster's Jeep came crunching up the frosted ground behind her.

Leila blinked in the bright headlights. Bianca had driven Foster's Jeep up the Elmhursts' drive and off-roaded it to the scorched earth by the barn, following the tracks of the fire trucks and cop cars from the night before.

Bianca hopped out. "Okay, I gotta admit, that thing is fun to drive."

Leila frowned. "Help me move him. We can use one of the blankets in the trunk and slide him over."

"And why would Foster need blankets in the back of his car, sister of mine?" Bianca asked innocently, opening the spare-tire door in the trunk.

"Shut up," Leila growled.

Bianca stopped in place, giving her sister a long look. "So, we're feisty now, huh?"

Leila groaned. "Just help me!"

She didn't like this familiarity with her sister, didn't like how Bianca had witnessed this big transformation Leila hadn't even had time to parse for herself.

Bianca made an annoying zipper motion over her lips and shook out a ratty plaid blanket next to Foster's body. They rolled his frame onto it, and Leila noted how much lighter Foster felt than before.

"Now we gotta shimmy him up into the car somehow," Bianca sighed. "Why does he feel way heavier than he looks?"

Leila shrugged. "Muscle is heavier than fat?"

Bianca shook her head in disgust. "I hate how hot he is."

"Bianca!"

"Yeah, yeah, I'll grab his legs; you grab his shoulders," Bianca said, waving off her sister's scandalized expression. Leila had known that Foster was attractive in a general sense but never knew her sister agreed with public sentiment. It was still shocking, though, to talk about something as banal as which guys they thought were hot. Just asking the other to pass the salt at dinner was excruciating.

Leila reached under Foster's armpits again, but before

Bianca could get a good hold on his legs, Leila was already dragging him up into the passenger seat.

"Whoa!" Bianca exclaimed. "Did you get super strength *and* a makeover?"

Leila pushed Foster into the car, then bent over to buckle his seatbelt. She yanked it hard, locking the belt in place to keep him from tipping over. Then she looked at her arms, marveling at how she barely felt winded.

"I *do* feel stronger," she admitted. She walked to the back of the car and gripped the bumper. She'd read somewhere that mothers got superhuman strength when their children were in danger. Maybe this was something similar.

She gripped the bumper, trying to lift it, and gasped with effort.

Nothing.

"Wow," Bianca said flatly, arms crossed over the hole in her sweater. "That was embarrassing."

"Oh my god, shut up, Bianca!" Leila said, exasperated. "Just give me the keys. Mom and Dad'll be home soon."

"What are you gonna tell Foster?" Bianca demanded. "That a fire demon knocked him out?"

Leila bit her lip. "I'll just tell him he fell asleep. You know . . . after . . ."

Bianca made a vomiting motion. "After you two did it in the back of his Jeep? Just write a country music song already."

Leila blushed, furious at Bianca for being so difficult in what was already an unbelievable series of events.

"Keys," Leila repeated.

Bianca tossed them to her, and Leila climbed into the driver's seat.

"Wait!" Bianca called out. Leila stopped, about to turn on the ignition. "Text me when you get there! I can pick you up."

Leila would rather clear her savings account on the town's one Uber than call Bianca for a silent, uncomfortable ride home. Better yet, she'd just take her chances with Shivani's Lexus and ask her for a ride. Shivani's driving was terrifying, but still, it wasn't as awful as sharing a tense ride with her twin.

"Fine," was all Bianca said, reading her face. "Don't call."

Leila reversed out of the field, her sister's face still frowning in the light of the high beams.

Heat surged through Leila's hands as she gripped the steering wheel. She knew, somehow instinctually, that there was a new fire simmering underneath her skin. Whatever had happened in the last hour had changed her, and she didn't feel the same.

Could she make flames dance the same way as the boy by the mountain? She found herself wanting to know, instead of compartmentalizing this power into some dark basement in her mind, like the rest of her questions about herself.

In that moment, Foster stirred awake.

"Babe?" he said, his voice thick. "What . . ." He trailed off, seeing that Leila was driving away from her house.

"You fell asleep, babe." Leila remembered to smile sweetly at him. "How do you feel?"

"Fine," Foster said, his expression still bewildered. He ran a hand through his thick hair, yawning. "Man, I must have been exhausted."

"Yeah," Leila agreed. "You must have been. Do you remember anything?"

Foster turned to her. Leila tensed, feeling his eyes on her.

"You look different," he said slowly. "Did I see the barn?"

Leila exhaled. He didn't remember the fire demon. "No, sweetie, you fell asleep before you got a chance to look." Inside, her heart raced. Did he remember the fire demon rushing him in his flame form? Did he see her disappear from the human plane?

"Makeup, huh? That stuff is like Photoshop." And then Foster promptly fell asleep again.

Leila exhaled, relief cooling the rising heat in her blood.

This is who you choose to stand beside? a small, petulant voice inside her began. *This fool?*

Leila almost bit her tongue. She was surprised to hear herself think those thoughts. Foster wasn't the smartest, it was true. But did she really think he was a fool?

She signaled to turn off their road and looked in the rear-view mirror. She squinted. There, in the field, Bianca was still staring after her, arms crossed.

Leila looked away, finally catching her own reflection. Foster was right: she did look different. She looked like someone strong, someone who radiated confidence and conviction. Her lips were redder, her cheeks sharper. She stared into her golden irises, and there, for a quick second, she registered a flicker of flame that almost made her swerve off the road.

She shook her head, pressing the accelerator. She didn't want to think about that mountain in the desert now, didn't want to think about what the djinn had said to her. Now that she was in the safety of the car, it all felt like a hallucination, a concussion dream that was surely made up.

Whatever you say, the voice inside her chuckled.

Part II

Indeed, we created man from sounding clay molded from black mud . . . As for the djinn, we created them earlier from smokeless fire.

—Quran, Surah Al-Hijr 26–27

BIANCA

Bianca watched her sister leave, breathing hard.

"Holy crap," she said to no one, her words falling flat on the charred field as Leila drove away. She finally caught her breath, and with the lower heart rate came a drop in adrenaline. Bianca shivered, the cold catching up with her. It didn't help that her sweater was basically useless now.

The demon hadn't just rushed them; it had combusted and disappeared. But where had it gone? Or maybe . . . maybe the demon hadn't left them at all. Maybe the demon had fled *into* someone. That must have been how Leila had gotten that super strength and vanished. That was why she looked so changed.

Nah, Bianca thought to herself, unwilling to believe this wild set of events. *There's no way.*

Still, Bianca trudged across the empty field toward home and ran upstairs to her laptop. Her brain buzzed with her unconfirmed hypothesis. She opened a search tab. "Demons made of fire."

The results ranged from a *Dragon Ball Z* index to a demonic encyclopedia. But one word kept popping up in all the different links:

Djinn.

Bianca read on.

"*According to the Quran, angels were made of light, humans were made of clay, and djinn were made of smokeless flame. Djinn have a natural aversion to iron.*"

"Hmm," Bianca said to no one, closing the laptop with a snap.

Iron. The same thing her ring was made from. She gingerly twisted the thick ring off her finger, expecting to see burned and pruned flesh beneath. The jewelry had felt so unbearably hot during the whole demon-on-fire incident, she was surprised it slipped off her finger so easily. Underneath, her finger was whole and unburnt. *How?*

She strode to the full-length mirror next to her dresser to inspect the giant hole in the middle of her favorite sweater. The evil eye necklace was still intact, and the skin beneath it looked warm and healthy despite the blistering heat. *What is going on?*

Bianca paced her room. This was her haven, her safe space. She had black lace curtains, dark wood furniture she'd scoured from various yard sales around town, and a blood-red comforter with black piping. It looked as if Hot Topic had a homewares collection, and just being in her room made her feel calm and relaxed.

But even her safe space couldn't soothe her now.

Bianca threw on a soft black cashmere sweater she'd scored at the local Goodwill and adjusted her iron ring and evil eye necklace. Whatever the jewelry was, it was clearly special. She'd never take them off again, not if she could help it.

She walked in circles, turning over everything that had happened in the last half hour. Was magic real? Did djinn really exist? And where had the demon gone?

She heard a thump come from Leila's room, next to hers. She must have gotten a ride back somehow. And then—

"It's the demon. The demon is still in me, I think." Leila stood at Bianca's doorframe, windswept and beautiful, her thick hair practically bursting out of her homemade scrunchie.

Bianca sat on her bed, completely frozen. When was the last time her sister had even opened her door? Still, she swallowed Leila's words. *The demon is still in me.* So, they'd come to the same conclusion. Maybe their twin telepathy wasn't as busted as she thought.

Bianca knew her sister was afraid, but in that moment, she really wished she didn't look so gorgeous. *Why am I surrounded by clueless, beautiful people?* Bianca thought bitterly.

Bianca grimly opened her laptop and pointed the screen at Leila. "I don't think it's a demon, Leila. I think it's a djinn."

"Djinn!" Leila yelped. She bent down to read the computer screen and gasped. "I . . . I didn't wear the ring. Or the necklace, so . . ."

"So that's why it screamed when it touched me, and

attacked you instead," Bianca finished for her. She scrolled down the page so Leila could read it. "According to this, there are different kinds. Ifrit made from fire, si'lat who can shape-shift, mareeds who are powerful and can grant wishes for a price. Plus dozens of others depending on whether you're from Indonesia or Iraq or Iran or . . ."

Leila whimpered. If they had been closer, Bianca would have put an arm around her. She felt terrible for Leila, yes, but also a tiny bit jealous. Finally, something interesting was happening! Something occult and mysterious and dangerous! But instead of happening to the goth sister with a penchant for the arcane, her sincere Wonder Bread of a twin had gotten first dibs!

Bianca patted Leila's thigh. "There, there," she said awkwardly.

"I can feel him, you know? I feel super strong, yeah, but also like my body temperature is higher. And he's in there, responding to me. Reacting to me . . ."

Leila sat on the other side of Bianca's bed, shoulders sagging. Despite her glow-up, she looked exhausted. Bianca couldn't remember when she'd seen her sister sit in her room before, not since they chopped their old bunk bed in half and moved to separate rooms in middle school.

"I'm sorry, Leila," Bianca said, trying to mean it.

"Thanks for . . . you know. Today." Leila played with a loose thread on her dress, not wanting to meet Bianca's eyes. Bianca wasn't sure what was more uncomfortable: almost being destroyed by an evil djinn or having a heart-to-heart with her twin sister.

Just then the front door opened. "Nenas!" a voice called out. "I brought takeout!"

Bianca's stomach rumbled.

Leila laughed. It was a small, husky laugh, but it broke the weird silence. "I guess fighting djinn makes you hungry."

Bianca smiled. "Come on." She stood up, offering a hand to Leila. She took it.

"Hola hola," Mamá greeted them. Baba clomped in after her, wearing a utility jumpsuit and carrying parts from the local auto store.

"I got Chinese," Mamá said, placing the bags on the dining room table.

Bianca's stomach rumbled again as the smells of steamed vegetables and jasmine rice wafted over. All the afternoon's excitement could wait. Right now, she was about to inhale some egg rolls.

She reached for a takeout container, but her mom stopped her.

"Now, before we eat dinner, there's something we need to talk about," her mother said, blocking Bianca's hand, her blue eyes narrowing. "Khosrow, I got a call from the school today. Bianca was sent to the principal's office. Again."

Bianca blinked. She had completely forgotten about her uneventful trip to the principal's office because of Señora Thompson today. All that Principal Wexler had done was chide her about respecting elders and given her a detention. After everything that had happened today, it felt like the least of her worries.

It was a miracle their mamá wasn't yelling in rapid-fire Spanish that only Bianca could understand, her hands flapping like crazy to emphasize every point. *I caught her on a good day*, Bianca realized.

"Mamá, Señora Thompson was giving me a hard time about my accent again. What was I supposed to do?"

Mamá's eyes narrowed at her daughter. Bianca could tell she was debating whether to punish her or congratulate her for upholding their heritage.

"Every day, I take classes where I already know the answers," Mamá said, sitting down. "Every day I have to listen to people who are less qualified than me tell me how to do my job. All because this country doesn't accept my degrees."

Bianca's heart hiccupped. Mamá rarely complained about work or her job. She just put her head down and got it done.

"And here you are, giving your teacher attitude, for the same reason. It doesn't matter if your Spanish is better or if she's being unfair. This is all a game, and you need to remember the rules."

Bianca slid further into her seat. She felt lower than low. Her mamá worked so, so hard. She hadn't even realized that the frustration she felt in Spanish class was how her mother felt all day, every day. Bianca now felt like an ungrateful brat.

"Lo siento, Mamá," she said quietly.

Just then, Baba cut in. "Alma, it's okay," he said, putting a hand on her shoulder. "Bianca just gets excited about languages. You know how she is. This is the last time, right, dokhtaram?" He gave Bianca a stern look.

"Baleh, Baba," Bianca said quickly, grateful for the backup.

He gave her an encouraging nod. Their dad was always the peacemaker. Mamá still didn't seem convinced, but she began shoveling lo mein onto Leila's plate, settling the matter.

Leila looked at Bianca and gave her a small smile. It was the smile of two people in on something together, of two sisters who had just gone through something huge and now had a chance to breathe. Bianca's heart lifted a tiny bit after being scolded.

She finally took a bite of her egg roll, the crackly paper skin giving way to seasoned cabbage and meat. She dipped it in spicy sauce and finished it in one more bite. Then came lo mein, steamed vegetables, and General Tso's chicken, the trifecta that her family always ordered.

The table was silent as everyone ate, with Bianca and her father shoveling food quickly into their mouths. Leila and their mother daintily picked at dinner.

Just then, Bianca's phone rang. *Who's calling me now?* She hit Accept on a call from June.

"What," Bianca asked, mouth full of noodles. Her mother shot her a glare.

"Bianca? You'll never believe this, but May said she just saw someone walk out of the old train station. And he was on *fire*."

Bianca's heart stuttered. She looked at Leila with wide eyes, and Leila froze, chopsticks halfway to her mouth.

"Een kieh?" Baba asked, reading the tense moment.

Bianca covered the receiver, thinking fast. "June . . . uh . . . Liam just broke up with her. Can I be excused? She's crying really hard."

Their mother's face softened. "Oh, poor girl. Yes, go see her. Does she want some Chinese food?"

"I'll be right there," Bianca said quickly into the phone before hanging up. "No, she already ate. Leila, can you come too? It sounds pretty bad." She gave Leila another meaningful look.

"Oh, um. Yeah, of course." Leila quickly finished her bite and gingerly wiped her mouth.

"Gracias, Mamá," Bianca said as she quickly cleared Leila's plate and her own. "We'll be back soon."

"I'll save you the leftovers!" their baba said. Bianca felt terrible for lying to them right after being taken to task about the principal's office, but June had sounded worried on the phone.

Bianca and Leila wordlessly slipped on their coats and shoes and headed out the door. It wasn't until they were turning off their driveway that Leila finally asked, "What's really going on?"

"I think June found another djinn," Bianca said grimly. "We'd better check it out."

Leila nodded, her jaw clenching. "Yeah, we'd better."

It took Bianca only ten minutes to get to the old rail yard where June was waiting for them. She stood outside the front gates in an old Ayers High basketball team jacket.

"Finally!" June huffed, her breath rising in cold puffs around her. "Oh. Uh, hey, Leila."

"Hi, June," Leila said, giving her a small wave.

"Show us," Bianca said dramatically. She felt like a detective on a police procedural, about to get a rundown from the officer on duty. It was pitch-black, the only light coming from Bianca's headlights, which she had left on.

"Here," June said, leading them to some old freight cars.

The rail yard was only for commercial use, since the newer, shinier Amtrak station had been built on the other side of town by the college. This one was a jumble of dead-end tracks and an old roundhouse that housed CSX cars and coal freight. It was completely ignored by the general population. May worked the line between Ayers and Bluefield, West Virginia, as an engineer. She made good money but was always on call for every possible disaster, rarely getting a day off.

"Where's May?" Bianca asked as they walked over the patchwork of railroad lines.

"Gone," June replied. "She was pulling out for Bluefield when she called me. I think she thought it was a prank or something, but she sounded worried."

Bianca grimaced. It wasn't a prank, that she knew for sure. June stopped at an orange caboose that looked completely rusted over. "Here's where she saw it."

Bianca braced herself, then took off her evil eye necklace. "Put this on," she told June. Leila, of course, wouldn't need a necklace. After all, a djinn was already inhabiting her, apparently. Leila shared a look with Bianca, as if she was thinking the same thing.

June started. "A necklace? Why?" She gripped the gold cross around her neck, the only jewelry she ever wore.

Bianca gave an exasperated sigh. "Just do it, okay? If you're not a necklace person, you can wear a ring instead."

June said nothing, just slowly put the necklace on. The evil eye looked strange against her wholesome, Americana, girl-next-door vibe. "Is this some Iranian superstition thing?"

She pronounced Iranian *eye-ranian*, despite Bianca's constant reminder that it was, in fact, *ee-ron*.

"Something like that," Leila replied cryptically.

June shrugged, then crossed herself for good measure.

Bianca's heart hammered for the second time that day, but this time, she felt prepared. An evil entity was attacking

Ayers. It might be a crummy town, but it was *hers*, dammit. All the anger and frustration from the afternoon came surging out of her. She grabbed a stick from the ground and hit the side of the caboose with a loud *CLANG!*

June and Leila jumped.

"What are you doing?" Leila demanded.

Bianca ignored her. "Hey!" Bianca shouted. "I know you're around here!" Her ring went warm, the way it had when she had been near the djinn in the field, though not as hot. *Interesting.* Whatever was out there was in the same family of djinn, if not the same exact Pokémon.

"Bianca, what the heck—" June began, but then she looked at her necklace, as if she could feel it heat up too.

"Beeya, shaytan!" Bianca shouted in Persian, which roughly translated to *Come on out, Satan!*

And then she heard it.

It was a crackly, rough sound, more like dry stones rubbing on each other than a human voice. June yelped, practically jumping into Bianca's arms. Leila gasped.

"You've got the necklace, okay?" Bianca whispered.

June just whimpered, clutching Bianca's shoulder. Leila assumed a fighting stance. *You don't even know how to fight!* Bianca wanted to yell at her.

Bianca cleared her throat instead. "What do you want, djinn?" she called out into the darkness. "State your business here!"

In that moment, a lumpy, misshapen thing the color of

an oil slick crawled out from behind the rusted caboose. June screamed, the sound echoing off the freight trains. Despite her terror, a small part of Bianca's heart soared. *Monsters are real. Magic is around us.* And then, *I knew it!*

She clenched her jaw and held her ground in front of the creature. She was horrified by the grotesque, oozing, sluglike thing heading toward them, but also a bit smug: her hunch was right. Ayers didn't have a demon problem; it had a very specific djinn infestation, and this one looked like one of the drawings she'd seen online.

"Bianca," Leila said, eyes wide. "It's not like the other one."

"There's another one?" June asked.

The thing stopped mere yards away from them, and Bianca could see its eyes glimmer back at her, more oily than fiery. Her ring smoldered now, though not as badly as before. As if sensing it, the thing kept away.

"Chee meekhai?" Bianca demanded, trying to ignore the feel of June's nails clawing into her arm, June's body trembling beside her. *What do you want?* She used the informal tense and wielded it like a weapon, her language skills coming in handy.

"Ghoosht," the thing said simply, its body quivering with anticipation.

"What?" June whispered, her quiet voice echoing across the thick, forbidding darkness.

"Flesh," Bianca repeated. The lump flickered with flame,

as if chomping at the bit, so close to its one desire. It oozed forward, but Bianca held up the hand with her ring, and it froze in place.

"Whoa," June breathed.

"Bianca . . . ," Leila said in a warning voice. "Be careful."

Bianca quirked a lip, trying hard not to smile in what was, undoubtedly, a very cool and witchy moment. "Why here? Why *our* flesh?" she added in English, hoping to finally get to the bottom of this.

"We were promisssssssed," the thing answered, inching closer, as if sensing Bianca's inexperience with this kind of interrogation.

"Stay back!" Bianca yelped. They stumbled away from the menacing lump. She wondered if they should run. But still, she needed answers.

"Bianca . . . ," June whimpered, threatening to bolt.

"*Who* promised?" Bianca demanded. "Who said you could take our flesh?"

The thing sniffed, the center of its face pulsing as if it had a nose instead of smooth, wet skin. "Your ancestor. It promissssed us."

"That's what the other one said . . . ," Leila whispered next to Bianca.

That didn't make any sense. How could a relative specifically promise Bianca and Leila to a djinn? All her family was back in Iran. She'd never met them before, and never would, all because of the country's strict policies. But she had picked the wrong moment to let her mind wander, and that was when the thing lunged.

June screamed. Its bloblike shape was suddenly aflame. It doubled in size, trying to consume them whole like a parachute that had just launched. Bianca punched it with her ring hand, and the second its grease-fiery flesh touched Bianca's, it was like water turning to steam.

The thing shrieked and writhed, its body losing substance. She opened her eyes, not realizing she'd closed them, only to see a thick, oily pool fall around the three of them like a halo. It was gone, the ground around them smoking in the cold.

She remembered to breathe.

June swayed on her feet, about to collapse. Bianca grabbed her arm just in time. Leila grabbed her other shoulder.

"Come on, Junie. Let's go sit in the truck," Bianca said soothingly, but her voice trembled.

Bianca's hands were shaking, though she felt better than she had after that first attack with a creature five times the size of this strange, misshapen thing. She ruefully noted the improvement.

June let herself be led, still in shock. Leila tucked her into the passenger seat and made her take a sip from her water bottle. Bianca pulled out her phone, itching to confirm what kind of creature she'd just fought.

Leila sat in the back and closed the door. June jumped at the sound. "Wh-what was that?" June finally asked.

"A ghul," Bianca said, reading from her phone screen. "It's

more of a Persian demon than a djinn, though. They haunt graveyards, apparently."

"Ghul," Leila repeated, rolling the word over her tongue. It sounded a bit like *ghoul*.

"Jesus, Mary, and Joseph," June said, crossing herself again. "This is where all those miners died, right before the mine closed. The ones that people say still haunt this place."

Bianca shivered.

This wasn't just a graveyard. It was a mass grave.

She reversed out of the haunted rail yard, eager to get the hell out of there.

The second the trains were in her rearview mirror, Bianca finally let herself exhale all the way. *This is not the Ayers I know*, she thought. This one was mysterious and dangerous and, she had to admit, much more interesting. It was only eight o'clock, but the road felt abandoned, the towering oaks and pines forming a dark tunnel back to June's.

Headlights soon lit up the truck's cab.

"Huh," Bianca said. Nobody used this road unless they were coming or going from the rail yard. The headlights on this car looked new, some electric vehicle with slick LED lights.

"What?" Leila asked, sitting up. Unlike Bianca, she hadn't relaxed yet. Meanwhile, June looked like a coiled spring, ready to jump at the slightest disturbance.

"Nothing," Bianca said, not wanting to worry anyone. But still, who would be driving this road in a fancy car at night? She looked closer in the rearview. It looked like a white BMW.

Hmmm, Bianca thought to herself. *This night keeps getting curiouser and curiouser.*

She turned onto the next road that would take her to June's neighborhood, and the white car continued on.

LEILA

They dropped June off outside her house, assuring her that they'd help her get her car back tomorrow. She had been trembling too much to get behind a wheel.

"I'm gonna have so many nightmares," June sighed.

"Keep that necklace on," Bianca reminded her. "I'll meet you early at school tomorrow, okay?"

June nodded and trudged up the stairs to her small home, which looked more like a cottage than the Tudors and Craftsman houses of Ayers. Leila moved up front. She had enjoyed spending time with June and was surprised by how easygoing a best friend of Bianca's could be. If Bianca was all mood swings and dramatic outbursts, June was the balancing force that kept the two of them level. Except, of course, when it came to supernatural djinn.

"So," Bianca said once they were back on the road. "Today has been . . . interesting."

Leila gave a harsh laugh, then stopped. She *never* gave harsh laughs. She felt gross, the skin of the djinn somehow still sticking to her. Was he watching her now, at this moment? Could he see and feel everything Leila did? That cackling sound must have come from whatever effects he had on her.

"Does it hurt?" Bianca asked. "Having the djinn . . . you know."

Leila chugged more water. Her mouth had felt dry all afternoon, her skin itchy and tight. "It doesn't *hurt*," she began. "I just feel wrong. Like I'm not myself. There aren't enough showers to get this weird feeling off me." She strained to hear that voice inside her head, that caustic, snide commentary she'd heard when she'd driven Foster home. Nothing.

She sighed, sinking into the passenger seat. "I don't feel anything now. But, Bianca, we gotta get this thing out of me. I feel disgusting."

Bianca nodded, her eyes still on the road. "I'll do some more research, okay?"

Leila's eyes fluttered. She was so, so tired. This single day had felt like a week. She struggled to stay awake the whole car ride, and Bianca went uncharacteristically quiet to let her rest.

Half an hour later Leila tossed and turned in bed, trying to get comfortable despite that unwashed, unclean feeling that coated her like a layer of grime.

There, on her nightstand, was the iron ring she'd gotten for her birthday from her parents. Had it really been yesterday? She leaned over, about to put it on, when suddenly it flashed bright red.

"Gah!" Leila cried, yanking her hand away. It throbbed painfully, as if she'd touched a hot poker, even though she couldn't see a visible mark.

She collapsed back in bed, clutching her hand. What did this mean? Was she a djinn who couldn't touch iron now, either? And why had her father given them iron rings in the first place?

Leila screwed her eyes shut, willing herself to go to sleep so she could deal with all this in the morning.

Needless to say, this was not how Leila had wanted her senior year to go.

The next day, Foster picked her up at the same time, whistling as if nothing unusual had happened the night before. Bianca had already left to meet June, and Leila wished she'd woken up earlier to check in with her sister this morning.

"Are you all right?" Leila asked Foster as she buckled in her seatbelt.

"I'm great, babe," Foster said, grinning at her. "Kind of embarrassed I passed out, though."

"It's fine," she said soothingly. "You probably didn't eat enough yesterday."

Foster nodded. "Yeah, I really need to up my protein."

She was lucky that Foster didn't remember anything. He wasn't even crafty enough to pretend he didn't remember just in case he was testing Leila for whatever reason. For better or worse, Foster Hutchins wore his brain on his sleeve, and Leila wasn't sure if she liked or disliked that about him.

They rode in silence the rest of the way to school. Leila noticed a white BMW sedan behind them, and she wondered who in Ayers had the kind of money to buy something impractical that would get dirty so quickly. When they pulled into the school parking lot, the car didn't follow, probably headed somewhere more exciting with fewer potholes.

The mundane routine of copying notes from the board, grabbing books from her locker, and trading hi's and hellos with her friends was enough to make yesterday feel like a dream. Here, in the harsh fluorescents of the senior hallway, was real life. Had she really gone to a mountain with a city in it yesterday? Had a djinn really wormed its way into her subconscious? She thought of the ghul in the pitch-black night, so eerie and strange. How could it have been real?

Without checking in with Bianca, it all felt so far away from her. She was tempted to write the whole thing off, like so many other parts of her life. She zoned out in class, struggling to bridge the magical world she'd witnessed and the normal one she currently occupied.

Leila diligently got out her notebook for science class, ignoring Shivani's pointed looks from the other side of the classroom aisle. Finally, when Mr. Gordon turned back to the board, Leila looked up.

"You still haven't told me if you're going to the

end-of-semester party tomorrow night," Shivani whispered urgently. "Spencer's brother got a mini keg. It'll be awesome."

Leila almost laughed in her face. A party? The second she got home she was going to brainstorm with Bianca about how to de-djinn her body. But there was no way Shivani would understand that.

"Maybe," was all Leila whispered back. She didn't drink, and she wasn't a big fan of being around drunk people. Besides, she'd probably have to help her dad pick out a Christmas tree for their mom. Even though Dad wasn't Christian, she could tell he secretly loved trimming the tree every year.

The bell rang. Shivani shot her a curious look.

What? Leila mouthed.

"Why are you being so weird?" Shivani demanded, waving a mechanical pencil threateningly.

My period, Leila mouthed desperately, hoping the lie would convince her.

"Bullshit," Shivani shot back.

Damn. "I'm just tired," she whispered. "I'll try to make it, though."

Shivani gave her a look as if to say *This isn't over!* She turned back to her notebook and Leila breathed a sigh of relief. Then she looked past Shivani's face out the windows that overlooked the school parking lot.

There, idling by the front entrance, was the same white BMW.

BIANCA

Bianca drove early to school to catch up with June, who she had a feeling would need a bit of emotional support after their harrowing night.

They sat on the bleachers of the swimming complex, watching the boys' team's last practice of the year while June took notes on the odds she'd be offering for the New Year's meet. Her hand trembled, making her usually neat cursive extra wiggly.

"How are you feeling? Did you tell May what you saw?" Bianca asked, sidling up next to her.

June looked up from her sportsbook. "What, and have her exorcise me? No, thank you. I just told her it was probably a senior prank and she bought it." June made another note. Rex Thornton's butterfly stroke was clearly the strongest on the team, and she marked his time. It was the last day of school before winter break, making this June's final chance to make some quick pre-Christmas cash.

"Hey, what are you girls doing over there? This is a closed

practice!" An assistant coach approached them, his whistle flapping against his crossed arms.

June froze. Liam usually helped her with boys' swim, being on the team and all, but he had a doctor's appointment that morning.

Bianca put on her best smile. "You're kidding, right? You know why we're here. These are the hottest guys at school."

The coach's face blushed bright red, but not brighter than June's. He wasn't much older than them. Bianca thought he looked familiar—probably a high school alumnus working a second job while going to Ayers College. She wondered if he was one of her mom's students now.

"I . . . well . . . ," he said, clearly thrown off.

"So hot," June repeated in a strangled voice, trying to sell it. Instead, she just looked constipated.

"We'll leave in five, okay? Just want to brainstorm more promposals together. Get a jump start." Bianca gave him her most innocent smile, at odds with her black lipstick and combat boots.

"June formal comes up fast," June added. Today's outfit was an Ayers cheerleading hoodie, and she pulled on the strings anxiously.

"Right . . . Well." And that was all the assistant coach said before awkwardly shuffling away.

"If you had a coat of arms, that's what it would say in Latin. *June comes up fast*. Winter is coming, et cetera," Bianca cackled.

June elbowed her. "Shut up."

"We gotta figure out how many of these creatures are here, though. The whole town could be swarming with them. It's not just djinn. It's all kinds of demons."

June closed her notebook, shaking her head. "Why do you care what happens here? I thought you were applying to every out-of-state school possible."

Bianca opened her mouth, then shut it, unable to come up with a good answer. Why *did* she care? It was no skin off her back if this town got infested with djinn. This was the place that had rejected her father's small business application to start his own garage. The college where her mom's degrees from Argentina were considered incomplete and she was made to retake classes here. This town could rot, for all she cared. So why did Bianca still feel a pull to rid it of monsters?

"Because someone has to."

And then she stomped off to the hallway, hating her answer.

As if the week couldn't get any more complicated, there was someone waiting at her locker. Winter break could not come soon enough.

"Bianca Mazanderani!" the boy cried, pointing an accusing finger at her, his nails painted dark blue.

"Oh my god," Bianca exhaled. "Not now, Steve, please not now."

"'Tis I, Steven Rosenberg!" He wore a cape, an honest-to-God cape, and used this moment to dramatically swish it behind himself. "Together, you and I can rule the underworld!"

June held in a laugh that turned into a snort.

"Listen, Steve, I'm late for . . . something I'm making up right now," Bianca said, irritated. She had a throbbing headache from smelling his cologne. And the fact that her town seemed to be plagued with supernatural beings.

"Just one yes, and we can make this town bow at our feet!" Steve punched his fist up into the air, like a singer reaching a high note.

From across the hall, Bianca could see some girls from the drama club titter at Steve's performance. *His little fan club*, she thought bitterly. It didn't work on her, though.

"When will you realize you want to go out with me?" Steve demanded, tossing his hair out of his eye, where it promptly returned. A junior by the water fountain swooned. It was annoying, having someone else at school cop her style. Bianca wore dark colors in a cool, goth, anime-obsessed kind of way. Steve wore them because he thought they made him the prince of darkness or something. His outfits felt like an act, while Bianca's were more like armor.

Steve's long shaggy hair and six-foot frame did well in the theater wing, with straight girls practically throwing themselves at any hetero male classmates. But his bright hazel eyes weren't enough to work on Bianca.

"I know an incredible sushi restaurant where they fly in the fish every day," Steve offered, as if this was the height of sex appeal.

"Tempting," Bianca replied flatly. Unfortunately, it *was* tempting, as Bianca loved sushi. Still, it wasn't enough to entice her to date Steve Rosenberg. "Maybe when hell freezes over."

"Jews don't believe in hell." Steve waggled his eyebrows seductively.

Bianca walked up to him, putting a finger on his chest coquettishly. He grinned, thinking he'd won her over. "You're blocking my locker," she said, then turned her finger into a flat palm, gently pushing him away from her personal space.

June, ever polite, jumped in. "Steve, maybe you should give it a rest. You know, let her come to you."

"Excellent idea, June!" Then Steve made a *rawr* noise, scratching the air like a sexy, gangly cat. "Let the woman make the first move."

Bianca made a vomiting motion.

"I'll catch you in the VIP section of the underworld, Mazanderani." He popped his sunglasses on, making a *call me* hand motion as he sauntered past. His gaggle of fans followed.

Bianca watched him go, not believing what she was seeing, but alas, it was real: Steve's sneakers lit up as he walked away.

"Well," June began, but Bianca cut her off.

"No."

"But I was just going to say—"

"Nope."

"Bianca—"

"Don't you have to get volleyball scores from Liam? That's what they're calling it now, right? *Volleyball scores*?" Bianca said sweetly.

It was June's turn to blush now. "He's out sick, remember? And he just helps me with the boys' teams, anyway," she mumbled.

"In the janitor's closet?" Bianca asked, raising an eyebrow.

"Gotta go, bye," June said quicky.

"Bye, Junie!" Bianca smiled, waving at her friend.

June shook her head. "See you at lunch, you monster."

"I'll take that as a compliment," Bianca said primly, closing her locker. "Besides," she muttered to herself, "everyone knows goths secretly love jocks, not drama nerds."

Instead of pretending to do schoolwork while secretly reading webcomics, like Bianca always did during her free period, she researched more of the strange demons that seemed to be plaguing her town. So far she knew about ifrits, mareeds, and ghuls, like the one she'd seen in the rail yard last night. But what about ones that had the power to possess her sister? What were those called?

In Indonesia there were shamans you could call if you suspected a djinn had overtaken a loved one. In Iran the previous administration charged a political group with consorting with djinn. There was so much noise and news that it was difficult to find actual classifications of djinn online.

Finally, she stumbled across a Quranic site that gave her more details. Along with mareeds, there were palis, disgusting djinn who sucked your toes and drank your blood from the feet up if you didn't cover your legs at night. Sleep paralysis djinn who gave you nightmares that turned your body into deadweight. Half-dog, half-human djinn called heen. There was even a guy who swore a djinn bit the inside of his lip one night and gave him a cold sore, stating there were even cold sore djinn. It was dizzying, the number of monsters there were, and even more disturbing how many real-life accounts were posted alongside each one. Ghuls weren't even classified as djinn, apparently. They were just bottom-feeders who walked in the same circles.

Bianca grimly took notes.

"And what do we have here, Miss Mazanderani?" Her free-period teacher, Mr. Ellertson, was peering over her shoulder. It bugged her how he still couldn't pronounce her last name right. Didn't Americans know that all Middle Eastern names were phonetic? It drove her crazy, having folks butcher her heritage.

Bianca gave him a bored look, the classic look of a teen underwhelmed by the accomplished adult in front of them. "The Quran," she said flatly. "Is that a problem?"

He gave her a cold look. "Focus on your studies, please."

It's the day before winter break! Bianca wanted to scream. *Who's actually working?* But instead she just said, "Yep. Will do."

Mr. Ellertson stalked off, and Bianca exhaled. If this was how people in this town reacted to mere pictures of djinn, how would they react to the real thing?

She hoped she wouldn't find out.

As soon as the bell rang, it felt like the last day of school in summer. Kids threw papers in the air, classmates whooped and cheered. Someone even shouted, "Go, Christmas!" and Bianca rolled her eyes so hard they almost got stuck there. People in Ayers didn't even pretend to admit that this break was for any other religion but their own. She wondered how Steve felt about it all.

She'd procrastinated all month, and now it was finally time to get everyone's Christmas gifts. Usually she just got Leila a gift card, but now she looked forward to buying her something more personalized. That was the nice thing about having a birthday right before Christmas: you could use all your birthday money for presents.

She slowly reversed out of her parking spot, noting how for a bunch of people who were so eager to leave school, her classmates dawdled around their cars, chatting with friends as if they were reluctant to leave. Bianca wouldn't be back for at least two weeks.

Good riddance.

She headed to downtown Ayers, knowing that Main Street would be having a bunch of Christmas sales. Parking under garlands of twinkle lights, she tried not to enjoy the sounds of Christmas music blasting from outdoor speakers. Alas, she couldn't help it. Ayers at Christmastime was hard to hate. Garlands of evergreen wrapped every light pole, candy cane decorations hung from the small brick buildings lining either side of Main Street, and vendors had hot chocolate stations and free samples outside every store to lure shoppers. The splash pad that usually had fountains for kids to play in over the summer had been converted into a small ice rink, and it all felt straight out of a postcard.

Bianca tried not to smile.

First up was the home goods store. Skillet Skillet was a staple in Ayers, with vintage cast iron pans, homemade spice blends, and just about every kitchen contraption you could ask for. Bianca opened the door, chiming the bell above.

"Bianca!" Mrs. Laughlin called out from the front register. "How are you? I saw your dad the other day." She wore a hand-knitted sweater and had cute purple charms attached to her glasses chain. Bianca wasn't surprised to hear her dad had been in recently; he was obsessed with this place.

"Hi, Mrs. Laughlin," Bianca said, perking up. Mrs.

Laughlin was always nice to her. "I'm trying to find him something for Christmas."

Mrs. Laughlin lit up. "He did mention he wanted a mandoline last time he was in here! Do you think that would make a good gift?"

"A mandolin?" Bianca asked. "Like, the instrument?"

"Here," Mrs. Laughlin said, gesturing her over to a table packed with ceramic eggcup holders, kitchen timers, tea towels, and other small knickknacks. She gestured to a box with the word *mandoline* on it, showing a picture of something that almost looked like a flat cheese grater, except instead of many holes it just had one in the center. "It can chop vegetables real thin. But you have to be careful; they're sharp!"

Persian food was notorious for the amount of dicing and chopping it required. She could definitely see her dad using this in the kitchen. "This is perfect," Bianca said, her heart cheering at the thought of her baba's face when she gave it to him. "Let's get it!"

Mrs. Laughlin beamed. "Great choice!" She bustled back to the register, and Bianca paid with some of her birthday cash. Mrs. Laughlin wrapped it up with eggbeater-and-whisk wrapping paper, and a curl of blue and yellow ribbon on top. "Go Apps!" she said, referring to the Ayers Appalachians, as she handed over the package. The blue and yellow colors were theirs, and Mrs. Laughlin was one of the college's biggest football fans.

"Go Apps," Bianca replied, smiling. Only Mrs. Laughlin could make her care about football.

"You let me know how he likes it, okay, hon? Tell your folks I say hi," Mrs. Laughlin added.

"Will do. Thanks, Mrs. Laughlin!" Bianca headed out of the cozy shop back into the brisk cold. Satisfied with her dad's gift, she made a beeline to Ayers Apothecary, where her mom liked to stock up on handmade soaps and beauty products. There, Mr. Farley helped her pick out some hand cream made from locally sourced goat's milk and shampoo bars with rosemary. He even threw in samples of their new hair oils, claiming they'd be good for Mamá's thin hair. Bianca clutched her purchases, feeling warm and fuzzy from all the store owners' thoughtfulness.

She stopped for a free cup of cocoa outside the Ayers Chamber of Commerce, loading the paper cup with marshmallows. She hated to admit it, but not *all* parts of Ayers were bad. It was days like today that made her wonder if she really hated the small town as much as she claimed.

Her last stop was the craft store for Leila. She would have tried to get June a gift too, but June always insisted on no presents and Bianca didn't want to make her uncomfortable. Instead, she turned in to Polite Sewciety and sipped her cocoa as she tried to parse through all the crafting materials.

On one side were bolts of fabric, and on the other hung homemade vintage quilts. Bianca didn't understand the appeal. Why spend hours and hours on a blanket? But still, she gamely tried looking through all the shelves on her own before giving up and asking an employee for help.

"Oh, hi, Leila!" an employee with a name tag that read JESSICA said. "Did you come back for that pattern?"

Bianca tried not to laugh. Rarely did people confuse her for her twin. It was almost nice. "I'm actually Leila's sister. What pattern was it? I'm trying to buy her gift."

"Oh!" Jessica startled. "Sorry, I . . ." And then she looked over Bianca's outfit: her black boots, her black trench, the black nail polish at the tips of the fingers clutching the cocoa cup. "I didn't know she had a sister," Jessica finally said.

"Don't worry, people confuse us all the time," Bianca lied. She was in too good of a mood to mess with this poor clerk.

Jessica gave her a relieved smile. "Here, she was looking at this zero-waste pattern the other day, but she said she didn't know which fabric to use. I could recommend some to you with the pattern?"

"Thank you," Bianca exhaled. "That would be great." Being in this store felt like trying to speak in a language she didn't understand. What were notions? Binding? Circular needles? She had no idea. She was glad Jessica had come to her rescue.

In fact, almost every shop owner had helped her with her purchases today. Their family had become fixtures in this town, making their own small mark. She resented the warm, glowy feeling it left in her chest. *Stop being so cute, town!*

She left the store clutching a fabric pattern for a pinafore dress and a couple of yards of pale blue gingham, just the kind of fabric Leila would wear.

She drove home humming along to "Jingle Bell Rock." After all, it was pretty catchy.

LEILA

The whole day, Leila's body buzzed. She felt different not just on the outside but on the inside too. She stirred with heat, and she could sense, rather than see, iron in the lockers and old foundations of the school, built in the 1910s after the first coal seam had been discovered in Ayers.

"What's your skincare regimen?" Shivani had demanded at lunch, interrupting Leila's racing thoughts.

"What?" Leila asked.

"Your skincare," Shivani repeated, almost angry. "You look like you bathed in retinol. I must know your secrets."

Was it that noticeable? She'd worn her hair down to try to detract from her glowing skin, along with glasses to hide the golden hue there was no way her prescription contacts could conceal. She looked even more owlish with her circular, wire-rimmed frames, but desperate times called for desperate fashion choices.

"Oh. Um," Leila began, struggling to think of something. "I did one of those face masks last night. The sheet kind."

"Which brand? Innisfree? Face Shop? Cosrx?" Shivani demanded.

"Uhhh, the last one," Leila replied, scrambling.

Shivani just gave an all-knowing nod. "The snail mucus one, right? I can tell. It completely brightened up your face."

"Yup." Leila nodded, buying into her lie. "The snail mask."

Shivani tapped out a few strokes on her phone, lightning fast. "'Kay, I'll start with ten and we can take it from there."

Leila blinked. Sometimes she forgot how wealthy Shivani was. Buying ten sheet masks at the drop of a hat was like spending Monopoly money to her.

Despite being one of the wealthiest girls at school, Shivani had always been nice to Leila. It wasn't hard to be well-liked when she threw the best parties, drove the nicest car, and was generous with her wealth. She was loyal to a fault, and even tougher to B.S. Leila was grateful her dramatic change in appearance could be chalked up to expert skincare, as far as Shivani was concerned.

A part of her wished she could tell Shivani everything that was happening, the way Bianca could confide in June. But it already felt like there was so much Leila hid from her best friend that she miserably added supernatural djinn to the pile.

Shivani turned back to their lunchtime crowd, where the group was strategizing about the big party tomorrow. "I'll bring the liquor," Shivani said definitively.

"And maybe we can find a nice quiet spot for Leila and

Foster," Shepherd added in a teasing voice, his varsity lacrosse shirt already stained with pizza grease.

The whole table burst into a chorus of "Ooooo," and Leila's face burned crimson. Foster just laughed and gripped Leila's arm tighter.

"Yes, please!" he chimed in.

That settled it. There was no way Leila was going.

The second Leila got home after school, she collapsed into bed. Foster hadn't even tried to pull anything on her during their drive home, saying he felt "super tired for some reason" and wanted to go home and sleep after dropping her off. Leila was relieved. She liked kissing him once she was doing it, but now, after lying to him about why he'd fainted, she felt guilty.

She knew she liked men, liked the undeniable attraction of *boy*. There were days when Foster's smell of soap and musk wasn't just attractive—the pheromones felt deeply real. Sometimes, in the back of his car, she could practically feel her pupils dilate with desire. But her heart didn't flutter around Foster the way women's did in the romance books she read. Was something wrong with her? Or was Foster just not the one?

She woke up from her nap with a start. She must have drifted off to sleep. Groggy, she shuffled to the bathroom, catching her reflection in the full-length mirror next to her sewing table. She froze.

There, in her eyes, was a flicker of flame.

And then that same voice spoke up. The one she had confused for her snarky inner monologue.

Together, we could be so much more.

The flicker morphed into a steady beam, filling her brown irises like a rising tide.

Leila wanted to scream. She wanted to gag. There was no tiptoeing around it: the djinn was possessing her, using her body like some sick puppet.

"What do you want?" Leila finally asked, looking in the mirror. The red in her eyes vibrated, as if he was thinking. Just admitting he was there was painful, but she had to know.

"*More,*" the djinn said simply. Only, it was Leila who uttered the words, the djinn controlling her from within. She gasped, covering her mouth. It felt like when she threw up, her body giving into the heaves. Having that *thing* speak from her throat was nails-on-a-chalkboard unbearable.

"*We want more,*" it repeated, and Leila's eyes watered in pain, her throat raw and singed.

Just then, someone knocked on her door. "What?" she snapped, then quickly covered her mouth again. She *never* snapped like that, couldn't remember the last time she'd raised her voice. Tears started to fall down her cheeks. *What is happening to me?*

"I just . . . I just wanted to see if you were okay," Bianca said through the door.

"I think . . . I think I need help," Leila finally replied in a strangled voice.

Her door flew open. "What is it?" Bianca stood at Leila's doorway, clutching a handful of shopping bags. Leila tried not to zero in on the Polite Sewciety one, with a gorgeous printed fabric sticking out of the top. *Did she get that for me?* she wondered.

Before she could tell Bianca what was wrong, her sister gasped. "I saw it! Your eyes were red!"

Leila felt the presence that was the djinn grow smaller within her, felt the unpleasant buzz of his consciousness recede. "He was here. He was speaking through me," Leila said miserably.

Bianca grimaced and held up her iron ring.

"Gah!" Leila cried. It felt terrible and cold, like dunking her face under ice water. She couldn't breathe, couldn't see—

"Whoa, whoa, I'm sorry!" Bianca cried, shoving her hand into her pocket. "I thought it would hurt him, not you."

Leila felt faint and woozy, her heartbeat sluggish, her eyes threatening to close.

"Okay, time for bed," Bianca said firmly. She led Leila to her beloved quilt, and Leila tried not to look pathetically grateful as her sister tucked her under the covers. It was the most affectionate she'd ever seen Bianca, but she was too exhausted to even say thanks.

"Here's some ice water," Bianca said, placing her own

water bottle on Leila's nightstand. "And I'm gonna plug in your phone. Text me if you need snacks or more water, okay?"

Leila gave a weak nod. She could already feel herself drifting off to sleep. She was so tired, so tired . . .

"Want me to stay?" Bianca asked.

Leila shook her head—she was already dozing. Bianca gave Leila a smile, then closed the door. Leila felt cozy and warm, and she liked how Bianca had swaddled her into her quilt. Then, like a cold iron around her neck, the dreaded feeling of not being in control of her own body was back.

"Come, let me show you. You were destined for so much more." The voice slithered out of her. She gagged.

"Nooo," Leila moaned, thrashing in bed. "Please, please leave me alone." She could barely scream, could barely speak, she was so exhausted. "Bianca," she whispered. "Bianca . . ."

She groaned as her body started to catch fire, her arms dancing with a light that moved up to her chest. Despite the red-hot flames, they didn't hurt, and they didn't seem to burn her blanket or clothes in the process. There was no smoke, and by the time the flames reached her head, Leila was so far past screaming that all she could do was watch as her body winked out of her bedroom like a burnt match.

She reappeared in a cave that looked vaguely familiar, only instead of hosting a crummy high school party, it seemed sinister and murky. A light came from deeper within, where flickering bodies of flame vibrated with voices.

She wasn't alone.

"Closer," the djinn spoke through her. That feeling of something speaking through her would never be less disgusting, but at least she didn't retch now. At the sound of her voice, the noises stopped.

"Who goesss?" a small voice called.

Leila couldn't tell who said it—she was having trouble seeing past all the random flames that seemed to float on invisible candlesticks.

"It is I," Leila spoke, shuddering. *I just want to go home,* she wanted to scream. *I just want to go to bed!*

The voices inhaled sharply. That's when Leila realized: the voices *were* the flames. A blue flame in the corner of the cave twitched and writhed; a darker-looking flame oozed shiny, oily tongues. There were small fires like the green of kerosene, the orange of birthday candles, and the deep red of embers. Suddenly, they stilled.

One by one, they began to transform.

The glistening flame turned into an oily black puddle no higher than Leila's knee. The red flame turned into a man so tall his head bent unnaturally against the cave ceiling, the slash of his mouth too wide to be normal.

Other strange shapes popped up: a small man who wouldn't stop licking his fingers, an unsmiling woman with green skin, and, lastly, a flame that morphed into an exact replica of Leila herself. She stepped back, repulsed. It wore a thin band around its neck. *Iron!* Leila realized. *But why would a djinn wear iron?* How *could a djinn even* wear *iron?*

The shape-shifting woman who had cloned Leila reached out to touch her. Leila screamed.

"Enough!" the thing inside Leila called out, rubbing Leila's voice raw. Leila's clone morphed into something else, a figure whose features were hard to pin down. It was a djinn made of flickering flames, its face spinning like a roulette wheel of different masks. She remembered Bianca's research: a si'lat!

And then, horror of horrors, the thing inside Leila began to slither out.

It felt like someone pulling a warm blanket out of her throat, a heating pad in the shape of spaghetti. She tried not to shudder again as the thing inside her finally released its hold.

It was the handsome boy from her trip to the mountain in the desert.

He wore that same royal uniform, complete with a fur-lined cape and jeweled rings. He grinned wickedly at her, his charming face disgusting Leila even more.

"See?" he simpered. "I'm not so bad."

He bowed to her, though it didn't seem in mockery this time. Leila, for all her surprise, was so relieved to have her body back she simply nodded. Her energy came flooding back, the exhaustion evaporating.

She felt scandalized, knowing this teen had been

possessing her without her consent. She had expected a thousand-year-old monster, not a peer.

But I'm me again, she thought to herself. Then: *I would do anything to stay this way*.

"Cyrus!" the other gruesome beings cried. They bowed low, as if synchronized.

Were these things from the desert with the mountain? Was Cyrus their ruler? It felt absurd, wondering about the hierarchy of these devils. But there was clearly some kind of order here.

Royalty, Leila thought ruefully. *These djinn have royalty*.

"Is thissss her?" the oily ghul asked, shimmering with excitement. Leila recoiled at the smell it gave off—putrescence and gasoline.

"There are two!" Cyrus replied gleefully. "She has a twin!"

At this, all the monsters in the cave grew excited. Leila's stomach churned to be spoken of like she wasn't there. *This can't be real. This is just a nightmare. Just a bad dream.*

"He didn't realize he had bargained away both," Cyrus continued. "We will have the sister soon, though she may be more difficult."

At the mention of Bianca, Leila jolted. She could no longer remain silent and cowed in the corner of this waking nightmare. It was one thing for Leila to feel helpless, but to let them plot against Bianca? Absolutely not.

"Enough!" she shouted. Well, she said it strongly. Leila really was not much of a shouter, and her voice trembled. It echoed through the cave, almost taunting her for speaking up.

The monsters froze.

"What is going on?" Leila demanded. "Who bargained us away? What about my sister?" She was breathing hard now, and she hoped the conviction in her voice hid how scared she felt.

"You don't know?" The thing that had tried to take her face cackled. "You're the bridge!"

"The bridge, the bridge!" the other djinn cried.

"All it takes is one," the tall man said, his gashed mouth moving excitedly.

"One promissse," another voice added.

"It's better if you go willingly," Cyrus said, as if confiding in Leila. "Then you can be crowned. Otherwise . . ." He gave her an exaggerated grimace, making a slashing motion across his throat. *Dead.*

"Those are my choices? Go with you to that place or die?"

Cyrus laughed. "Oh, you won't die. You'll live for a very, very long time. Just not as you anymore. And no longer human. We'll take the town too. We can finally expand!"

At this the other monsters in the cave grew excited.

"Fresh soulsss," they crooned.

"Souls of innocentsss!"

"The bessst kind."

The chorus grew overwhelming in Leila's ears. "But why? What's a bridge? I don't understand!"

"A bridge," the ghul sighed contentedly. "Someone from your world must give us permission. The more people we possess, the stronger we grow."

"These are the bodies of the people we took lassst," the very tall man said, his flesh hanging unnaturally off his bones like a coat that was too big for him. It was rotting and patched in places, with fire peeking through.

Leila flinched, putting the pieces together. These djinn were just wearing the bodies of humans they'd made deals with before. Its unnatural smile looked even more disturbing as Leila realized it was one that belonged to someone else. She'd be turned into a living flesh puppet, just like these poor people.

"But I didn't agree to anything," Leila said simply.

"You were promised to us before you were born," Cyrus said, patting her on the shoulder. "All we need is one person who was born here to take over. Two people would be even better. You'll be taken care of, of course. You'd get to rule this side of the bridge." He made it all sound so reasonable, as if they were deciding what to have for dinner and not the fate of the town.

Leila wrenched his hand off her shoulder. "Never!"

Cyrus's cackling stopped mid-laugh. His good-natured smile turned menacing. "I don't think you understand, khosh-keleh," he said, his voice low and threatening. "Your soul has already been bargained."

Leila flinched at the way Cyrus used her father's pet name against her.

"My soul is *mine*," Leila growled through gritted teeth. Even though Cyrus wasn't currently possessing her, she could still feel her skin heat up, could still feel that bubbling tidal wave of anger threaten to course through her. Did this mean she had powers even when he wasn't possessing her?

"Do you really think your body is yours?" Cyrus tilted his head, giving her a pitying look. Then he grabbed Leila's shoulder, and she watched in horror as his hand melted into her body.

"Nooo," she moaned. It was worse than tinfoil on a filling, worse than nails on a chalkboard. It felt like every nerve in her body had been exposed and was being scrubbed with steel wool.

All around her the djinn were cheering, hissing, and chanting. "Cyrus! Cyrus! Cyrus!"

Slowly, painfully slowly, he melted back into her skin, and Leila had to stop herself from shrieking out in pain.

"*Fighting me is useless,*" her voice said out loud, without her permission.

In that moment, Leila finally let herself scream.

BIANCA

Sometimes, when Bianca was especially bored, she'd pull up Leila's secret Instagram account, the one Leila thought no one knew about. Almost all the accounts she followed were crafting, homesteading, or family accounts, all of them with this weird, muted color palette of sad beige.

Who is Leila Mazanderani? Bianca wanted to know. *And why is she obsessed with dresses that make everyone look Amish?* She thought of her sister, of the way her eyes had flashed red, and how she had seemed too exhausted to even speak. It had felt good caring for her in a way that Bianca hadn't been able to all these years. Maybe this was the start of something new, a chapter where they might not be besties or anything like that but at least someone they could each rely on. Tonight, she'd spend more time researching how to exorcise djinn out of a loved one.

Her phone buzzed. **I KNEW HE WAS A SCUMBAG**, the text read. She quickly opened the message.

Bianca gasped. It was a photo of Foster and a girl from the volleyball team, the two of them hiding behind the school's equipment room as they sucked each other's faces off, practically dry humping. June must have been grabbing scores and stumbled upon them in the act.

Bianca wondered what she should do with this new information.

If she and Leila hadn't just had their serious djinn bonding experience, she would have pocketed the information and secretly gloated over her sister. But Bianca could feel the iron weight of her ring on her finger, could feel the thrum of excitement she'd earned after successfully fighting a ghul. She felt closer to her sister in this moment than she had in years. Surely, she owed her the truth?

Besides, Leila deserved better than Foster Hutchins.

Just then, she heard a thump come from Leila's room. "Gah!" Leila cried, her voice muffled.

"Leila?" Bianca knocked on their shared wall. "You okay?"

"What?" Leila asked. Her voice sounded rough and strained, as if she'd been screaming. Bianca pushed open Leila's door and stilled.

Her sister looked *horrible*. Despite the glowing skin and golden-flecked eyes, Leila looked wretched, as if she'd spent the last half hour thrashing in bed. *Does she already know?* Bianca wondered. *Did someone else tell her about Foster?*

"What is it?" Leila said gruffly. Bianca was taken aback: Leila might be aloof, but she was never *rude*.

"Are you okay?" Bianca asked. She was getting worried now. Leila breathed heavily, her eyes wild with panic. What was going on?

"What's that?" Leila asked, pointing to the photo Bianca had kept up on her phone. *Crap*, Bianca thought. *Maybe now is not the best time to show her.*

"Oh, this? Nothing, it's—"

Leila snatched the phone out of Bianca's hand. She didn't seem like Leila at all. *Is she the djinn right now?*

Leila stared mutely at the screen in her hand like it was playing a movie that she wasn't watching. It was clear she was seeing this information for the first time.

Bianca shifted uncomfortably. "Do you . . . do you want to talk about it?" *That's what sisters say to each other, right?*

Leila blinked, as if having forgotten Bianca was there.

"*Talk?*" Leila sneered, her face doing a one-eighty. Suddenly, all the energy in her face came roaring back, the fire seeping into her skin. Leila never, *ever* raised her voice, but in this moment, she had clearly reached a breaking point. "After four years of the silent treatment, you suddenly want to *talk?*" she spat.

Bianca held up her hands defensively. Maybe Leila was just feeling vulnerable after being cheated on, especially since the information had come from her. Plus, she *had* just had a supernatural run-in with a djinn this week. Bianca couldn't blame her for freaking out, but still, this wasn't her fault.

"Whoa, I'm sorry! I just . . . I wanted to help."

"First you ditch me in eighth grade for not being cool enough, and now you want to talk about boy problems?" Leila almost screamed. Flames popped up on her arms, more like welts than fires.

Bianca took a step back, shocked. "What are you talking about? *You* ditched *ME*!" She knew she wasn't being fair. Knew her sister wasn't entirely herself. But still, those memories were *Leila's*, not the djinn's. Whatever was happening to her must have pushed them to the surface.

Leila scoffed. It was a cruel, caustic sound.

It was Bianca's turn to get mad now. "You *hated* that I wanted to listen to weird music and watch random movies and be loud! You HATE that I want to leave this shitty town! You're the one who got popular and left *me*!"

They'd finally said it out loud: their reason for the aching chasm between them. Bianca had thought it would feel good to have it out in the open, especially after years of tiptoeing around each other. Instead, she just felt even angrier, the pain of Leila's indifference and cold shoulder after all these years boiling over.

She stared at her twin, at her long hair that she curled with old-school fabric scraps every night, at the gingham shirt she wore, at the way her nails were painted blush pink to match her lip gloss. *How could I have ever thought we were growing closer?*

"You used to like the way I dressed, Bee," Leila whispered, as if registering Bianca's disgust with her outfit. "You even used to wear the same clothes as me. And then suddenly, they weren't good enough."

Bianca's heart broke. This was too much. She hadn't asked for this, hadn't thought that one afternoon of trying to be a normal sister and do the right thing would become a referendum on Bianca's behavior for the past four years.

"Good luck with your boyfriend," was all Bianca said, snatching back her phone.

Then she closed the door, walked into her room, and sobbed silently into her pillow. *Even if I figure out how to exorcise the djinn,* Bianca thought miserably, *my own twin will still hate me.*

Bianca woke up the next morning, her first day of winter break, with a strange, wet feeling on her toe. Her eyes were puffy and tight from crying all night, but this feeling on her feet was different.

"Mmmfff," she said, rolling over, dismissing it as a dream. But her roll was stopped. She couldn't move her leg. She cracked an eye open, her face painfully swollen.

There, on the edge of her bed, was a plump, scarlet-colored demon sucking on her toes with one extremely long tongue.

She screamed, then morphed the scream into a yelp. If she woke up her parents, would this thing attack them, too?

Bianca tried to kick the demon off her feet, silently and furiously. It was no use; it was like its tongue was cemented to her foot.

"Be gone, you beast!" Bianca whispered angrily. She pushed the iron ring at the monster and felt it pulse with heat. The second the ring got close, the thing unlatched and whimpered.

"But your flesh tastes bessst," the small man moaned sadly, horns jutting out of his head.

"Did you not hear me? Get the hell out of here!" she whisper-shouted. Then she yanked her ring off her finger and threw it straight at the demon's red skin.

Pffft, hisss!

Bianca watched, satisfied, as the monster evaporated into steam, leaving a crusty silhouette on her carpet.

"Gross." Bianca tried not to retch. She hoped she hadn't woken anyone. If Leila had heard anything through their shared wall, she certainly hadn't rushed over to help.

Bianca hobbled to their bathroom, careful not to let her slimy toes touch the ground. She stuck her foot under the faucet, where she scrubbed furiously, all the while whispering, "Gross, gross, ack, blergh, yuck!" to herself.

Once she had rubbed each foot raw, she dove back under the covers and got out her laptop. She'd get carpet cleaner when everyone else was awake.

"Palis are a kind of djinn that enjoy sucking on the toes of their victims, slowly devouring them from the feet up."

"A pali!" she exclaimed. That's right, she had read about those.

Bianca launched out of her bed and inspected the rug where the pali had been. Whatever jewelry Bianca wore, it clearly hadn't been strong enough to prevent the djinn from sneaking into her room and attacking her feet. Her ring and necklace sat on the upper half of her body. Would she need to wear something on her feet to protect her lower half too?

She began googling things that could protect her from evil spirits, which led her down an occult rabbit hole. Esfand, a kind of incense she was pretty sure they had somewhere in the house, helped ward away evil spirits; bright red colors and fruits helped, and so did reciting certain du'as from the Quran. Bianca wrote them all down as she began the process of turning her bedroom into a djinn death trap. Should she place wards throughout the rest of the house too?

But then what will happen to Leila? Isn't she . . . Doesn't she have . . . ? If she concentrated on her ring hard enough, she could feel *something*, some kind of warmth from the room next door. She shivered.

Bianca couldn't face the fact that her sister now had something in common with the creature who had just licked her foot like a lollipop. It was enough to make her pity Leila, despite their huge blowup yesterday. *Maybe her powers aren't all they're cracked up to be*, Bianca realized.

She snapped her laptop shut. She would djinn-proof her room and her parents', nothing more.

Just then a text message from June buzzed through. **You wanna go to the bonfire party tonight? Liam's begging me to, but I won't go if you don't.**

She thought for a second. Normally over winter break she would hunker down into a reading spree. But the thought of being at home with Leila after their fight was not appealing.

Count me in, Bianca replied.

LEILA

It was the first day of winter break and Leila was unraveling. She'd spent all night tossing and turning under hot blankets with dreams of fire and cruel, harsh laughter. The nightmares had left her shaky and clammy. The thing inside her, all the djinn in the cave, the specter of a bargain she never made— it was all too much. And now, on top of it all, sat Foster's betrayal. Thank goodness it was a Saturday and she wouldn't have to see him.

She longed to knock on the shared wall between her and Bianca's rooms, but the thought of having to swallow her pride after their fight felt like one more thing to add to her pile of misery. She felt disgusting, knowing Cyrus was somewhere beneath her skin. Better not to let anyone see her like this. Better to just suffer alone.

So, Leila did what she always did whenever she wanted to shut out the world: she made things. She slowly got up, stretching and popping all the joints that felt tense after her nightmares. She brushed her teeth, trying not to look in the mirror, and threw on a long-sleeved dress she'd made from a thrifted linen tablecloth.

Sewing, crocheting, journaling: Leila found comfort in it all. Leila_Makes_Do was a crafter's social media heaven, and she followed everyone, from pattern makers and illustrators to embroiderers and fiber artists. She scrolled through her feed, all the images of handcrafted items giving her a sense of calm and control in a life that was slipping out of her grasp.

These distractions are just that: distractions, the voice in her head said. The djinn prince was trying to poison her thoughts and turn her into pliable clay to be molded for whatever he wanted.

Shut up, she seethed.

Leila pushed him out of her mind. A free sewing pattern she had always wanted to try had just popped up on her feed. She downloaded the PDF, printed it out at her desk, and slowly began to piece the shirt pattern together, being careful to mark every notch and dart.

She had a couple yards of woven fabric in her stash, so she laid each pattern piece on top of the fabric and pinned it down. Sewing garments was so fiddly that she had to hold every pattern piece in her head, the multiple components threatening to unravel the second she broke focus. It was the perfect way to block everything out.

Foster and Shivani kept texting her, but Leila couldn't bear to open her messages. What was worse: Foster admitting he'd done something wrong, or continuing to act as if everything was okay? She didn't want to talk to him, didn't want to face the reality that the past year they'd spent together was a lie.

She had thought she could shoehorn herself into this picture-perfect life. But being quiet and agreeable had gotten her nowhere, and she felt at fault for a boyfriend who cheated on her. Not because she deserved it; she knew she didn't. But because she hadn't been true to herself in the first place.

Yes, Cyrus wriggled in. *Unleash your true powers.*

She shook her head, blocking out his voice, blocking out the image of Foster sucking face with Kinsley Wheeler, blocking out Shivani's endless questions about how to dress sexy in 20-degree weather for an outdoor party happening tonight.

Instead, she got out fabric scissors and began to cut around the pattern pieces. Soon, the voices in her head quieted, and all her pattern pieces were cut out. Now came the fun part: sewing.

She prepped her sewing machine by gently cleaning it. She ran a pipe cleaner through the nooks and crannies and checked to make sure her bobbin was full of thread. Then she slowly wound the thread through the sewing machine and poked it through the needle, being sure that the needle was in securely. She hovered her foot above the sewing pedal, took a breath, and began stitching the pieces together.

As she double-checked her stitches and pressed each seam, all the buzzing in her head turned into a gentle roar in the background. All the problems of her life fell away, and even if Cyrus tried to talk to her, she doubted she'd hear it.

She attached the collar, then sewed the side seams. From there she placed the sleeves into the arm holes and gently coaxed her machine around each turn and curve. Halfway through she put the shirt over herself to check that it fit, adjusting the sizing a bit. She kept going.

By the time Leila finished the shirt, it was getting dark outside. *When did that happen?* She looked around her room, confused. There, on her dresser, was a plate of lunch her father must have left out. *When did he come in?*

Her family knew better than to interrupt Leila while she was sewing, but she hadn't realized just how late it was. She fumbled around for her phone and winced at how many missed texts and calls she had. The party must have started already.

Shivani had even left a voicemail, something she *never* did. "Leila? Where are you? Are you coming to the party? Something weird is happening. . . ." and then the voicemail abruptly cut off with the sound of someone screaming near Shivani's phone.

Leila frowned going through the rest of her texts.

Foster: Babe? Are you okay?

Foster: Are you coming?

Foster: Are you mad at me

Shepherd: Leila can you please come Foster is being all mopey and pathetic and it's throwing off the vibe

Then her phone rang. Bianca.

Leila pressed Accept, her mouth going dry. They hadn't spoken since Bianca had shown her the photo of Foster and Kinsley together. Hadn't spoken since Leila had finally let out all her hurt and anger at her sister in one single, horrible conversation.

"Leila?" Bianca gasped. She was breathless, and her voice sounded thin and strained.

"Bianca?" All thoughts of their fight went out the window. "Are you okay?"

"You'd better get down to this party," Bianca said, gulping down another swallow of air. "It's crawling with djinn."

Somewhere behind Bianca, Leila heard another scream. The sound of people running was clear through the phone.

"I'll be right there," Leila said grimly.

Inside, Cyrus cackled.

BIANCA

Bianca wasn't supposed to be "working" tonight. Tonight, she was just supposed to help June at what would undoubtedly be an awkward party near the cave that Ayers High students sometimes used. Still, Bianca had stashed a packet of esfand incense in her purse and wore a new evil eye chain she'd bought online. June could keep her other one. She had a feeling her best friend would need it.

She parked her truck near the trailhead and followed the music down the path that led to the Appalachian Trail throughway. "The Cave" was an open secret in Ayers, and the Park Service turned a blind eye to the teens partying there so long as they picked up after themselves and lit fires only in the wetter months. After all, many of the park rangers had grown up here, doing the exact same thing they were doing now.

The gathering reeked of beer. Bianca wrinkled her nose, glad she'd brought her own Cokes. To her, beer tasted the way dishwater smelled. There wasn't any point in pretending that she liked it.

She recognized pretty much everyone at the party. There was Shivani, holding court from where she was perched on a rock and regaling a group of girls with some stupid, shallow story (probably). Shepherd was by the tree line trying to do a keg stand, his Afro squashed on the mini keg. And there was Foster, sitting next to Kinsley Wheeler on a split log in front of the firepit. Bianca's eyebrows flew to the top of her forehead. *Have they no shame?*

June's "bookie assistant," Liam, had his arm around her as they stood under a giant pine. Bianca tried not to feel territorial about it. Liam had an Ayers High Swim hoodie on, and June wore a sweater with miraculously zero sports teams on it.

"Bianca!" June called out.

"Hey," Bianca said.

"Hey, Bianca," Liam replied. Bianca liked Liam. He was nice and polite. But she would always like June more, and she considered her friend "on loan" to this boy, even though they were both going to Ayers College and would probably be married one day. "Hey, do you have a cousin here?" he asked. "I thought I saw someone who looked like you."

Bianca stilled. There were very few, if any, other Iranians in Ayers. She shook her head at Liam. "Nope, don't think so."

Liam just nodded. Then he kept nodding, as if bopping his head to the music. The silence that followed was awkward.

"Want a Coke?" Bianca asked, breaking the silence.

"What kind?" June asked.

"I got Coke, Sprite, ginger ale, and a diet."

"Gimme a Sprite. Thanks."

Bianca handed it over and they cracked open their cans, surveying the scene. Liam excused himself to go talk to his friends on the swim team, another reason he would always be a tad suspicious to Bianca. Why did he have so many friends? Surely no one was that likable.

"So," Bianca said, taking a sip.

"So," June said, doing the same.

"Some party, huh."

"We're seniors. This is what seniors do now," June said sagely.

"So cool," Bianca answered flatly.

"Yup," June agreed.

"Why am I here again?" Bianca asked.

"Because you love me," June explained. "And I didn't want to come without my bestie."

"Right. That."

And then someone screamed.

It took Bianca a second to understand what was happening. One moment, she was chatting with her friend, and the next a stream of classmates ran toward them like a stampede, everyone sprinting to the parking lot.

She and June had hightailed it to their cars like the rest

of the party, figuring it would be better to run first and ask questions later. "Cops?" Bianca asked, breathless.

"I don't think so," June replied.

Bianca's ring suddenly seared—red-hot, just like it had with the djinn and the ghul. The same voice screamed again. Bianca sprinted back to the trailhead, trying to get closer.

"Bianca?" June shouted from the crowded lot. "Where did you go?"

"You go on!" Bianca called, her body filling with dread. *Here? Right now?* But it made sense. This was a party full of young, vibrant people. If she needed a human meat puppet, this was the first place she'd go too.

The path was empty now. She picked her way back to the party scene, where discarded cups and cans lay scattered on top of the pine needles. The rangers would not be pleased.

"NO!" a voice cried.

The voice sounded familiar but was too distraught to place. Bianca took a deep breath and took off her new necklace. She started swinging it in front of her like a lasso. Clutching her packet of esfand incense, she made her way closer to the cave and gasped. There stood a tall, fiery being bent over someone crouched on the ground.

"No," the person moaned.

And that's when Bianca recognized him. It was Steve Rosenberg.

She got out her phone.

LEILA

Leila borrowed her mom's car. Her mother was only too happy when Leila asked if she could use it for a party.

"It's good for you to get out," her mom said, eyeing Leila's housecoat and slippers. "Maybe you should shower?"

"I will when I get back!" Leila said breathlessly, throwing on a sweater and a coat. She shoved her muck boots on and made for the door.

The whole drive over, her head swam. What were djinn doing at a party? Why did her friends insist on drinking near that stupid cave? She hadn't realized that the big outdoor winter break shindig was going to be at the same cave that the djinn had been hiding out in.

The djinn hadn't just attacked the party; the party had practically been on top of their headquarters.

The voice inside her chuckled. *Who are we to turn away flesh on our doorstep?*

Leila accelerated, trying to shake off the voice. *I have to help my friends.*

Soon, she pulled up to the trailhead, where she could see

a bunch of Ayers High students huddled in small groups by their cars, looking anxiously at the woods. She saw Foster at the other end of the parking lot with Kinsley Wheeler, and her blood seethed in a way she'd never felt before.

Leila slammed her car door. "What happened?" she asked him sharply.

"Leila! Hi! Where have you been?" He and Kinsley sprang apart, even though they technically hadn't been doing anything. Leila just added it to the evidence she already had.

"Leila! About time you showed up!" Shivani joined them. She was clad in skintight Lycra, looking like a trendy ski bunny. Shivani was always dressed for the occasion. "Just in time for the party to end, of course." She pouted.

"Where's Bianca?" Leila repeated to Foster.

"Bianca? How should I know?" Foster shrugged. "I think there's a bear or something up there, though. We're debating calling the police."

"I left my phone up there, ugh," Shivani added.

Leila turned around, hoping to find someone else who had answers.

"Leila, wait!" Foster said.

Leila gave him the coldest look she could muster. "Shut up, Foster. Go hang with *Kinsley*."

Foster's face went pale. Shivani recoiled, confused. Kinsley looked away, ashamed. It all would have been hilarious if it hadn't been happening to Leila herself. She spun on her heel and found June, shivering for warmth next to Liam.

"June?"

"Leila!"

"June, where's Bianca?"

"You better go up there," June said, her eyes sorrowful. "I think . . . I think it got someone."

Whatever "it" was, it wasn't a bear, though she wasn't sure how much Bianca might have told June. Leila strode off to the trailhead.

"Wait!" Shivani called out, indignant. "What are *you* going to do about it?"

Leila ignored her and strode up the path.

"Can you at least grab my phone?"

It was eerily quiet in the woods. No sound of foxes or squirrels rooting around, not even a branch creaking or a twig snapping. Leila followed the trail of empty cups and trash to a clearing that faced the mouth of the cave. Her mouth went dry. It looked exactly the same as the ambush she'd had last night, the cave where she had been introduced to all those horrible, creepy djinn.

Something inside her bristled at her disgust, but she ignored it. She needed to find Bianca.

A shout broke the silence.

Leila sprinted to the sound, jumping over split logs and embers, until she found her sister.

Bianca wasn't alone. She stood in front of multiple djinn,

like a paper boat in front of a tidal wave. At her feet was Steve Rosenberg from school, completely terrified, backing up against Bianca's legs as the whites of his eyes shone.

Bianca held up a single iron ring against what looked like dozens of djinn, all different shapes and sizes, some with horns and some with fangs, all of them advancing on the two of them. It was like a scene from a horror movie, the creatures gnashing their teeth and howling like a pack of wolves.

One of the djinn looked exactly like Bianca. It was the shape-shifter who had tried to mess with Leila. Bianca swung her necklace pitifully against it.

"STOP!" Leila yelled. The djinn froze.

"Well, well, well," a sly voice said. The shape-shifter. It was unnerving to see Bianca's face sneer back at her, her limbs unnaturally long, her teeth pointed and menacing.

"Is . . . is this a golem or something?" Steve whimpered. How Steve Rosenberg had ended up in this mess, Leila didn't know. But Bianca towered protectively over him all the same.

"No, a djinn," Bianca said through gritted teeth. She held her iron ring between her thumb and index finger, pointing it at the horde. It clearly wasn't enough.

Steve moaned. "How is that possible?"

And then Leila felt it. That throat-searing voice that came out of her before.

"*Be quiet, boy,*" she snapped. Only it wasn't Leila. It was Cyrus. Her voice was deep and booming, and every word felt like it was being dragged out of her chest.

"Leila?" Bianca whispered. "Is that you?"

The djinn that had been living inside Leila poured out of her body like she was a magician's top hat and he was the rabbit. She went rigid, hating this feeling but loving the relief she felt when her body was completely free of this parasite. Standing there, djinn-free, she suddenly felt ashamed. She could feel Bianca's eyes searching to meet hers but didn't dare look up to see whatever disgusted expression Bianca probably had.

Next to Leila now stood Cyrus, the djinn prince, in full regalia. His skin glowed even more than the last time Leila had seen him in his true form. His jewels glittered, his midnight hair shone, and his smile grew even wider.

"Oh my god," Bianca gasped. "I didn't realize how bad it was . . . I didn't know . . . ," she babbled.

"Put down your ring, girl," the prince crooned. "Tell her, Leila jan. You can barely feel my presence, no?"

The rest of the djinn panted around them in a circle, eager, waiting for something. But Leila's head felt the clearest it had been since this whole ordeal began.

"No," she finally growled.

"W-why do you need us?" Steve asked, his voice shaking. Cyrus turned sharply to Steve.

"What's this?" Cyrus asked, his smile growing. He sniffed the air in front of Steve, getting right in his face. "Another human from our continent. You smell like home."

Steve turned his face away from Cyrus, looking like he was holding back a scream.

"We cannot exist on this plane for too long," Cyrus continued, answering his question. "We need a human host."

"Then go back to your world!" Leila spat, her courage roaring back, the dull haze of possession truly gone. "You don't need to take over ours!"

At this, Cyrus laughed. The other djinn joined in. Instead of sounding like normal chuckles, they were hisses and splutters like a crackling fire.

"Didn't you see our mountain, Leila jan? We are outgrowing it. That is the only home we have. It is time for us to expand."

"But why us?" Bianca asked, trembling. "Why here?"

The djinn were closer now. The circle that had formed around them was now a pressing mob, and Leila could see the tongues and teeth of a dozen or so djinn.

"We were promisssssed," whispered a human-shaped bonfire. "The debt must be paid."

"What debt?" Bianca cried. "Why are you guys always talking about some debt? I didn't take out this debt! So why do I have to pay it?"

The djinn flinched away from her wrath. Bianca in her full fury was a thing of wonder.

"Assssk your ancesssssstorssss," another wriggly ghul close to the ground finally said, its voice slithery. "You musssst pay the pricccccce."

"This makes no sense!" Bianca shouted.

"ENOUGH!" Cyrus boomed. "Do you think this life is supposed to be fair? Before humans, we roamed the earth.

And then your kind oozed up from the clay and destroyed our way of life , forcing us into hiding. We have paid the price for your kind, but now we have a chance to thrive."

Leila had been standing near Bianca, trying hard not to show any fear. She tried to absorb Cyrus's words, but they just wouldn't sink into her skull. What did they mean? Would she ever understand?

Then she watched as Cyrus changed form. His smart double-breasted coat and brass buttons began to melt into tongues and flames.

"I'm done talking," he said, his voice pitching lower, more menacing. The djinn around him followed suit, the one looking like Bianca morphing into fire, the odd-shaped humans melting into their true forms.

Leila recognized what was happening. After all, it was what had happened to her that day in the Elmhursts' field when Cyrus had advanced on her too.

They were trying to possess Steve and her sister.

The monsters wanted to be that same voice Leila had inside her. That same urge to scream and yell. That same feeling of nausea and dizziness and exhaustion.

She couldn't let that happen to her twin, much less Steve, who was innocent in this whole mess.

Bianca and Steve backed away from the slithering flames, but it was too late. The fires of the djinn were too close.

A small fire began to crawl up Bianca's pant leg like a spider. She screamed, and Leila's heart broke.

Nobody deserves this.

"STOP!" Leila shouted. Only, instead of just words, something else happened. She poured everything inside her, all her anger and fear, her frustration with this situation and her heartbreak from Foster, into that one moment. And all those emotions unleashed themselves on the djinn across from them.

Flames flew out of Leila Mazanderani.

They poured out of her like water, heading straight for Cyrus and his band of monsters. Instead of looking like the deep red, blue, and green flames of the djinn, Leila's flames were lighter and brighter, with more oranges and yellows swirling around.

The demons screamed, the fire burning them in a way their own flames didn't.

"Leila!" Bianca gasped, amazed.

Leila kept the djinn at bay by holding up her hands and letting the fire spew forth. It was incredible. It was wonderful. She felt such a rush expelling all this heat out of her that she never wanted to stop.

"Bianca, come on!" Steve scrambled up and was now leading Bianca away while the djinn were distracted.

"Go!" Leila shouted, waving them on. She had no idea how much longer she could do this, and she didn't want to find out. The djinn howled, flinching from her spray of flames.

She had never felt so alive before, so in control. She relished the feeling.

I could get used to this, she thought, surprising herself.

She watched to make sure Bianca and Steve had a head start. Once they disappeared down the path, Leila gritted her teeth and concentrated on making her flames even hotter, more scalding.

They were met with high-pitched shrieks and screams. She didn't want Cyrus to keep leaching from her, didn't want to have to deal with these horrid creatures and their quest for domination. She held the flames for a second longer, then extinguished her inferno. She sprinted for the trail, not bothering to turn around and get a good look at whatever pain she had doled out.

Leila raced through the forest, trying to keep to the path. She could hear the howls of the creatures behind her, snapping twigs as they gained ground. Leila jumped over tree roots and leaned through switchbacks until she stumbled into the parking lot, empty except for their mother's car and Bianca's truck. Bianca had their mom's car running and threw the door open.

"Come on, Leila!" she screamed. "Get in!"

Leila slammed her body into the passenger seat, her lungs aching for air. "What . . . about . . . Steve?" she gasped.

Bianca reversed out of their spot just in time to see a streak of red fire make its way to the edge of the lot.

"He's got my truck. We have to go, *now*." She threw the car into drive, Steve bringing up the rear, and Leila watched in the mirror as an unruly-looking bonfire waited by the edge of the parking lot, its flames vibrating with anger.

We did it, Leila realized. *We beat them.*

Leila knew that it was a temporary win. These creatures knew where she lived, after all, and Cyrus knew how to possess her. But right now, she was just relieved to be safe and sound with her sister.

"Did you know you could do that?" Bianca finally asked once they were on the main road, her voice filled with wonder and what sounded like a tiny bit of fear.

"No," Leila insisted. "I had no idea."

She held her hands out in front of herself, marveling at how wonderful it felt to be completely in control of her own body after the past few days. She opened her palm, and a spark danced across it, surprising them both.

"Careful!" Bianca yelped from the driver's side.

Leila shut her hands. "But . . . Cyrus isn't inside me anymore. How can I still have powers?"

Bianca bit her lip. "I don't know. You're the one attracting all the supernatural forces around here, not me."

"Let me see your ring," Leila said. She could feel the presence of the necklace and the ring in the car, but they no longer stung like a bad toothache. She wanted to see for herself how changed she was without Cyrus in her head.

"My ring?" Bianca blanched, sneaking her eyes away from the road to quickly make sure Leila wasn't joking. "Are you sure?"

"Yes," Leila said firmly.

Bianca handed over the ring. Miraculously, Leila took it from her without any pain.

"I can sense the iron inside it," Leila began, still puzzling it out. "But it doesn't hurt." Did this mean she could wear her iron ring? And not worry about iron anymore?

"Whoa," Bianca replied. "Maybe when Cyrus possessed you, he left some of his powers behind."

"Maybe," Leila said, chewing the inside of her cheek. She didn't feel as changed as she had with Cyrus controlling her, but she still felt *different*. She wondered what she'd see in her mirror back home.

Bianca went quiet, her eyes glued to the road. She opened her mouth, then closed it.

"What?" Leila asked, finally breaking the silence.

Bianca shifted uneasily in the driver's seat. Leila could see her sister trying to form her next sentence carefully, her eyebrows furrowed in what was her thinking face.

"Well," Bianca began. "It's just . . . if you didn't know you could shoot flames, then what else can you do?"

Leila leaned back, the question flooring her. *What else can I do?*

She looked back at her hands. There, on her ring finger, sat Foster's promise ring. She gently pried it off.

"I don't know what else I can do," Leila said. "But I know that I want to find out."

Bianca looked at her, and her grim face cracked into a grin. "All right, then."

Bianca parked their mother's car in The Grove, leaving the headlights on so they had a light source. It felt like an unspoken understanding that they were too wired to go straight home and try to sleep after all the night's excitement.

"Okay," Bianca said, clapping her hands together, very businesslike. "We saw you throw a fireball. Does that mean you can throw them whenever you want? And you can hold my ring now. Does that mean iron doesn't affect you when Cyrus isn't around? Let's figure this thing out."

"Wow," Leila said, surprised by Bianca's interest. "You're really into all of this, huh?"

Bianca's face drooped the slightest bit. Just enough for Leila to notice. "Well, I can be your man in the chair. You know, help you with your powers and stuff. Even if I don't have any of my own."

Leila thought she saw a flicker of disappointment there, but knew that couldn't be right. No way could her sister be *jealous* of her powers.

"Okay," Leila said. "Let's do this."

Bianca pointed to a faraway tree. "Try shooting a fireball there. It's just close enough to hit but not so close to send sparks back in our face. It's so damp it shouldn't hurt anything."

Leila nodded, glad Bianca had thought this through a bit more than she ever could. They exited the car and stepped into the cold air. Leila inhaled as she summoned up all that heat and intensity and rage from before and let it swell in her body, her new fire sizzling under her skin. She lifted her hands and unleashed two jets of flame at the tree, not quite hitting the bark but getting close. Bianca gave a happy squeal.

"Wow," Leila said out loud. "I still can't believe that's me doing it. It still feels like someone else." She looked at her hands again, unable to process that each palm was able to produce fire. It felt surreal, like part of the waking dream that this whole week had seemed to belong to.

"Believe it," Bianca replied. "Too bad we can't tell Baba, or he'll finally make that tanour oven he's been begging for, now that you can heat it."

Leila laughed. It had been more than twenty-four hours since that sound had come out of her naturally and not as Cyrus's cackle. She could just imagine her father asking her to hold her flames *just so* to make his beloved sangak flatbread in the special oven. "Dad wouldn't stop there. He'd ask me to roast a whole lamb on a spit if he could."

Bianca chuckled. Were they ... *joking* with each other? Leila couldn't remember the last time the two of them had cracked a joke. It almost felt as miraculous as her fireballs.

Bianca waved the laughs off, regaining her breath. "Okay, we gotta focus. The last thing we need are djinn storming in and ruining Mamá's Christmas Eve dinner, or she'll go ballistic."

Leila nodded. Her mother didn't cook often, but when she did, she went all out.

"What else do you think you can do?" Bianca asked her.

Leila's laughter died in her throat. What *could* she do? She remembered that day in the field, how Cyrus's flaming figure had approached her. How she had seen that city on the mountain, its jewels shimmering back at her.

"Wait," Leila said. "That day Foster passed out. I disappeared, remember?"

"Right . . . ," Bianca said. "You said you saw the djinn city."

"That was when Cyrus was possessing me. But maybe I can go on my own?" Leila asked, partly to herself and partly to her sister.

Bianca's eyes lit up. "Oh man, that would be amazing. But what if you get stuck?"

Leila hadn't thought of that. What if she *did* get stuck? She'd have to go crawling back to Cyrus for help, and she didn't know if she could do that alone. She held out her hand. "Come with me?" she asked. Whatever happened, Leila had faith they could figure it out together.

Bianca gave Leila the biggest smile she'd received from her in four years. "I thought you'd never ask."

Leila held her hand out, and Bianca clasped it. Her skin was surprisingly soft compared to Leila's calluses from sewing and knitting, but her grip was strong. Leila concentrated on the city in the desert, on the way the mountain loomed above them.

"It's working," Bianca gasped, gesturing to the flames at their feet.

Leila focused on the desert, on the feel of the shifting sand underneath her boots, on the dry air and the ever-pressing heat. She felt the flames tickle her entire body, and when she closed her eyes, she saw their destination loom over them.

She opened her eyes. It was dark here, nighttime just as in their own plane, but she could still see the mountain, lit up from within with thousands of flames.

"Whoa," Bianca said, her voice tight. "Can you get tele-portation sick? Because that is how I feel right now."

Leila looked up at the mountain towering over them. She didn't know what to say. She had done it all on her own, with-out Cyrus's help, all with her own mind and body.

"I did it," she repeated, still in shock. "Do you think any of the djinn will see us here?"

"It's pitch-black. Who's gonna notice?" Bianca said, whip-ping her head around to get a good look. "So, this is the djinn plane," she continued, her voice filled with awe as her face danced with light from the nearby city. She turned back to Leila, her eyes growing wide, a new idea flashing across her face. "Leila . . . ," Bianca began, her voice growing even more excited. "If you can teleport us here, what if you could teleport us to other places too?"

Leila froze. *Other* places? "You mean, like, other planes?"

She saw Bianca shake her head in the dark, a soft figure in the faint glow of the city. "No, like, to DC, or New York. Nowhere fancy. Just, you know, in our dimension."

Leila hadn't even thought of that. Other cities. Maybe even other countries. After all, how far *was* the djinn plane from Ayers? If she could travel this distance, could she do larger jumps at home?

Leila gulped, her throat dry from the whirling sand. "Where do you wanna go?"

Bianca gave a low chuckle. "Oh, I've got a couple ideas."

BIANCA

Bianca had never been on a plane, much less left the state. Their class field trip to Washington, DC, to see all the monuments didn't count.

"Bianca?" Leila prodded her. "Where to?"

Bianca held up her phone. There was no service in the djinn plane, obviously, but her phone's wallpaper would do just fine. "Here," she said. "The Sydney Opera House." The unique scalloped roof of the building glowed in the dark of the desert. She'd read about their special production of *Sweeney Todd*, where they handed out free ponchos and sprayed fake blood on audience members. She'd been obsessed ever since.

Leila shook her head. "Wow, you really picked the place farthest away from Ayers, huh?" Leila looked at Bianca's phone clock. "Australia's way ahead of us. It'll be broad daylight!"

"There's a tree over there in the photo. Just port us behind that," Bianca huffed. Why did Leila have to make everything so complicated?

"I'm still in my muck boots," Leila protested.

Bianca could tell Leila was stalling, that her sister was scared of seeing just how far she could push herself. "Leila," she said, gripping her sister's shoulders. "You can do this, okay? You just took down a dozen djinn, told off your boyfriend, and teleported us to the djinn plane. Australia will be a piece of cake."

Her irises began to grow gold with power. "Okay," Leila exhaled.

"Okay," Bianca repeated for moral support.

"Lemme see your phone." Leila held out her hand and stared at the screen. She clenched Bianca's upper arm. "Sydney, Sydney, Sydney," Leila repeated to herself.

Bianca watched their feet. Sure enough, flames began to dance over their shoes. "Oh, hell yes," Bianca said, more to herself than to her sister. "Sydney, here we come!"

And then they were gone.

Bianca blinked, her eyes adjusting from the dark to the hot December sun.

"Gah!" a jogger yelled, surprised by the twins stepping out from behind a tree. But the jogger kept chugging past, shaking their head as if Bianca and Leila were just mere annoyances and not supernatural appearances.

"Phew," Bianca said. "That was close."

Leila said nothing, her jaw slack, her eyes wide. There

stood the Sydney Opera House in all its glory. Leila looked fresh off the turnip truck, gawping in her cold-weather farm getup as a truly surprising number of joggers flowed past them.

Bianca followed Leila's gaze to the building, but instead of feeling as awestruck as her sister, she just felt *wrong*. Maybe it was the same teleportation sickness she'd had when they'd gone to the djinn plane, but instead of feeling elated, Bianca just felt unmoored. This wasn't Ayers, this wasn't Virginia, this wasn't even the United States. Everything felt too bright and overwhelming, the hot sun making her dizzy, the shining water behind the opera house twinkling too brightly. Where were the kudzu vines? Where were the mountains to orient her?

"Excuse me!" another jogger shouted. The twins quickly stepped off the sidewalk and onto the grass. They stood right where the photo from Bianca's wallpaper must have been taken, yet instead of marveling over the fact that they had gone thousands of miles in a matter of seconds, all Bianca could think was *Even the grass feels weird here*.

"Come on," Leila said, noticeably more psyched than Bianca. "Let's go take a look."

"Okay," Bianca said, trying to sound positive. But she couldn't help it. Leaving Ayers was supposed to solve everything, so why did Bianca feel the same? "Let's go."

They walked up to the opera house steps and looked at the harbor. It was odd seeing Christmas lights strung up in the sweltering heat. She'd never seen Santa in a swimsuit, but there were ads and decorations with a very sunburnt St. Nick. She flinched at the parrots in the trees, which felt unnatural to her. Everything felt off, and even the poster for the *Sweeney Todd* production couldn't cheer her up.

What is wrong with me? she wondered. *I finally get out of Ayers and all I want is to go back.*

"Bianca?" Leila prodded her, her eyes still sparkling from all the new sights and sounds. "You okay?"

Bianca shrugged. "Can we go back now? I don't feel great." She gestured to the pools of sweat under her long-sleeved black shirt, making it seem like the heat was really the problem, and not this empty feeling of getting what you wanted and realizing it wasn't what you thought it would be. Not even a little bit.

Leila gave her a concerned look. "Okay." She stared longingly back at the harbor, at the glittering boats and the gorgeous bridges and at one girl who had an entire eight-pack on display as she jogged past them. Bianca stared too. What was it with Australia and its joggers?

Leila led Bianca to a tiny alcove around the side of the opera house. It was already the morning of Christmas Eve here, and the building still hadn't opened. She found them a tiny crack in the shade. "Home," Leila said to herself, closing her eyes. Bianca did the same, grateful for this seasick feeling to finally go away.

LEILA

They reappeared in The Grove next to their mom's car. Leila's blood hummed the way it did whenever she sewed something she loved or baked something particularly delicious. Traveling to a new country had felt like a revelation. All the new sights and sounds and colors and even just the smell of that corner of Sydney had lit up parts of her brain that had felt long dormant. When was the last time she felt so alive?

Meanwhile, Bianca wordlessly trudged to the car, her shoulders drooping.

"Bianca?" Leila asked, buckling in next to her. "You okay?"

Bianca nodded. "Just tired."

"Okay," Leila said, not entirely believing it.

Bianca guided them through the back entrance to their gravel driveway. Their parents had long given up on having a curfew for their girls. Not because they didn't trust them— more because their kids never went anywhere.

Leila doubted her parents would be waiting up for them. Bianca turned off the car and slowly got out, silently walking to their house.

Instead of gushing about how wonderful the colorful parrots in the trees had been or the surprising number of people exercising in the sun on the morning of Christmas Eve in Australia, Bianca just shuffled up the stairs to her bedroom. "Goodnight," she said to Leila. "Glad you kicked the djinn prince's butt." She smiled at the last part, but Leila could tell it was halfhearted.

"Goodnight," Leila replied, unsure what else to say.

Bianca gently closed the door, and Leila stood there, wondering how someone who had wanted to go to a place so badly she'd made it her phone's wallpaper could be so disappointed after visiting it.

By the time Leila had washed her face, brushed her teeth, changed into pajamas, and stopped pacing her room, it was one A.M. So much had happened tonight. From Cyrus almost taking Steve and Bianca at the party to learning she could shoot fireballs and teleport, Leila felt completely different from the broken shell she'd woken up as earlier that day. But that wasn't what kept her awake.

No, she couldn't go to sleep because suddenly the world felt so much bigger than before. Ayers had been her everything, her whole life, and suddenly it had all been shrunk by one outing to another country. Her picture-perfect life with Foster had crumbled before her eyes, but she found that she didn't even care anymore. There was so much more out there, so much to see. How could she have ever thought staying here, in this town, would be enough?

She got out her laptop and snuggled under her covers. Where should she go next? Opening Google Maps no longer felt like some disorienting exercise; now it was like being a kid in a candy store, getting to choose whatever she wanted. *Argentina*, she wrote down at the top of her list. She wanted to see where her mom had grown up. *Iran*, so she could finally meet the country that matched her face. *South Korea, Mexico, Sweden, Zimbabwe*—with her new power, she could do it all.

Her phone buzzed with another text she'd probably ignore.

Shivani: Leila . . . I need to talk to you. I saw Foster do
     something at the party last night.
Shivani: Where the duck are you??
Shivani: duck
Shivani: duck
Shivani: ugh this new phone's autocorrect!!

Leila's heart cracked just a tiny bit. Shivani had probably seen Foster kiss Kinsley again. The fact that he felt so comfortable doing it in front of everyone at the party hurt even more.

She felt like she was staring at a snow globe of her life from the outside in, watching an unhappy Leila with an unhappy Foster pretend to play house. Could Foster tell that Leila's heart wasn't in it? Or would he have always been a cheater? Leila had no idea, but she knew she deserved better.

Leila: It's okay, Shiv. I already know.

Her phone immediately buzzed again.

Shivani: Want me to kill him for you? Or I could pray to our shrine that he gets a really bad case of jock itch?

Leila laughed. The truth was, she was relieved. Now she could explore the world and her life outside Ayers without feeling crushing guilt. She felt like twenty pounds had been heaved off her chest.

Leila: It's okay. Kinsley has braces. I'm sure he's already gotten cut a bunch of times.
Shivani: This is why we are friends.
Leila: G'nite Shiv. Love you.
Shivani: Love you too. But seriously. You let me know.

Leila smiled and plugged her phone into her charger. Yes, she still didn't know what to do about Cyrus. True, she had a horrible boyfriend she would need to officially break up with.

But right now, she could picture a life after this djinn problem. A life after prom and graduation. A life after *Ayers*. And that gave her the sweetest dreams to slide her properly into Christmas Eve.

She rolled over in bed, gave a contented sigh, and fell asleep.

BIANCA

Christmas Eve. Bianca woke up that morning with a groan, her body aching, her sheets still sweaty from last night's ordeal. She glanced at her phone, relieved that no new texts had come in. She lay there for a moment, blinking, thinking about how lucky she was to even be here today after getting mobbed by angry demons, teleporting to the djinn plane, and going across the world to Australia.

Australia, Bianca remembered with a pang. It wasn't what she had thought it would be. She'd figured that when she went abroad, everything would click into place. That she'd instantly feel at home with her surroundings. But the plaza in front of the opera house had felt too bright and too exposed, the trees there disturbingly different from the ones here in Virginia. Where was the greenery? The lush hills and meadows? The feeling of not knowing anyone there, in either the city or the continent, had felt strangely discombobulating.

She had finally been a small fish in a big pond, and she

did *not* like it. She felt ashamed over her failed jaunt around the world. Where was the cosmopolitan Bianca now? The girl who was famously going to leave Ayers and make something of herself? Hiding in Ayers, of course.

"Bianca? Estás listo?" her mamá called up.

Bianca quickly rolled back under her covers, pretending to be asleep just a little longer. Maybe if she stayed quiet, her mother wouldn't come in to check on her.

She was not looking forward to all the Noche Buena cooking her mamá would rope her into. As an Argentinian, Alma had a strong Italian heritage, and that meant cooking the Feast of the Seven Fishes every Christmas Eve. It was tough to get seven different kinds of seafood without breaking the bank though. Bianca hoped her mamá would spare them this year and cook only one or two kinds of fish.

Christmas was a Christian holiday, and her mother's domain. After celebrating Shab-e Yalda last week, a Zoroastrian holiday from before Persia converted to Islam, Bianca found it easy to switch between the two. Spanish and Persian. Christian and Zoroastrian. Argentinian and Iranian. Having her mother home from work this week meant cortados instead of chai, panqueques con dulce de leche instead of flatbread and feta cheese for breakfast. Her mouth watered, her stomach weighing the pros and cons of eating a good breakfast against being forced into Christmas chores.

She shifted in bed, hearing dry leaves and twigs crunch beneath her. She'd been so exhausted that she'd collapsed into her sheets, not bothering to take off her clothes, or, it seemed, the pile of leaves that had stuck to her from the forest bonfire. She sighed, her mind racing with everything she was up against now.

The fact that no djinn had breached their unprotected home before she could put up any wards seemed like a Christmas miracle. Maybe the djinn were too busy licking their wounds after her sister basically torched them. She wasn't sure, but she wasn't going to make the same mistake twice. She had all the tools she needed. Now it was just time to trim their house like a bizarre Christmas tree.

Bianca slowly got out of bed and opened her drawer.

Inside were the surplus anti-djinn accessories she'd purchased online. Evil eye pendants. Tasbihs. Esfand. Dates were another recommendation she'd learned about, but they'd been hard to find—the local grocery store didn't seem to carry them. Pure iron rings were surprisingly expensive, so she'd had to make do. She hung an evil eye pendant over her bedroom door, and again over her window, using duct tape to hold them up. She did the same with Leila's door, assuming that if iron didn't affect her now, an evil eye wouldn't, either.

Slowly, she walked down the stairs, careful not to stir her mother into the chore-addled frenzy she'd enter soon enough. Bianca laced up her boots, zipped up her jacket, and slipped out the front door. She had a package of loose esfand and began crushing the dried leaves and seeds between her fingertips, the cold making her hands ache. Slowly, slowly, she made a thin line around their home, pouring the small seeds of wild rue like gunpowder for a fuse.

Once the first bag of esfand ran out, she opened the next one. By the time she made it all the way around the house, she couldn't feel her fingers. She ran back inside, sticking another evil eye pendant above the front door. She left a tasbih that looked so much like her dad's that she hoped he wouldn't notice it in the bowl of keys by the coat hooks.

Her mamá's voice rang through the house. "Bianca? Is that you? Help me get the cartilage out of the squid!"

Great.

Bianca sighed and walked over to the kitchen. She hoped Leila would wake up soon and help. Plus, she wanted to talk to her about last night.

Mamá stood at the sink, her dirty-blond hair in rollers, her arms up to her elbows in squid. Bianca eyed the gloopy tentacles in the bowl and washed her hands. It looked disgusting, but it would soon turn into sopa de mariscos, her mamá's famed Christmas seafood soup.

Christmas music played on the small kitchen radio, perking Bianca up a bit. She plunged her hands into the bowl, feeling around the tentacles for the hard bits of cartilage.

She unstuck all the cartilage and washed her hands again. Mamá handed her a small coffee cup, and Bianca smiled.

"Thanks."

"You will need it," her mamá said darkly.

Bianca took a sip and perked up. They only busted out the

stove-top espresso maker for special occasions, and Alma's cortados were better than any of the fancy lattes at Cup of Joe on Main Street.

"Ahhh," Bianca sighed. Despite the roller coaster of last night, she was glad to be here in their warm kitchen with her mom and a cortado, next to a bowl of dead squid.

"So, how was your party?" her mamá asked as she began deveining some shrimp that had thawed overnight.

Bianca took another sip of coffee, buying herself some time. What should she say? How could she skirt the fact that they almost got themselves possessed?

"Were there any boys there?" her mamá prodded. She had on a thick bathrobe and slippers, along with a matching pajama set. Even while deveining shrimp, her mother still looked put-together.

"Oh," Bianca replied. Her mom was just snooping. She just wanted to know about their love lives. Well, that was much easier to handle. "Yeah, there were a bunch of boys from school." Which reminded her—she needed to get her truck back from Steve.

"Any you like?" she wheedled some more.

Bianca considered the question. Were there any boys she liked at school? No, not really. But she did like how it felt to protect Steve, to step in front of fire and see the awe in his eyes when she had shielded him. That, she had to admit, felt pretty good.

"Not really," Bianca said, though it still felt like lying.

Just then, Leila shuffled down the staircase into the kitchen. Normally it was Leila who woke up early and helped get food ready for the day, but today she looked like she'd had a late night. There were bags under her eyes, and her glossy hair looked flat and dull. Whatever glow-up that freakish djinn had given her, he'd taken it away.

"Buenos días," Mamá said. She handed Leila a cortado and then motioned to a pile of herbs that needed to be cut for the sabzi khordan. Even though tonight was an Argentinian feast, they couldn't resist adding a few Persian touches. Sabzi khordan was a pile of fresh herbs, radishes, flatbread, feta, and walnuts that accompanied just about every meal, giving the kitchen an herbaceous smell along with the aroma of coffee and desserts baking in the oven.

Leila gratefully took the cortado and sat down, taking small sips.

Are you okay? Bianca mouthed to her.

Leila smiled at her sister, some color returning back to her face. *Just tired.*

That was the last private conversation they got to have.

The rest of the day was spent cooking and cleaning, with their mom barking out orders the second they finished each task. They unearthed Christmas decorations, swept and steam-mopped the floor, and washed the rice. Mamá made Leila iron the nice linen tablecloth and had Bianca figure out how to open the flue in the chimney so they could light a real fire. Meanwhile, their baba puttered in and out, stringing fairy lights on the outside of the house with a ladder and a staple gun, or making trips to the root cellar for supplies. If he saw the evil eyes, he didn't say anything. Whenever there was a spare minute, everyone would sporadically run up to their room to wrap last-minute gifts without anyone else prying.

Even though they had no family here, Mamá always invited students who had nowhere else to go over the holidays, and Baba would invite anyone who was remotely Middle Eastern in Ayers or the surrounding area to come over. Both parents took hospitality very, very seriously.

Bianca vacuumed and scrubbed using their dad's homemade vinegar spray to wipe down windowsills and doorhandles. It was her job to polish the banisters and then wrap them in pine garlands, wash the quilts on the couch, and move all their shoes from the front door to their respective rooms. All thoughts of last night were banished in exchange for this cleaning frenzy that happened once every year.

Leila didn't have it much better. Since Bianca wasn't much of a cook, her twin was the one who ended up assisting both parents in the kitchen.

The turkey that their father had soaked in brine overnight had to be dressed and roasted. The trout needed to be gutted and cleaned. The combination of Argentinian and Iranian celebration foods meant chopping, so much chopping that the sound of the knife on the cutting board began to make Bianca's head throb.

Then there was the rice. Baba had soaked it in huge tubs

overnight, and Bianca helped him strain each tub so that they could keep the starchy water for their plants and for the garlic shoots overwintering out back. Iranians were fastidious about washing rice, and by the time they were done it had probably gone through three or four full cleaning cycles.

There was so much rice that instead of cooking it inside, Baba placed a big camp stove on the back patio and boiled it in a pot that could have fit an entire toddler. Before pouring the drained rice back in, Bianca watched, mouth watering, as he covered the bottom of the pot in a few inches of oil, then placed sliced potatoes on the bottom. When the rice was done, the bottom of the pot would reveal crisp, perfectly steamed potatoes that were both crunchy and soft. Potato tahdig was what Christmas tasted like to Bianca.

The sun set without the family noticing, they were so busy with preparations. Guests were invited for six P.M., though of course that meant seven P.M. for their crowd. There was just enough time for everyone to clean up and put on their nice clothes. Bianca chose a sleek black dress that gave her perfect Wednesday Addams vibes. Leila went with a traditional red dress that helped make her pale complexion glow a bit more, though Bianca noticed her sister still looked exhausted. Today's marathon of party prep probably hadn't helped.

Someone knocked on the front door. Bianca wondered if they'd seen the evil eye she'd put over the threshold. Then their dad turned on the music, and all thoughts of djinn and horrible creatures evaporated. It was Christmas Eve, Bianca was hungry, and she was safe and happy with her family's Persiantinian celebration of Christmas.

"Nenas!" their mother called out. "Come grab everyone's coats!"

"That's our cue," Leila said at the top of the stairs.

"We haven't had much time to talk," Bianca began. "Are you okay?"

"Yeah," Leila said, her eyes crinkling as she smiled. "For the first time in a long time, I feel really good. I'm just tired."

Bianca registered Leila's small, confident smile, the general air of contentment surrounding her. Her sister looked less tortured somehow, less like a tightly wound spring that threatened to pop at any moment.

"I'm *starving*," Leila added.

Bianca chuckled, her heart lifting a tiny bit too. "Same."

Tomorrow, they could deal with the monsters knocking at their door. But right now, they would enjoy Christmas Eve.

LEILA

Maybe it was the rush of having survived a djinn ambush, or maybe it was the adrenaline of realizing her future could be even more expansive than she'd realized. Maybe it was just the happy feeling of being snug inside with her family on a cold, crisp night filled with twinkle lights and stories. But Leila couldn't remember a happier Christmas Eve.

Their mother had invited a few students from South America who all had nowhere to go for Christmas. Javier was Colombian and studying engineering at Ayers College. Valentina and Marcelo were Argentinian like their mom, and their excitement over all the Argentinian food was infectious.

Bianca grabbed coats, and Leila served drinks. She was truly enjoying herself for the first time in days. It didn't hurt that Bianca slipped Leila more wine, either.

The table was set to its absolute limit, the legs buckling under turkey, grilled trout, seafood stew, jeweled rice, ashe-reshteh, pomegranate salad, Waldorf salad, and—as a concession to their adopted American home—mashed potatoes.

Instead of gravy there were sides of salsa golf (a ketchup and mayo mixture from Argentina) and yogurt with cucumbers and mint. If the foreign students were hoping for an authentic American Christmas, they'd have to go elsewhere.

Leila's mouth watered. Her appetite had been poor while Cyrus had been dwelling inside her, but now she was ravenous. She heaped her plate with rice first, then layered turkey, trout, yogurt, and salad on top, letting the rice absorb all the flavors above.

Once she inhaled her plate, she filled a soup bowl up with sopa de mariscos, chewing the squid, shrimp, clams, and tender chunks of whitefish that had simmered in a tomato and saffron broth. Then, she refilled the same bowl with ashe-reshteh, a Persian stew of herbs, chickpeas, and noodles that tasted the way you wished a salad would.

"Whoa," their dad said, pointing to Leila's empty plates. "Slow down there!"

Leila stopped chewing. The entire table was looking at her. She swallowed.

"I'm just really hungry," was all she said.

"Dalé, Leila! You look like you need it," Marcelo said, nodding approvingly.

"Buen provecho," Valentina added, raising her wineglass.

Javier just groaned. "This dinner is soooo good," he said. "The food in the cafeteria is garbage." Then he tucked back in to the plate of jeweled rice.

Bianca gave Leila a small smile and then went back to her

bowl of ash, slurping the noodles with abandon. Their father beamed.

Later that night, much, much later, after the goodbyes had been said and the Tupperware for the students had been filled and the dishwasher was running, Leila walked around the dark house. They'd be doing presents tomorrow morning, but she wanted to fill everyone's stockings up with some small homemade gifts she'd been working on.

A black silk scrunchie for Bianca. A jar of sourdough starter she'd been feeding for her dad. A crocheted hat for her mom.

She sat there in the dim living room, the glow of the Christmas tree twinkling and giving her a pleasant, cozy feeling. It was the most relaxed she'd felt since their neighbor's fire turned her world upside down.

She took a deep breath and sat in their squashy armchair.

I'll do whatever it takes to protect Ayers, she thought to herself. *Even if I don't want to live here anymore.* It surprised her to finally admit it to herself. There was just no way she was going to stay here, not after her life had been cracked open, not after she learned she could go anywhere in the world with the snap of a finger. But still, this was where she'd learned to ride a bike and where the owner of the craft store had taught her how to sew. It was where her family was, along with all her memories. This town was too precious to her. She had too much to lose.

She prayed Cyrus would simply leave them alone, though her hopes weren't high. Today had felt like the calm before the storm, and she had sucked the marrow out of the calm as much as she could.

And then she saw it: the evil eye Bianca had placed over the front door.

Leila flinched, but instead of the talisman hurting her, she didn't feel anything.

That gave her an idea. She tiptoed upstairs to her room. On her nightstand was the jewelry box. It sat heavy, the cute box somehow menacing.

She opened it now. The iron ring twinkled in the moonlight, begging her to put it on. It didn't emit a cold ache like it had before. This time, it seemed warm and inviting.

She slipped it onto her finger and flexed her hand.

"Time to fight back," she whispered.

BIANCA

Today had been another typical Christmas Eve celebration, but somehow, because of the outrageous turn of events of the past few days, the mundanity of it all felt *good*. It had felt like putting down an exciting novel to go and get a snack, knowing you could dive back into your swashbuckling story later. Ayers no longer felt stifling and oppressive; it felt comforting and solid, the only thing keeping her afloat after this wild week.

That night she put on her favorite red reindeer pajamas, looking forward to pancakes and presents tomorrow on Christmas Day. Her parents usually gave them some pocket money, and Bianca had her eye on a couple more anti-djinn talismans.

Crack! The sound echoed through her room. She flinched. *What was that?* Then it came again, another loud *crack!* that came from her window. She climbed out of bed and tentatively inched across the floor, clutching her evil eye necklace. Should she get the esfand? She peeked outside, drawing apart her bloodred curtains.

There, below her windowsill, was Steve Rosenberg in a surprisingly normal outfit, about to launch another pebble at her bedroom window.

Bianca opened the window. "Steve!" she hissed. "What are you doing here? It's Christmas Eve!"

"Do you wanna get some pie?" he whispered back up to her. "I promise it's really good pie."

Out of all the things she thought he was going to say, inviting her to eat pie was not one of them. She looked back at her room, thinking. Steve wasn't what she'd expected. The way he'd pulled himself together after the djinn attack and wordlessly taken the keys to her manual truck had impressed her. Plus, Steve Rosenberg wearing gray sweats and a hoodie intrigued her after seeing him in all-black getups for four years at school.

Pie sounded good.

"What the hell," Bianca said back to him. "Sure."

"Yesss!" He fist-pumped as quietly as he could.

She hastily threw on some clothes and tiptoed her way down the stairs. It felt like their whole home was holding its breath on Christmas Eve, even the glowing Christmas tree. It felt comfy and right, and Bianca basked in this feeling.

She met Steve in their gravel driveway, where, even more surprisingly, a gray Honda Civic sat along with her truck. "This is your car?" Bianca asked, confused. "I thought you drove a hearse or something."

Steve shrugged. "Nope. Leighton drove my car while I

drove your truck back." His eyeliner, she noticed, was gone. He handed over her car keys.

"Leighton?" Bianca asked, grabbing them.

Steve shrugged. "She was in the one-acts with me. Junior. Sweet kid."

Bianca rolled her eyes, feeling weirdly jealous over Steve's theatrical fan club. She got into the passenger side of the Civic and buckled her seatbelt. "So," she said, changing the subject. "Pie. At midnight."

"Pie." Steve nodded back, completely serious. He didn't elaborate, which added an air of mystery to the whole thing that Bianca had to admit she found, reluctantly, attractive. *If only June could see me now.*

"Any reason you threw pebbles at my window instead of texting me?" Bianca asked.

"Just felt like it," Steve replied.

Well. This was the least talkative Steve had ever been in her presence. Instead of searching for more answers, Bianca was content to just sit and watch the shadows of trees fade past as they made their way to downtown Ayers. He pulled over on the quiet brick-lined Main Street, where Bianca recognized Granny's Pie Shop.

"They're open this late?" Bianca asked.

"They are for me," Steve replied cryptically.

"Not a real answer, but okay."

Bianca followed him out of the car and into the biting winter night. But she wasn't cold for long—Steve quickly opened the folksy front door and they stepped inside. The warm, cozy pie shop held a glass case where multiple kinds of pie glimmered like precious jewels.

There was blackberry, pumpkin, apple, lemon meringue, and ones she hadn't seen before with intricate latticework on top. Her mouth watered. For some reason, they were the only people in here, and she couldn't see any staff or servers.

Steve, however, did not seem as entranced by the pies. In fact, he stepped right behind the empty counter and, in a completely different voice from Drama Club Steve, said, "Hi, welcome to Granny's Pie Shop, can I take your order?"

Something in Bianca clicked. "Wait, you *work* here?"

Steve bowed dramatically. *Ah, there he is*, Bianca thought to herself. "My family owns it."

"So, there's no granny?" Bianca asked.

"Bubbe lives in Naples, Florida, and would keel over if she saw what we've done to her rugelach recipe," he answered.

"Whoa," Bianca replied. She had seriously miscalculated Steve Rosenberg.

"What?" Steve replied.

"Nothing," Bianca said, trying to regain her footing. She eyed a blackberry pie. "I just . . . well . . . you're surprising, that's all."

"I contain multitudes!" Steve shouted into the empty shop, using his theater-projection voice.

Bianca winced. "Don't do that," she said.

"Do what?" Steve asked.

"Put on that Shakespeare front! There's no audience. It's just me, okay?"

Steve chewed the gray tie of his hoodie, something Bianca could have sworn he had never done in his life if you'd asked her yesterday. He just said, "Yeah, okay."

The silence this time was awkward, but not in a bad way.

"Blackberry pie, please, with extra whipped cream," Bianca said.

"Coming right up."

Bianca watched, fascinated, as Steve expertly cut a slice of pie, plated it, and added whipped cream like he was on autopilot. It felt similar to finding out your friend knew how to drive stick or was secretly fluent in another language. She tried not to stare at his forearms while his back was to her. *I can't believe I'm on a date with Steve Rosenberg.* Then—*Wait, is this a date?*

He set the plate on the two-person table by the window, where they could watch Main Street, and the twinkle lights gave the pie shop a warm, romantic glow.

"Aren't you going to eat?" Bianca asked, sitting down. The pie looked seriously delicious, and she found she still had room despite a heaping Christmas Eve feast.

"Nah," Steve said, sipping a cup of coffee. "I ate way too much pie over Hannukah."

"Fair enough." Bianca took a bite and moaned, finding a second stomach to tuck the pie into after all her Christmas Eve desserts. It was so, so good. The tart blackberry mixed perfectly with the flaky, buttery pie crust. Topped with whipped cream, it was perfection. "Yum," was all she said, forgetting to be self-conscious on this maybe date.

Steve looked on approvingly. "My mom's favorite is blackberry too. She doesn't like things to be too sweet."

"Same." Bianca nodded. "This is seriously incredible."

Steve smiled. "Thanks. I made that one this morning."

That's really hot, Bianca begrudgingly thought to herself. *Multitudes, indeed.*

"Any reason why we're having pie in the dead of night?" she asked casually.

Here, Steve shifted in his seat, his back stiffening. "Well, I wanted to say thank you."

Bianca frowned. "For what?"

He gave a hollow laugh. "Are you kidding me? For saving my life!"

Bianca froze, the cozy moment evaporating. Right: djinn had practically kidnapped Steve at the party. So, this wasn't a date. This was a thank-you meal.

"Ah," was all Bianca said, disturbed by how disappointed she felt.

"I mean, that was wild, right?" Steve asked, getting animated. "I wanted to ask you about it but didn't know how. I mean, I can't exactly text you that kind of stuff."

Bianca, completely deflated, just replied with "Yeah."

"So, what were those things? Genies?"

Bianca exhaled. *Snap out of it, Bianca! You don't even like this guy!*

"Djinn," she corrected, launching into her two-second definition. "They're beings made of smokeless flame. There's a bunch of different kinds."

"The satanic gates have opened!" Steve bellowed. He punched his fist in the air, projecting his voice into the small space. Every time Steve pretended there was an invisible audience, it felt awkward. Bianca shifted uncomfortably.

"Why do you act like that?" she asked, her mouth half-full.

"Like what, exactly?"

She put her fork down and leveled one of her trademark scathing looks at him. "You look like you're in a one-man soap opera."

Steve looked away, embarrassed. "I thought you liked it."

Bianca blushed. *So, he* does *like me?* "Why would I like it?"

"You know," Steve began. "Trying to stand out in this boring town. Like you." He gestured to her all-black outfit, her black boots, and trademark black lipstick she had hastily swiped on.

"But . . . this isn't an act, Steve. This is just how I look."

It was Steve's turn to give her a scathing look. "Uh-huh."

"What? It's true! I'm a winter, Leila's a summer. These are the facts."

Steve sighed. "I really do like theater. There just aren't many opportunities here. I was just hoping to make my mark."

"You don't have to be that way with me, though, okay?" Bianca said softly. Even if she and Steve only stayed friends, she wanted him to know that.

"Okay," Steve said. "But I look really good in eyeliner."

"Let's not ruin the moment."

"And a cape," he added.

"Aaaaand the moment is ruined."

They both laughed. For Bianca, it soon morphed into a belly laugh. Then it turned into a weird, desperate cackle where she couldn't stop, the absurdity of the week's events taking over. What else could she do *but* laugh?

Steve gave her a worried look, his chuckles ending much sooner. Bianca finally caught her breath and dabbed at the tears forming in her eyes. Were they from laughter or fear? Who knew.

"Do you . . . want to talk about it?" Steve asked.

Bianca toyed with her fork. "It's all been so weird ever since our birthday last week."

"Happy birthday," Steve said, with a flourish of his hand.

"Thanks," Bianca replied. "The Elmhursts' barn caught on fire, but we're pretty sure it was because of a djinn. Because of *us*."

"Aha!" Steve said. "There is foulness afoot."

"Foulness indeed," Bianca said, grimacing. "Can I have more pie? It's a long story."

Steve saluted and hopped up from his chair. She watched as he cut another slice of pie, his shoulders illuminated in the fluorescent glow of the pastry display. She could feel the back of her jaw start to salivate all over again.

Because of the pie. That's all. Just from the pie.

Steve slid the new plate in front of her. "Okay, pie has been refilled, now the show must go on."

Bianca tried not to laugh. Steve was *funny*. It felt good to just chuckle and decompress with someone. She shoved another forkful of delicious blackberry into her mouth instead.

"Okay, so, at the barn fire there was this demon thing, which we now know is a djinn, and he kept talking about some *debt*. And then he totally rushed Leila with his fire and like, possessed her the whole week!"

Steve shivered. "It just poured out of her. At the party, the dude walked out of her skin like he'd been there all along."

Bianca shook her head. "I should have been a better sister. A better *friend*. I wish I knew how to help her, but now, I don't think she needs my help anymore." She said the last part a bit glumly, her shame from her failed jaunt around the world adding to her internal list of failures.

Steve gave her a sad look. "You had no idea what you were dealing with. You can't blame yourself."

Bianca warmed to his words, but still, she *did* blame herself. All those moments when Leila looked strange, her eyes glassy. All those instances of Bianca wondering if something was going on, the times she let herself be convinced by Leila's "fine." She felt lower than low, in that moment, and vowed to be a better family member.

Her *family*. Bianca gasped and looked down at her hands.

"What? What is it?" Steve asked, his face coming closer to Bianca's.

She swallowed, looking back at him. He smelled like sugar and pine, like the coziness of the indoors and the wild winter woods behind them. Bianca gulped.

"My ring," Bianca said, gesturing to the iron band on her finger. "This all started with the birthday present our dad gave us. He has the same one."

Why had their father given them an iron ring that had suddenly become incredibly useful? What did he know that Bianca and Leila didn't?

Steve bit his lip, deep in thought. "Come on," he said. "I'll drive you home."

Bianca nodded, knowing she had better get back. She needed to ask her father about the rings. About *all* of this.

The second Bianca sat in Steve's car, she felt all the adrenaline she'd been buoyed by flee her body. All she felt was a deep, bone-weary exhaustion now.

I think I just went on a date with Steve Rosenberg? Bianca texted June while Steve backed out of their spot.

June called her immediately, despite it being the middle of the night. Bianca quickly declined the call.

Hold your horses! I have so much to catch you up on, Bianca texted back.

June just responded with a knife emoji and the words **You better call me!**

They sat in companionable silence as Steve led them onto the dark roads that would take her home. Bianca was comfy and sleepy, her body full of pie and whipped cream.

"You awake over there?" Steve chuckled.

"Barely," she replied.

She looked out the window, letting her thoughts drift. Then she saw it: a quick burst of flame in the forest, keeping even with Steve's car like a galloping horse. Bianca sat up quickly, peering into the dark.

"What the . . . ," she began.

"Did you see a deer?" Steve asked, worried. Out here, it was common for deer and cars to collide.

Bianca thought fast, not wanting to freak him out anymore. "Yeah, but it went the other way."

"Phew," was all he said.

But Bianca knew what she saw.

It was more djinn.

LEILA

Leila *woke up well rested* for the first time in a week. She cracked her eyes open under cool covers, looking forward to Christmas morning.

Her phone buzzed with a text.

Foster: Babe? What's going on? Did I do something wrong?

Foster. During the madness at the party, followed by frantic Noche Buena prep, she'd completely forgotten about him. Above his latest text were a dozen unanswered ones.

Leila thought back to how happy she'd been when Foster had asked her out junior year. How thrilling it felt to feel his arm around her shoulder in the middle of the cafeteria, where everyone was watching. How delicious it had been to disappear into dreams of their future together.

But then she thought about all those times she'd felt empty whenever they were alone. How bland her thoughts and expressions had to be to stay on the same level as him. Her fingers tickled with fire, and she watched as the flames danced across her knuckles over her covers, even while wearing her ring.

No. She was different now. Even if he hadn't cheated on her, she knew it had been over for a long time. She didn't want the same things now. That wraparound porch on her own homestead was no longer a fantasy but an anchor weighing her down.

It's over, Foster, she texted back. Then she set her phone to Do Not Disturb, ending the conversation. He didn't deserve anything else.

It was done.

Leila took a deep breath, then looked at herself in the mirror. Maybe instead of wearing a dress today, she'd wear something different. She rummaged around in her chest of drawers and came upon a pair of jeans.

Jeans. When was the last time she'd worn those? She slipped them on, surprised they still fit, and assessed herself in the mirror. She looked like Leila, yes, but somehow stronger and fiercer. The jeans showed off her long legs and wide hips, something that had been tough to showcase in her modest ankle-length dresses.

She looked *good*.

She headed into the Jack 'n' Jill bathroom she shared with Bianca and scrubbed her face with cold water, relishing the feeling of having her body back to herself. She scraped her long hair into a scrunchie and looked in the mirror. Her skin still looked a bit gray, but at least she didn't look haunted.

Losing her glow was a small price to pay for having autonomy again. Still, a flicker of gold winked back in her irises. *Interesting.*

She threw on a doe-colored sweater and gently made her way down the stairs. Bianca's door, she noticed, was still closed.

"Hi, baba jan," her dad said from where he stood at the stove. Christmas Day was pancake day, and she watched as he expertly flipped them onto a stack.

"Mi amor, que te pasa? You look pale," her mom asked from the breakfast table, where she'd been reading an academic paper. She stood up and felt Leila's forehead. "Hmm, a little warm."

You have no idea, Leila wanted to say.

"I'm okay, Mom," Leila said instead, shrugging her off. Her mother looked at her daughter's sallow skin and said nothing. Thankfully, her dad slid a plate of pancakes over, along with a steaming cortado, ending the conversation.

"Bokhor," he said, passing her the dulce de leche. *Eat.*

She eyed the pancakes hungrily, the powdered sugar flecked across the thin, rolled Argentinian-style pancakes. She took a bite, savoring the way her dad never made the panqueques too sweet, like the Waffle House in town always did. That was where Foster would take her on dates nights: the Waffle House.

Leila took another bite, and another, adding dulce de leche to the remaining stack, chewing hard as she tried to banish all memories of Foster from her brain. Of Foster with Kinsley, of her and Foster tangled in the sheets of his bedroom with his parents out of town on an Alaskan cruise.

Maybe it's better this way. Then she felt her cheeks redden with the pain of being rejected, of being cheated on, and she tried to think of something else.

She took a sip of cortado, enjoying the way the strong espresso made everything seem a tiny bit better, a tiny bit less pathetic.

Just then, Bianca stomped down the stairs. "Morning," she yawned, still in her pajamas.

"Buenos días," Mom replied.

"Sob bekheir, Behnaz jan," their dad added.

Bianca just gave a gruff nod, her arms weighed down with gifts. She put them under the tree, where it was easier to see how hastily they'd been wrapped.

"Okay, what's the plan today? Presents, then bed?" Bianca asked, pouring herself a cortado from the stovetop espresso maker, looking way too tired to have gone to bed at the same time as everyone else.

Their mother frowned. "You want to go back to sleep already?"

"The party didn't let out until eleven P.M.!" Bianca yelped.

Mom's eyebrows rose. "In Argentina, we would stay up until four in the morning then go to work at nine."

Their dad coughed.

"Okay, ten!" she conceded.

"I could use some help at work today," Dad said from the other side of the table. "There's a Mercedes with a spark-plug issue from the Johnsons." Even on Christmas Day, their father had to work. After all, he didn't get time off or paid vacations. If he didn't work on his cars, he didn't get money, and today was no exception.

"Pass," Bianca said quickly. "I have a date with my duvet."

Leila put her coffee down, thinking. When was the last time she helped her dad in the garage? It was mind-numbing work, handing her dad tools and holding lights under the hood as her dad fiddled around in the engine. But she loved the smell of engine oil and orange Gojo, and the feel of opening a fresh pack of shop rags.

More importantly, she had questions for her father. Questions she wasn't sure he would want to answer. But sometimes, when he was under the chassis of a car or puttering around his garage, he was a bit more talkative, telling tales of Iran, though he rarely brought up his past life. This was her chance to ask him about the iron rings.

"I'll help," she said.

"Merci, Leila jan," he said gratefully. He cheersed her with his mug.

Bianca turned their Bluetooth speaker on to a Christmas station. "All right," she announced. "Present time!" She grabbed her lumpy packages and began handing them out at the breakfast table.

For their mother, Bianca had gotten new hand cream and

organic soaps. For their dad, a cutting mandoline that she warned was dangerous.

"Yes!" he cried, his eyes lighting up. "Now I can prep torshi in half the time!"

For Leila, Bianca had thoughtfully gotten a zero-waste pattern she'd been eyeing and the fabric to make it. She'd clearly been talking to Jessica at the craft store. "Thanks, Bianca." Leila smiled.

The sourdough starter Leila had made for their dad was a big hit, as was her mom's crocheted hat. Leila had made a photo album as a joint gift for both her parents, and the two quickly began tearing up as they looked through the old photos Leila had scoured off their computers, full of baby pictures and awkward school photos.

For Bianca, Leila had gotten even more evil eyes. She'd found a place online that sold the charms in bulk and used jewelry wire and beads to thread them into necklaces, rings, and bracelets. She wordlessly gave the pile to her twin.

"Is this design very popular at school?" their mom asked, eyeing the large pile.

"Yep," Bianca said, cheerfully raking all the jewelry toward her. "They're all the rage. Thanks, Leila!"

"No problem," Leila said solemnly. She watched for her father's reaction, noting how his eyes went wide, his face pale. She added it to the list of things to casually ask him while she helped him work on cars.

Then, their dad handed out envelopes to both girls: fifty

dollars each. It might not have seemed a lot to girls like Shivani, but to Leila and Bianca, their yearly Christmas cash was a small fortune.

"Thanks, Mom and Dad," Leila said.

"Gracias, Mamá. Merci, Baba," Bianca repeated.

"Okay!" their dad said, clapping his knees. "Garage time!"

Bianca scuttled up the stairs. "Merry Christmas, bye!"

"I have some reading to catch up on," their mom said quickly, not wanting to volunteer for any garage work. She made for her bedroom, already in "work mode." Both women's doors slammed at the same time.

Leila followed her dad out to the garage. It was detached from the house, set back on the property where the gravel driveway ended. It had originally been a barn, but their father had converted it when they first moved here, adding electrical wiring and pouring the concrete floor himself. Even though it fit three cars, there were still other vehicles parked on the grass, some on blocks, some so rusted out they should have been towed away years ago.

Leila had on her chore coat and muck boots, along with a thermos of chai. No open-toed shoes were allowed in the garage, and without a working heater, she needed to keep her jacket on.

Her dad turned on the cage lights that swung from the exposed beams in the ceiling. Moths and small birds flew away, annoyed at being disturbed.

"Okay," her dad said, clapping his hands and rubbing

them together excitedly, his bushy eyebrows practically flying off his head. "This car's got an interesting problem. Whenever it rains, the car alarm goes off. I think it's because of the spark plugs under the rear seat, but we won't know until I pour water on the car!"

He said this like it was the most delightful thing to happen in weeks. He went to the old black boom box in the corner and turned on the radio, where reruns of his favorite show, *Car Talk*, played from the tinny speakers. He gazed at the beige Mercedes parked out on the gravel like it was a fun puzzle waiting to be solved.

"I need you to get the hose. I'll pull the car up front and we can start to spray it."

"All right," Leila said, trying not to smile at her dad's dorky glee. Nothing excited him more than a car with a weird issue. Oil changes and tune-ups were fine, but car forensics was his specialty.

Leila grabbed the hose around the back side of the barn, listening to the thick Boston accents of the radio hosts arguing about a Subaru that had a gear-shift issue. This truly was her father's heaven.

Her dad pulled the Mercedes into the drive. It was a diesel car, the engine percolating pleasantly. He rolled down the window.

"Okay, as soon as I roll this window back up, spray me!"

He quickly closed the window and Leila opened the spigot, letting the water fly. She hosed it on the driver's side, then arced it so it fell right on top of the roof. That's when the car alarm went off.

HONK! HONK! HONK! The noise pierced Leila's skull, too loud this early in the morning.

"AHA!" she heard her dad cry from inside the car. He held up his palm, motioning for Leila to stop. She quickly turned off the water.

"It *is* the spark plugs in the back!" he yelled over the car alarm as he hurried to the rear passenger side, showing Leila where water was leaking through the window and onto the back seats. He lifted the beige cushion, revealing a panel of spark plugs beneath.

"Voilà!" he said with a flourish, his hand gesturing to the slow leak of water entering the spark-plug tray. Leila still had her hands over her ears, the noise deafening.

"GREAT!" she shouted. "Now can you turn it off?"

Her dad yanked the offending spark plug out of its socket and held it up like it was a rotten tooth. The car alarm stopped instantly.

"You rascal," he chided to the offending plug. He held it so close his mustache practically tickled it. "You're the reason the Johnsons have been having so much trouble!"

Leila tried not to laugh. He talked to his cars like they were his children. He moved the car back into the garage, and then she watched as he felt along the back window seal, trying to see how water was getting in. He winced as his ring got caught.

"Baba," Leila began. She *never* called him Baba, always preferring the term *Dad*. But this was her opening, and she was going to take it for all it was worth.

"Mm?" he said, either not noticing she had switched to his name in Farsi or being too absorbed in his car work.

"Why do you wear that ring? Even though it gets caught all the time?"

Her dad just shrugged, his eyes still on the bank of spark plugs. "Because I can't take it off."

Then he froze, as if realizing how weird that sounded. He slowly turned to Leila. *Busted.*

She didn't want to spook him, though. Her father was on high alert now. Better to act casual about the whole thing.

She turned around, pretending to rummage in the drawers of her father's meticulous tool chests. "Why can't you take it off?"

She couldn't see his expression, but she could feel the stillness of the garage, feel the loaded weight of her question.

"Because . . . ," her dad began quietly. "Because I made a promise."

Too vague. That promise could mean anything from his wedding vows to whatever kick-started this whole mess of djinn. She decided to try a different angle and waited until he started to lower the rear passenger window to fix the seal.

Silence.

"Did that promise involve me and Bianca? Is that why you gave us rings for our birthday too?" she asked casually. She pretended to examine a wrench closely. Her father said nothing. She didn't push. She didn't turn around. She waited for him to be the one to explain.

Then she heard a ragged choking. She faced him.

"I'm sorry," he said, tears streaming down his cheeks.

Leila's heart stilled. Her sneaking suspicion was correct, and instead of feeling triumphant, she felt horrified.

Leila's throat went tight. "Sorry for what?" she whispered, still hoping that her dad wasn't the reason all this was happening, praying that her father was going to apologize for not getting them a car for their eighteenth birthday or that the rings weren't actually from the Atlas Mountains, or, or, or—

"A long time ago, I made a deal," her father whispered. His eyes met hers, and Leila could see how sorrowful they were. How completely and utterly miserable just talking about this was making him.

But she had to know.

"What kind of deal?" Leila asked, voice cracking.

"It wasn't supposed to happen to you," her father finally said, his eyes unable to meet hers. "When I made the deal, I didn't know it would be you."

"Dad, what was the deal? What are you talking about?"

"There's a price for every wish," he said, tears now streaming down his face. "And you were the price I paid."

Part III

And some men used to seek refuge with some djinn—
so they increased each other in wickedness.

— **Quran, Surah Al-Djinn 72:6**

TEHRAN,
35 YEARS BEFORE

He had always known it was illegal to consort with djinn. It was an old law, back when Persia had kings and dynasties. Everyone knew it was wrong, even if nobody believed in djinn anymore. But the government had collapsed years ago, and a newer, stricter government was in place. He was running out of options.

It was a bad time to be a political dissident. It was a bad time to be a young man of age who could be easily drafted into Iran's new theocratic army.

It was a bad time to be a bad Muslim.

He hid all the evil eyes in the house and aired out the smell of the esfand incense his family lit every day. There was no way the djinn would come if those were still out, those traditional methods of warding evil spirits away. He looked at his acceptance letter again, the one that said he'd gotten into an engineering program in the United States.

He already had a visa guaranteed to study there, something called a J-1. All he needed was the passport that his country was reluctant to give its citizens. They'd denied him, of course, citing that he needed to serve his mandatory army time. They'd turned a blind eye to the wealthier young men who had already fled the country, though.

I'd do anything to go to that university, he thought to himself. *Absolutely anything.*

But with the student protests and the government's violent crackdowns, it was near impossible to leave. The black market had dried up, and all counterfeit passport shops had shut down.

This is the only way.

He winced as he took one of his mom's sewing needles and pricked his finger, letting the blood draw. He threw her tasbih into the other room.

Then, he did the last thing he ever thought he would do.

He tried to summon a djinn.

BIANCA

It had been no use. Bianca couldn't fall back asleep after Christmas morning. Instead, she watched a Studio Ghibli movie in French. It helped her grasp of languages to watch a movie she'd seen before in another language. If she aced her AP French exam that spring, then she would be able to fulfill her foreign language credits at university and take another, newer language that wasn't offered at Ayers High. Besides, *Totoro* was awesome no matter what language you watched it in.

Does it matter how many languages you speak if you don't wanna leave anymore? a small voice inside Bianca asked herself. *What is even the point?*

Then she heard it.

"*WHAT?*" Leila's voice screamed from the backyard.

Bianca snapped her laptop shut and peered out the window. It looked like Leila was facing off with their dad outside the garage. What was worse, her body was so full of flames she looked like she had the night of the party, about to throw a fireball. Meanwhile their dad looked positively white, not even bothering to fight back or call for help. Mamá, who usually listened to music while reading for work, had mercifully not heard.

Bianca sprinted downstairs and threw the back door open. She ran out in her ridiculous red reindeer flannel pajamas. "What's going on?" she shouted. "Leila, what are you—"

But Leila cut her off, pointing a finger at their father. He shrank away. "Did you know *he's* the reason all the djinn are here, Bianca?"

Bianca froze. "How?"

Leila laughed. It was a cruel, harsh sound. "That was how he escaped Iran after the revolution. He made a deal with a . . . with a . . ." She looked accusingly at her father, whose tears were now running down his face.

"A mareed," he whispered.

"Baba?" Bianca turned to him, horrified.

Instead of answering, their father slowly took off his iron ring and placed it on the ground. His left hand looked strange without it, and the flesh underneath was pale and pruned after so many years of wear. He sank to his knees and bowed his head.

"Please," he said, his voice a bit stronger now. "Take me instead."

"You think it's that simple?" Leila cried.

Bianca had never seen her sister like this, never seen her emotions spew out so quickly, even when she had told her about Foster's infidelity.

"Leila . . . ," Bianca warned.

"I can't just *give* you all the crap that you dumped on me, Dad! All the weird looks about our last name, all the politics, our strange food! And now you want me to give this extra burden back? Like I can just take it off and hand it over?"

Their dad said nothing, head still bowed, tears falling. He looked like a boy standing before a parent, about to be slapped. Bianca's heart hammered, her confusion morphing into concern.

"Leila—" Bianca said, stepping toward her.

"STOP," Leila shouted. Only it wasn't Leila. It was something else. Her eyes were bright gold, her skin searing with flames. Bianca stood still, the ring on her hand aching with pain. She tried to take another step toward their father.

"DO NOT MOVE," Leila intoned again, this time in a voice that sounded deeper, richer, one that echoed of a dozen other languages. Bianca stilled, her mind racing. Hadn't they banished the djinn inside her? Wasn't Leila her own person now? But then . . . where was that voice coming from?

Unless . . . unless it was all Leila herself. She was changing, becoming more djinn-like every day.

Leila's golden gaze turned back to their dad. Bianca had no idea what to do next.

"How dare you gamble with our future," Leila uttered in that deep, creepy voice. Their father was quiet, a puddle of tears spreading on the gravel beneath his bowed head.

"Take me, please," he whispered.

Leila stalked closer to him, flames licking her hands. She wasn't herself—she wasn't the sister Bianca had grown to know this past week. Whatever she was planning on doing, it wouldn't be good.

Bianca's limbs finally thawed, her mind made up. In that moment she yanked off her own ring and threw it at their father, the iron band landing in his bent lap. If only she'd run down with all the evil eyes Leila had gotten her for Christmas, then she could have covered Baba in those life-saving amulets. Back when Leila had been her sister, that is, and not the cruel, heartless monster before her.

"NO!" Leila roared the second the ring fell into their father's lap. Flames poured out of her, the fireballs launching from her fingertips. Bianca acted quickly, throwing herself in front of their dad. He still hadn't looked up; he still couldn't face the choice he'd made all those years ago.

Bianca jumped and the flames hit her instead. This fire burned, charring flesh and sending pain shooting across her body. She screamed, the heat too much to bear.

And then everything went black.

LEILA

It happened in slow motion. Her father had been sitting in front of her, head bowed as if in prayer. Then she'd felt rage pour out of her, searing hot. Suddenly Bianca was there, intercepting the fire, the fire Leila had pushed all her feelings of betrayal and hurt into.

How could he have done this to us? How could he have bargained with the lives of his children? Every question seemed to flow from her fingertips in the form of a flame. And instead of hitting her father, they hit her twin.

It hadn't felt like she was the one doing it. Leila had been floating above herself, watching it all unfold. She couldn't even claim she'd done it because she was possessed; this was all Leila, years of pent-up frustration with her family and their Otherness bursting out of her. And now this bargain.

Bianca lay on the ground, her pajamas charred, the hot pink reindeers turned to gray ash. There weren't burn marks on her, but her eyes were shut, and she was unresponsive. Her father's endless supply of tears just flowed even harder.

"Naaaaaaah," he moaned, cradling Bianca's head. "Dokhtaram. Janam. Jiggaram." He mumbled the words over and over, *my daughter, my heart, my liver*, a term of endearment in Farsi. And all Leila could do was watch, dumbstruck.

Finally, she blinked, as if coming out of a trance, and poured cold water from the spigot onto a clean shop rag. Wordlessly, she sat next to her father and placed it on Bianca's head, their fight forgotten, his tears falling as they joined Leila's.

Please let Bianca be okay. Please let her have fainted like Foster.

"Baba?" Leila whimpered, as if offering a truce. "What do we do?"

He scrubbed his face with the back of his hand, then looked at Bianca again. Something flickered across his face— Recognition? Fear? Hope?

"Get the esfand," he told Leila, his voice suddenly stern.

Leila's stomach roiled at the word. *Esfand*, the incense used to keep evil spirits away, what they called wild rue seeds in English. She'd noticed how Bianca had circled it around the house and how she'd had to walk over it carefully, the seeds putrid even when they were unlit. But she ran to the house anyway. Her hand trembled as she gently opened the kitchen drawer where they kept the candles, matches, lighters, and esfand. Just picking it up made her skin crawl. She ripped a sheet of tinfoil, and she didn't bother grabbing a lighter.

Leila sprinted back to the yard and threw the plastic packet of esfand to her father. She exhaled, glad to not be touching it anymore. Just holding it through plastic had made her feel strange.

Bianca's face was now chalk white.

"Here," Leila said, handing her dad the tinfoil so he could form a shallow plate for the esfand. They switched places, Leila now holding Bianca's body in her lap. Bianca's breath was shallow, and she could feel the clammy sweat of her sister's palms. *What have I done?* Leila thought miserably. And then: *What am I becoming?*

Dad poured the dried rue and placed it on the gravel. He looked at Leila expectantly.

Leila gulped. It felt weird using her flames in front of her father, felt strange sharing this new part of herself. She could feel the cold weight of the esfand on the ground, the menacing thing inside her shrinking away from it, but she held out her hand anyway and lit a small flame under the foil packet.

Slowly, thin strands of incense smoke wound their way up as the seeds cracked and popped. But the second the smell touched Leila's nose, she dropped Bianca's head with a thud and ran to the other side of the garage. She had to get away from the smell, had to get away from the toxic fumes as they wafted. Why this affected her and not iron, she wasn't sure.

Her reaction had been automatic, as if a doctor had hit her knee with a rubber mallet. The stinging December air was nothing compared to the pain, the torture, of having to smell the esfand that kept evil spirits away. Evil spirits like the one Leila had now become.

From the other side of the yard she heard Bianca cough and splutter, the strong scent acting like smelling salts, and Leila sagged with relief. *Bianca is going to be okay. She wasn't hurt, she was just knocked out, Bianca will be all right—*

And then Bianca was suddenly standing next to her, breathing hard, her skin color back to normal, no, *better* than normal, and her eyes—her eyes, they looked—

"Oh my god," Bianca said with disgust. "That incense smelled *horrible.*"

And then she threw up.

Leila held Bianca's hair, rubbing her back as she heaved in the weak December light. The sound of footsteps crunched closer, then there was their dad, his face lined with worry as he watched Bianca retch.

Bianca stood up, wiping her mouth. Leila gasped.

It was Bianca, but a new version of her. Her skin looked so bright it practically shone under the gray Christmas sky. Her hair was glossy and strong. Her eyelashes, already long, looked even thicker, if possible. And her eyes . . .

"Bianca," Leila gasped. "Your eyes are blue."

"*WHAT?*" Bianca clutched her face, horrified. "What

happened? You were about to take out Baba, and then I woke up with the worst combo of orange juice and toothpaste I've ever tasted in my life."

The esfand, Leila thought numbly. Now Bianca stood before Leila, just as damned as her. *What have I done?*

"But . . . you had your ring . . . ," Leila said, clawing for an explanation.

Leila's eyes met her father's, and his expression crumpled, his already swollen face threatening to cry more as he stood there. He wordlessly held up the iron ring Bianca had thrown him.

"Behnaz jan," he said. "Beeya, it's too cold." Leila watched him place Bianca's ring on a rusted car, as if deciding he didn't care about its protection anymore.

Bianca shook her head, dazed. "I'll be right in, Baba. I don't feel cold."

Of course you don't. Leila wanted to cry. *Of course you don't feel cold.* Their dad just nodded sadly and shuffled back to the kitchen. "I'll pour you some fresh chai," he said, as if chai could solve everything.

"I feel so weird," Bianca said, holding her hands in front of her face.

"Bianca," Leila began. She'd have to be the one to break it to her, but her throat had gone dry. It was her fault. Leila had done to this her.

Leila instead held up her phone, turning on selfie mode. Bianca's eyes went wide at her image, her hands roving over her even-sharper cheekbones, her redder lips, her fuller hair, and now, her bright blue eyes. Leila's eyes looked more gold compared to the brown eyes she had before her transformation, but nothing as stark a change as Bianca's.

"Holy crap," Bianca breathed. "I look incredible!"

Leila lowered the phone. "Huh?" This was not the reaction she'd been bracing for.

"Did I get a power too?" Bianca asked excitedly. "Hold on, let me try to shoot flames."

Leila watched in disbelief as Bianca scrunched up her face, then shouted, "Flame-ee-yo!"

Nothing happened.

"You look like you're trying to take a huge dump," Leila said, trying not to laugh. But secretly, she was relieved. Bianca hadn't gotten a power, she had just gotten some weird physical changes. *Okay*, Leila thought. *We can work with that. That's not so bad.*

"Dang," Bianca said bitterly. "I really thought I was gonna get to be like you."

"You *want* to be like me?" Leila asked, surprised.

"I mean . . . being able to shoot flames has to come in handy." Bianca was looking at Leila like she was a bit dim.

"You know I can't eat red meat anymore, right? It has too much iron. I can wear the iron ring, but ingesting it is too much. I found out the hard way at lunch this week."

That did it. Bianca gasped. "No cheeseburgers? But . . . but . . ."

Leila sighed. "Or spinach. Be glad you didn't get any of this stuff. Just keep away from that ring, to be safe."

Bianca turned back to the house, resigned. "Come on, we'd better go talk to Baba."

For the second time in ten minutes, Leila was incredibly relieved. Yes, she'd thrown flames at her sister, but Bianca was alive and unburnt somehow. Yes, she'd been transformed to look like the best plastic surgeon in the world had worked on her, but she didn't have any weird powers. They were going to be all right.

Bianca stumbled in the dirt, her legs still wobbly, and Leila instinctively steadied her. But when she gripped Bianca's hand, she felt something. Not quite a static shock, but a crackle of energy.

Bianca looked down at their hands, and her blue eyes began to glow.

"Bianca?" Leila asked, panicking. What was going on? What was her sister doing? Leila tried to remove her hand, but Bianca's grip had turned to stone. Leila began to panic, her breath coming in rapid gulps.

"Bianca?" Leila repeated, her voice frantic.

Bianca didn't answer, and her blue eyes glowed even brighter. Leila watched as a blue flicker of static formed between their hands, then turned into a tiny flame, no bigger than a pilot light. Leila looked, mesmerized, as it climbed up her own arm, like a bright blue vein.

"Don't fight it," Bianca whispered. "It won't hurt."

"Bianca? What won't hurt? Let go!" Leila demanded.

But Bianca wasn't there. Her eyes bored into Leila's, but they weren't focusing. Her grip on Leila's arm was like a bear trap.

Leila's body suddenly seized. It felt like when she'd had sleep paralysis and that demon really had been sitting on her. Her body was frozen, and all she could see now were Bianca's bright blue eyes boring into her own, like a serpent hypnotizing its prey.

"Nghhh," Leila moaned. The static current had taken over her whole body now, like limbs that had been woken up and had that pins-and-needles feeling.

Turn around, a small voice inside Leila said. It wasn't the cackling, menacing djinn. It sounded gentler, like a pitcher of water being poured into a pond. *Turn around*, the voice said again, this time more insistent. Leila's body began to ache, but when she turned around, a wonderful, cool feeling washed over her again.

Pat your head three times, the same voice said again. Leila did it, tapping her hair. She'd do anything to feel this blissful, mind-numbing relief.

Whistle! And Leila did, whistling a long, clear note. It felt incredible. How could she feel like this forever?

"Oh, hell yes," she heard Bianca say, as if she were speaking in another room, somewhere less cozy and comfortable than Leila's brain had now become. Leila waited for another command, eager to please the voice, but none came.

"All right," Bianca said. Slowly, Leila felt the cold of the backyard seep back into her. The calm feelings dissolved, and the fuzzy outline of Bianca became clearer. There was no mistaking it: Bianca's blue eyes were iridescent.

"Bianca?" Leila whispered. "What did you do?"

Instead of answering, Bianca just grinned.

"My turn."

BIANCA

It *hadn't occurred* to Bianca when she jumped in front of her sister's flames that there'd be a good chance she would get sprinkled with fairy dust too. If she had, she would have asked Leila to strike her down days ago.

Bianca had done it. She'd finally figured out how to get a power of her own. Was it piping hot flames that would smite her enemies? No, but it was *something*. She flexed her fingers, marveling at how her body had just imposed its will on Leila's. Leila stood across from her, horrified.

"Did you just . . . possess me?" Leila asked, breathing hard.

"Looks like it," Bianca replied breezily. "I guess that calls us even, after you tried to kill me, huh?" she joked.

She hadn't *meant* to do it, but the second Leila had reached for Bianca, it had felt like a new pathway had opened, a door that Bianca had never seen before in the form of her twin. And she'd taken that door and plunged her mind into Leila's.

It had felt surreal, opening up a human and seeing the remote control that Bianca could now command. That's when she'd felt the extent of her power. She could make Leila move and talk, could feel her sister's emotions and, if she wanted to, do worse things, like Cyrus had. All Leila's memories had been like tadpoles, swishing around her consciousness, ripe for the plucking. But Bianca hadn't wanted to mess with that.

Leila tilted her head as she looked at Bianca, reassessing her. Then: "What do we do about Dad?"

Baba. Bianca had totally forgotten it was his fault they were in this mess in the first place.

"What did he do, exactly?"

Leila shook her head. "He made a deal with a djinn to leave Iran. In exchange for his firstborn."

Bianca sharply inhaled, remembering Cyrus's words about how they were "promised."

Part of Bianca pitied her father. He'd probably been the same age she was now, about to start college. Bianca couldn't fathom having kids of her own, so she would have felt fine making a blood oath on her descendants' lives since it felt like an impossibility. But another part of her was furious. Who makes a deal with a djinn in the first place? Who gambles away something they don't even have yet? If June were here, she'd be shaking her head, the odds were so crummy. And now his two daughters were given weighty powers with serious consequences, all because their dad had run out of options, so he'd bought futures instead.

"Behnaz?" Baba stood in the doorway, wringing his hands. He'd seen the whole thing. "Are you . . . I mean . . . has it . . ."

Are you a monster now too? Bianca could tell he wanted to ask but didn't know how.

"Baba . . . I . . ." He'd seen what she could do. Had witnessed her possessing Leila for himself. How to tell him out loud how she felt, though? How a power that probably made her baba want to cry was something she'd been secretly hoping for?

"Bianca?" Mamá joined Baba in the doorway, clutching a thermos of hot water and a gourd full of yerba mate, her drink of choice when she'd already maxed out on coffee. "Que esta pasando?" *Had Baba even told Mamá what he'd promised when they'd become parents?*

Before Bianca could process everything, she heard the crunch of gravel in their driveway. *Who would be here on Christmas morning?* Bianca wondered.

"Come on," Leila said.

They walked around the house, Bianca nimbly avoiding the lines of esfand she'd poured around their home, instinctually jumping over the disgusting powder, and made their way to the front.

There sat a white BMW.

The thing about being Iranian is that you can just tell when you see another Iranian, Bianca thought to herself. *The same crick in the nose. The same big eyes.* Bianca had never seen another Iranian in Ayers until the owner of the white BMW exited the car.

"Whoa," Bianca breathed. This chick looked *cool*. She was tattooed up to her neck with enough marks to ink a whole book. She had the same dark hair as them, and the same copper-colored skin. She wore a leather jacket and tight-fitting black jeans that made Bianca want to ask where she'd gotten them from. Bianca heard Leila give a sharp inhale as if she, too, was caught off guard. Was this the "cousin" Liam had asked her about at the party?

Maybe she was a long-lost relative of their father's. Or a family friend. But as the tall, lanky woman stomped her way up the drive, Bianca had a feeling this wasn't a social visit.

"You!" She pointed to the two of them. That was when Bianca noticed the markings on her body weren't *just* tattoos. They were evil eyes and lines from the Quran, along with drawings of djinn and other monsters she didn't recognize.

"Uh, can I help you?" Bianca asked.

"Reveal yourselves!" the woman shouted.

"Bianca . . . ?" Leila asked from beside her. Bianca saw the panic in Leila's eyes and knew it was mirrored in her own. "Do you know her?"

"No." Bianca shook her head. The woman was advancing on them now, but Bianca still had no idea why.

"To kieh?" their father asked, his face still puffy from crying. *Who are you?*

Mamá stood next to him, her face hard. "Nenas, get back in the house."

The stranger ignored them, turning to Bianca and Leila instead. "Take off their faces, dirty si'latah!"

"This is my face!" Bianca cried back, offended.

"Si'latah?" Their baba balked from the doorway. "These aren't djinn! These are my daughters!"

"Bebakhshid, agha," the stranger said, finally turning to their father. "These djinn have been parading around with your daughters' faces. They're not safe."

Before their father could say anything, Bianca rounded on the woman.

"What is *wrong* with you?" she cried. "This is *our* house. You can't just come stomping up here, making wild accusations!"

Leila said nothing. Bianca gave her a look as if to say, *Come on, Leila! Speak up!*

"Yeah," Leila added unhelpfully.

"What's wrong with *me*?" the woman snarled. "I've been hunting djinn all up and down the middle of nowhere because you two chuckleheads couldn't pick a city to terrorize that's closer to an airport!"

"Huh?" Leila asked, turning to Bianca. Bianca shrugged.

"Enough talk," she snapped. They watched mutely as the stranger got out a lighter and lit what looked like a metal sphere. Smoke poured out of it, and she began to swing it from a long chain.

Their father ran out the front door, about to stop the intruder from hurting his daughters.

Iron, Bianca realized. *She's trying to destroy us.* She could feel the metal's cold from here. But that wasn't the only iron she wore. With a sinking feeling, Bianca registered the iron rings, necklaces, and earrings practically dripping from the woman's body. And now she had a powerful iron ball in her hand, with incense pouring out of it. Bianca already knew what burned inside.

"Get away from them!" their father shouted. "Boroh!"

"Stand back, agha!" the woman cried, rolling up her sleeves to reveal even more tattoos. "I don't want to hurt you!"

"Que esta pasando?" their mother screamed from the doorway. "Khosrow, quien es? Porque esta aqui? Que quiere?" Their mother was rambling, frantic, forgetting her husband's Spanish was almost nonexistent.

"Uh-oh," Bianca said to Leila. "Mamá's going full Spanish."

"What do we do?" Leila asked, panicking.

Bianca glanced back at the house. Her father still looked like he was about to go into old-school fisticuffs with this fellow Iranian who dared besmirch his daughters' honor.

"Come on, let's get out of here. We can lead her away," Bianca said, thinking quickly. "Hey, jerkface!" she cried to the woman, mid-swing of the iron chain. "If you want us that badly, you'll have to catch us!"

Bianca grabbed Leila's arm and the two began to run, sprinting to the back field that led to The Grove.

"Get back here!" the stranger cried, still swinging the ball. Bianca caught a whiff of the esfand inside it, and her stomach roiled.

"Behnaz! Leila! Don't!" Baba cried. But Bianca couldn't bear to have her parents involved in whatever this was. For the first time ever, Bianca realized she was more powerful than her dad. He'd always seemed so strong, with his bushy mustache and huge hands full of cuts and scars from working on cars all day. But now the roles had reversed, and Bianca needed to protect her parents, despite the promise her father had made.

The twins sprinted to the tall trees that shielded them from their parents' view, their assailant's footsteps pounding close behind them. This was the kind of physical exertion that normally would have winded her, but Bianca found she was barely tired. In fact, she could do this all day. Leila pumped her arms as she easily ran alongside her, the two of them making incredible time.

Still, Bianca slowed down once they reached the near side of The Grove. Whoever this was, she already knew where they lived. They could only run so far.

Leila stopped next to her. "What now?"

"We have a little chat." Bianca turned to face their mysterious stalker and summoned that staticky, lightning-bolt feeling again. Her hair crackled, her pulse quickened, and she clenched her fists as the woman stopped about ten feet away from them, squaring off under the tall hickory and oak trees that had stood here since before this country had even been born.

"Stay right there," Bianca growled.

"Or what?" the woman taunted them, swinging the ball of esfand like an evil priest. Bianca tried hard not to inhale it, but just one whiff sent her coughing.

Leila responded by letting her flames build, the fire licking the bottoms of her boots. She held up her hands, each palm dancing with red and yellow tongues. "Or I barbecue you," Leila replied evenly.

Bianca nodded approvingly. *That* was the kind of comeback their duo needed!

Leila's response had been enough. The woman's eyes went wide, and she stumbled backward, tripping over a rotted log on the soft pine floor.

Bianca shouted across the clearing. "Who are you? What do you want?"

"Si'lat can't throw fire," the woman replied, dumbstruck.

"Your name, jerkface!" Bianca reminded her.

"Zahra," the woman spat. "Don't pretend you don't know who I am."

Bianca gave Leila a look like *Can you believe her?* "So you just come stomping into our home on Christmas wielding esfand? That's not very nice."

From the corner of her eye, Bianca saw Leila put her head into her hands, mortified by Bianca's poor bantering skills.

I'm new to this djinn thing, okay! she wanted to shout.

"What's not very nice is holding this town hostage! Now stay still while I banish you back to oblivion!" And then Zahra strode forward, swinging the esfand like a ball-and-chain weapon.

Bianca couldn't help but notice how this woman was all stoicism and puffed chest, all projection and pomp.

Steve could learn a lot from Zahra.

Just then, Zahra withdrew a handful of evil eye chains from her pocket. She was already reciting lines from the Quran, approaching the girls as if she were about to lasso a wild horse.

"Gahhhh!" Bianca cried, inhaling more esfand. It smelled like torture, both metallic and sulfurous. Leila gagged next to her.

In that moment Bianca yanked off the evil eye necklace she herself wore and threw it back at their assailant. "Leave us alone, you freak!" She knew that wasn't a very nice thing to call someone, but her better insults were for when she could breathe cleaner air and not feel like she was inhaling noxious swamp gas.

Zahra stilled, looking at the evil eye necklace Bianca had thrown at her. "Wait . . . why haven't you dissolved yet?" she wondered out loud, looking at the two of them.

"Because we're human!" Leila screamed back at her.

Bianca nodded vigorously, her throat too choked with smoke to say anything smart.

Zahra fumbled with her esfand holder and took a step back. Bianca chugged fresh air.

"But this doesn't make sense . . . ," she mumbled to herself. "How could they have powers and wear the Nazr?"

"Because they are weak," a deep, chilling voice said from behind them.

Bianca turned. She knew that voice. She'd heard it at the party, the voice of the thing that had tried to take her and Steve, the thing that had originally possessed her sister.

There stood Cyrus, handsome and terrible, in his full royal uniform. He glittered in his fur-lined cloak, glowing gems, and golden buttons, making Bianca's Christmas Day pajamas and Leila's muck boots look laughable. Now, a jaunty golden crown sat atop his midnight hair.

"Hello again," Cyrus said, bowing low.

Bianca and Leila scuttled backward as Cyrus's djinn subjects all flamed into the clearing. Green flames, blue flames, oily flames, and tiny flames no bigger than a twinkle—The Grove was filling up fast.

"You!" Zahra cried.

Bianca watched as Zahra began opening the many pockets of a strange leather holster she wore. The bandolier had more evil eyes and esfand, along with dates and red-looking fireworks. Zahra was going to fight this huge host on her own. After trying to battle Bianca and Leila, it was laughable of her to take on this djinn army.

Zahra wasn't going to make it. She would fail, and Bianca

would have another consequence of her father's actions on her hands.

Zahra doesn't look much older than us, Bianca realized with a start. This impressively tattooed girl looked like she could still be in high school.

Still. *The enemy of my enemy is my friend.* She turned to face Cyrus, and Leila did the same.

"We can't stand by," Bianca whispered to her. "We gotta help."

"Yeah," Leila said, her voice still sounding a little unsure. "But what happens if we help and then she still comes after us?"

"Let's burn that bridge when we get to it," Bianca replied.

Leila shook her head, but she let her body ignite regardless. "Not how that works."

Bianca snorted. "Don't care."

The two faced off to meet the evil djinn prince as he bore down on them.

LEILA

Seeing another Iranian in Ayers was almost as startling as the djinn army now approaching them. The djinn appeared between the trees, their menacing flames dancing between bark and cold dirt. But even as she tried to track the growing horde, Leila kept finding herself sneaking looks at Zahra.

She couldn't help it: Zahra's sharp jaw, amber eyes, and tattoos hypnotized her. Leila had always associated being Iranian with being unattractive somehow, following Ayers's lead in worshipping tall, thin, and hairless women. But here was a beautiful Iranian girl, and Leila couldn't stop staring at her.

She was everything Foster wasn't.

"What?" Zahra asked, catching her gaze. It was no longer a hostile *begone, djinn!* kind of look, but she still seemed wary. "Do you need another evil eye?"

Leila didn't know what to say, so she just nodded. After being on opposing sides five seconds ago, they were suddenly united against a swelling army of demons, all without needing some big conversation about it. Zahra expertly tossed her a necklace, then turned back to the swell of djinn, some of them shifting out of their flame forms and into their flesh ones.

Leila tried not to be disappointed by how businesslike their transaction had been. *Focus, Leila!* she chided herself.

She tried to count how many djinn flames she could see. Ten, twenty, thirty—they appeared too quickly for her to keep track.

"If you will not join us, then you leave us no choice," Cyrus said from the front, like a military commander giving terms. He gave another menacing bow, then stood up and smiled, revealing his pointed teeth and sinister sneer.

"Attack," he said with a lazy wave of his hand.

The dancing flames that had looked like will-o'-the-wisps suddenly morphed into evil creatures of ill-fitting flesh. Djinn with horns on their heads and djinn with long, lashing tongues. Djinn in the form of beautiful women and others as old crones. There were close to fifty djinn now, and Leila's heart leapt into her throat. These djinn also had thin collars around their necks, as if marking them as part of Cyrus's army. What did that mean? How could evil djinn wear iron and still have their powers?

She shook her head, trying to focus. She prayed her father hadn't done something stupid like follow them to The Grove.

Quickly, the djinn closed the gap between Zahra, Bianca, and Leila.

Leila's adrenaline flooded her body with panic. *What do we do? What do we do?* Their eyes were red, their smiles menacing, their limbs at odd, incongruent angles.

"LEILA!" Bianca screamed across the clearing. "Fireball!"

Right. Leila willed heat to surge through her body and felt her hands light up with flames. She released a red-hot ball of fire at a djinn with a long tongue next to a slithery, oily ghul. The two screamed as the fire made contact, dissolving their bodies into ash and oil.

Before Leila had time to relish how she had just defeated two djinn in the blink of an eye, more surged forward. The trees that had looked brown and gray in the winter now reflected the reds and yellows of the fight below. Pine needles and twigs crackled underneath Leila's feet as she punched the air in front of her with more and more fire, sending demons dissolving into screams. But it was no use—they just kept coming.

Leila's shoulder suddenly blazed with pain. A ghul no taller than her knee had snuck up and splattered some of its oil at her, like an octopus shooting ink. She shot it down, but her shoulder throbbed where the ghul's oil had burned through her chore coat.

She stole a glance at Bianca and Zahra next to her, and they didn't seem to be faring any better. Bianca's power meant that she could only control demons she touched, and with such a large mob it was no use trying to do one-on-one combat. Instead, she swung some evil eyes in an impressive figure eight, trying hard to banish the closest djinn with less efficiency than Leila's fire.

Zahra seemed to be using the same moves as Bianca but echoing them with lines from the Quran. This seemed to help the demons dissolve more quickly, but still, Leila could tell that it wasn't enough. There were only three of them, and they'd maybe defeated ten djinn out of what was now a hundred. The odds were against them.

We're not gonna win, she realized. *There's just no way.* What little gap there had been between them and the djinn had closed quickly. They were surrounded now.

We have to get out of here.

"Bianca!" she screamed. "Come on!" She had an idea, but she wasn't sure if it would work with all three of them.

"Leila!" Bianca shrieked, punching a horned pali in the mouth. "What now?"

"We retreat," Leila said grimly.

"Retreat?" Bianca gasped, throwing an evil eye into an ifrit's face. It screamed as its fiery body turned into hissing steam. "To where?"

Good question. Where *should* they go? They could retreat back to their house with its wards and protections, but then they'd be trapped, the djinn circling them outside like vultures, their parents trapped with them. School was closed. There was no mosque in town. Leila had no idea where to go.

"Zahra!" Leila shouted. "We have to go!"

Zahra glanced up from the si'lat she was fighting, which

must have been especially difficult considering the si'lat had taken on Zahra's face. Still, Leila could easily tell the real Zahra with warm amber eyes apart from the smoldering, red-eyed twin opposite her.

"Go?" she repeated, as if Leila was being ridiculous. "We can't leave!" The si'lat with her face erupted into a pile of screaming steam. Zahra barely blinked before turning to another djinn.

"We're losing!" Bianca shouted, hitting a ghul with her boot. She'd tucked an evil eye into the laces, and Leila gagged as the thing turned into bubbling oil. "Come on, jerkface! Read the room!"

But to Leila's dismay, Zahra simply ignored them. Leila frowned, scanning the battlefield. *Where is Cyrus? Where has he disappeared to?* Typical of the spoiled prince to run off and not get his hands dirty.

Just then a huge djinn, taller than the tallest tree in The Grove, thundered into view. The ground beneath them shook. Birds took to the sky in angry squawks. The djinn army cheered, as if rallying.

"A giant?" Zahra gasped, momentarily forgetting to fight the thirsty bloodsucking djinn in front of her. It bit her arm, and she screamed before hitting it with a talisman.

"A giant?" Bianca repeated, incredulous. "Those are real?"

"Bianca!" Leila screamed. "Get Zahra. We have to go. NOW!"

Bianca looked at Leila. Leila gave her a meaningful nod.

"Do whatever it takes," Leila added, trying to steady herself on the quaking ground.

It felt like a small earthquake had reached Virginia. Leila's teeth clanked as the ground under them buckled.

Bianca understood. Her eyes burned bright blue, her hair lifting with static electricity. Then Bianca grabbed Zahra's shoulder, and Zahra's body suddenly went limp, her trademark scowl turning into a pleasantly empty smile. Her brown eyes turned blue.

"I smell the blood of a debt!" a low, thundering voice roared. It was the giant, gazing down on them. Only it didn't look like the giants in books, with thick legs and brown scruffy beards. No, this one was like a set of redwood trees strapped together, its scarlet skin shifting with glowing embers. Two eyes of coal glittered, and Leila watched, horrified, as it reached a smoldering arm toward them, tree branches cracking against his bulk.

They must be coming here from the djinn plane, Leila realized. And then she remembered: She knew how to get there. Knew how to transport herself to that other dimension. Maybe, just maybe, she could find a safe place for them there, while their enemy was busy.

"NOW!" Leila screamed, grabbing Bianca's and Zahra's hands. Zahra's grip felt floppy. Bianca's eyes glowed electric blue as she made Zahra stop fighting.

Leila concentrated, their destination crystal clear in her mind. The giant's hand came closer and closer, the fire of

Leila's power licking their feet. Just as the giant's fist tried to close around them, they disappeared.

They reappeared in the desert, standing before the same sunlit mountain Leila had seen twice before—except it was devoid of djinn. *All of them must be invading Ayers now*, Leila thought bitterly. *Thousands and thousands of them.* After Leila had seen so many hundreds, maybe thousands, of flickering lights on the mountainside previously, it now seemed so empty a tumbleweed could roll through what had become a ghost town.

Bianca let go of Zahra, and Zahra's eyes returned to amber.

"What!" Zahra spluttered, still clutching her talismans. "Where are we? Where did they go? What did you do to me?" She said this last part accusingly at Bianca, who simply gestured to the mountain with a *ta-da.*

Zahra stopped, jaw dropping as she gazed at the mountain. "Is that . . . ? Are we . . . ?"

Leila nodded grimly. "This is the djinn plane."

Zahra fell to her knees in the sand, gazing up at the mountain peak. "I never thought I would see it," she whispered. "All our generations of fighting them, and I never knew."

"You knew this place would be empty since they were all in our backyard. Smart," Bianca said approvingly. She cut her gaze up to the city in the mountain, eyes scanning for anyone else. "Still. We can't stay here forever. What are we going to do?"

At this, Zahra seemed to shake herself out of her trance. "*We?*" she asked, turning to the twins. "*We* aren't going to do anything. I'm going to call my family and they're going to come down and sort out this mess."

Bianca crossed her arms, staring Zahra down. "Okay, and who are you again? The girl who almost got her butt kicked by a giant? And who is this family?"

Zahra exhaled, and Leila could see she was trying to be civil. "First off, I'm nineteen. *Girl* is not appreciated. Second, we're djinn hunters. That's what we've been doing for hundreds of years. And when my father decided he wanted to move to America, we found plenty of djinn to fight here too."

"Is that why you've been trying to find us?" Leila asked. "What are you going to do now?"

At this, Zahra deflated, the bravado leaving her. "I . . . I don't know. I still don't understand what you two even *are*. I thought you were just a couple of si'lat hiding out in a small town."

"Well, we're definitely not si'lat," Bianca snapped.

Leila swallowed. Zahra sounded like someone who knew much more about this world than they did. "Have you met people like us before, though? Humans with djinn powers?"

At this, Zahra looked down at her leather boots, which were now coated in mud and sand. "No," she whispered. "I've never met people like you before."

Leila sighed, disappointed. They were out of their element, away from their world, and still without answers.

"What about Mamá and Baba?" Bianca asked, cutting through the grim silence. "What if the djinn get to them?"

Leila shook her head. "Dad made the deal, remember? They can't hurt him. If Mom's with Dad, she'll be safe." Plus, she was pretty sure Bianca had hung evil eyes on every possible exterior wall of the house. That, and the caustic line of esfand she'd had to step over on her way to the garage that morning meant the house was warded within an inch of its life.

Leila tried not to sound bitter when she mentioned her father, but it still hurt. They were in this mess because of him, and now his daughters and their community would have to pay the price. "The djinn are probably heading into town now. That's what Cyrus said he needed. More flesh, more ways to expand."

"Whoa, time out," Zahra said, making a T shape with her hands. "Your dad made a deal with *Cyrus*?"

Leila nodded.

Zahra's eyes went wide.

"That's how he got out of Iran," Bianca whispered. "He promised his children in exchange for safe passage to the US."

Zahra looked back at the swirling sand, squinting at the mountain. "Man," she said after a while. "That's the most messed-up thing I've ever heard."

Bianca gave a hollow laugh. Leila found herself chuckling along. After all they'd been through, burnt clothes and all, it felt almost hysterical that they were in this position. To think, Leila had been mourning the loss of her high school boyfriend only hours ago! And now here she was, in a universe parallel to her own, with no clue how to stop an invading djinn army from taking over Ayers.

"What do we do?" Leila finally asked, looking Zahra in the eye. Her amber eyes met Leila's gold ones, and Leila found herself blushing all over again. Zahra, too, seemed momentarily caught off guard.

It's not just me, Leila wanted to shout. *She feels it too!*

Zahra recovered quickly. "First, we have to see what we're up against. Then I have to call for reinforcements."

"Reinforcements?" Bianca asked. "Like, more amulets?"

Zahra shook her head. "No. We need more djinn fighters. I've never seen this many djinn at once. Usually, I just deal with one or two hiding out somewhere, but this is massive. Your dad's the bridge that let them come into his world. He promised them blood and flesh, and now they're going to get it however they can, even if they can't get you."

Leila's heart broke. Ayers, which she loved so much, was now under attack, and it was all because of their family. Would the djinn slowly possess everyone there, the way Cyrus had tried to overtake her? Or would they just slash and burn, cutting people down and turning them into si'lat? Leila's chest heaved as she thought of the destruction the giant could wreak on downtown, of how Shivani and her classmates weren't safe.

"Leila," Zahra said, breaking her out of her spiral. "Can you transport us anywhere? Or just back home?"

Leila froze, balking under the weight of Zahra's full attention. *How much should I tell her?* The thought of Australia seemed so far away now.

"Could you take us to New York City?" Zahra pressed.

"Do you have a photo?" Leila asked. "Somewhere to point me to?" She didn't want to let on that they'd teleported much farther than New York City. She didn't want to make Zahra any more suspicious than she already was.

Zahra got out her phone and scrolled to an image of a swanky loft-style apartment, the concrete floor covered in Persian rugs. "Here," she said. "This is my place. It's in Harlem."

Leila gave her a blank look.

Zahra pulled up a subway map and pointed to where her apartment was, near the top of Manhattan. "There."

"Okay." Leila nodded, trying not to feel overwhelmed. The Sydney Opera House was a landmark, a classic destination that had always been familiar to her. Someone's house felt much, much trickier, and way more specific. "I'll try."

She held her hand out to Bianca, who grabbed it instantly. Zahra followed her lead, and Leila tried not to think about how warm and callused Zahra's hands felt, how strong her grip was. Instead, she pictured the apartment with the beautiful rugs and tin ceilings, and concentrated on being there, on that leather sofa, as if it was the most normal thing in the world.

Flames began to lick the bottoms of their feet, snaking their way up their legs.

"Uhhh," Zahra said, "is this normal?" Zahra hadn't been fully conscious when they'd dragged her to the djinn plane, but Leila was thinking too hard about their destination to answer.

"Just relax and enjoy the ride, Yankee," Bianca snickered.

And then they were gone.

BIANCA

They reappeared in the apartment from the photo, though it was decidedly messier and filled with many more takeout containers than the picture had shown. The air inside was still, the feeling of an empty space that had been left in a hurry. Outside, the sounds of cars honking and the air brakes of buses gave the teleportation a surreal soundtrack. Bianca remembered to breathe.

Leila lifted their held hands. "You can stop digging your nails into my skin now."

"Sorry." Bianca unclenched her hand from Leila's.

Zahra took a second, glanced around the room, and nodded. "Okay, then."

Bianca moved to the window. Zahra's apartment had a view of New Jersey, her building at least eight stories tall. Down below there was a café, and she watched as people of every color walked with purpose, their strides fast and sure, even on Christmas.

Just then, something pricked the corner of her

consciousness, like she was receiving a text message directly into her brain. Then she felt another. And another. Bianca stood there, reaching back out to the gentle pings in her mind. Just like she could sense the blue spark inside her, she could *sense* other djinn too. She could feel a si'lat a mile and a half south of them. If she let her focus expand, she could feel ghuls in a cemetery in Brooklyn, and an all-powerful mareed across the water in New Jersey.

It was too much. As soon as Bianca quested with her mind, trying to see more, she felt the connection open, as if they felt her too. Tortured, powerful beings who cried at the intrusion on their consciousness. Had she not felt it before because there had been no other djinn who weren't controlled by Cyrus? These djinn felt different, more capable, and also so, so lonely on their own.

And who are you, little girl? The mareed's mind brushed against hers.

"Gah!" Bianca cried, severing the connection. She stumbled to the couch and hugged her knees.

"Bee?" Leila asked. "You okay?"

Bianca nodded, saying nothing as Zahra shot her a suspicious look. Bianca felt unmoored again, like the whole building was swaying beneath her crowded brain. It was dizzying, having all these thoughts pressed up against her. She found herself wishing for the relative quiet of Ayers, even when it was being attacked by djinn.

Zahra's phone rang. "Baba?" she asked into the receiver.

Then: "I'm back." Bianca watched as Zahra gave her and her sister an appraising look before switching to Persian.

"It's crawling with djinn. I'm with two of them now. No, they won't hurt me. Okay. Okay. Yeah, I'll explain later. I don't know what to do with them. Yes, see you soon. Be well."

People always thought because they were only half-Iranian that they couldn't speak Persian. Well, Leila couldn't, but Bianca was annoyed.

"How do you know we won't hurt you?" Bianca smirked the second Zahra hung up.

Zahra pinched the bridge of her nose. "This wasn't supposed to happen. I was supposed to go down on my first-ever solo trip, get rid of two djinn, and then drive back up. Now my family has to help me clean up this mess. This is humiliating."

Zahra flopped onto the butter-soft leather couch next to Bianca and sighed, looking up at the tin ceiling. Bianca hadn't seen many Iranian Americans in the media or on TV. Was this how the cool ones looked?

Leila still hadn't said anything. She kept stealing glances at Zahra, as if she knew she shouldn't be looking.

Does Leila have a crush on Zahra? Bianca wondered. God, she hoped so. Zahra was a huge improvement from Foster, even if Zahra *had* tried to kill them.

She felt pieces of her twin slot into place. The gingham and lace, the domesticity, the pairing with a solid bet like Foster. She knew that Leila wanted to be a mom, but did Leila think she needed a man to have the life she dreamed of?

Suddenly, a memory of Leila staring hard at Shivani's older sister when she came to pick Shivani up from a sleepover flashed before her eyes. How Leila had turned crimson, how she'd turned away from Nandani's cute dimples and easy smile.

How long has Leila been torturing herself? Bianca wondered.

Leila daintily sat on the other side of Zahra. "So . . . you've hunted djinn before," she began.

Wow, Leila's flirting is rusty. Bianca watched, like David Attenborough observing two young people engaged in a mating ritual. Still, she was glad her sister was trying. Seeing someone not live their truth was painful, and she was relieved to see Leila go after someone who knew how to pronounce their last name properly.

"Ever since I was a kid, I've hunted djinn," Zahra answered, shrugging. "It's all I know."

"So, do you just travel the country looking for baddies?" Bianca interjected. She was curious now too.

"A long, long, long time ago, one of my ancestors made a deal with a djinn too," Zahra began. She got up and walked to a bookshelf with a very, very old Quran. Gingerly, she flipped to the first page, where families often noted births and deaths.

There, at the top, Zahra pointed to a name so faint Bianca could barely read the inscription.

"My great-great-great-great-great-grandfather Mortezah Esfandiari," Zahra said. "He made a deal with a djinn to save his village from invaders, but he lost his only son in the bargain. Once the debt was paid, he spent the rest of his years hunting them down so no one could ever make a deal again. His daughter took up the cause, and she passed it down."

"That's how we got wrapped up in all this too," Leila said quietly. "Because of our dad."

"He bargained *us*," Bianca said. She looked at the family Quran, with all those names. How wild that one man's decision could shape the fate of his entire bloodline.

All the events of the day suddenly caught up with Bianca. It still seemed impossible that the father who baked her homemade bread on Sundays had gambled with her future. She felt like Steve in the pie shop, too tired to put on a front at two A.M. She felt tears prickle the corners of her eyes. *How could Baba do that to us?*

Now that she was far from Ayers, she missed it already. As much as she'd dreamed of visiting New York, she found that she didn't want to go down to the crowded sidewalk and see it for herself. She felt claustrophobic, aching for her town's calm space. "What's going to happen to Ayers, Zahra?"

Zahra exhaled and put the book back on the shelf. "I'm not sure. If your dad has an outstanding debt, then that means the djinn can basically do whatever they want until the debt is fulfilled. The people in your town are all at risk. Including your parents."

Leila looked at Bianca, and she could see her own horror mirrored in her face. "Bianca, what do we do?"

"How is the debt *not* paid?" Bianca asked. "I mean, look at us!" She gestured to her violently blue eyes, to her glowing skin. "I feel like we paid a pretty big price here."

Zahra shook her head. "They want people they can slowly take over until there's nothing left of them. Bodies. They want to live in this world."

"We have to go back," Leila said to Bianca, her eyes pleading. "We have to help them, and our parents."

Zahra held up a hand. "We're not going anywhere until my family comes. We have way more experience handling djinn than you do. Besides, we need to get more supplies."

"Supplies?" Bianca perked up. Was there some secret djinn-fighting warehouse here in the city? *That* she wanted to see.

"Come on," Zahra said. "The store's only a couple blocks from here. We can walk, instead of . . . you know." She gestured vaguely at Leila, as if afraid to mention the teleportation again.

"Bianca's still in her pajamas," Leila pointed out.

Bianca looked down at her singed reindeers. She hadn't even remembered to put on a bra.

Zahra shrugged on a backpack. "It's New York. Nobody cares."

Leila looked at Bianca. Bianca looked at Leila. It was Bianca's turn to shrug. "When in Rome."

Zahra led them into the elevator where, true to her word, none of the other neighbors batted an eye at Bianca's getup.

They headed out the building's front door, and Bianca was hit with a wave of smells and sounds. Music blared from someone's stoop. Throngs of people walked on the sidewalk: students, families, and just random people Bianca couldn't place out and about on Christmas Day.

She'd never seen so many types of people before, so many races and ethnicities in one spot. Her ears pricked at the sound of different languages she didn't recognize, more tantalizing than the smell of suspicious meat wafting her way. It was dizzying, even more dizzying than looking down from Zahra's apartment.

Who are you? The mareed pressed against her consciousness again. Did the walls of Zahra's building shield her a bit? Because now she felt even more exposed.

One of us, another djinn said into what now felt like a conference call. *I can tell.*

Bianca shot Leila a panicked look, but Leila seemed blissfully unaware. If anything, Leila looked like she was *enjoying* herself. Leila, who claimed she never wanted to leave Ayers. Leila, who said she needed grass and ground beneath her feet. Now she looked like a kid in a candy store as she soaked up the street and her surroundings.

"Wow," Leila said from next to her. While Bianca's body felt tight and ready for something unpleasant, Leila looked at everything with wide eyes and open arms, her entire face lighting up. "Did you see that, Bee?" Leila said. "There's a guy with a Messi jersey on over there!"

Bianca whipped her head to where Leila was pointing and, sure enough, saw a man with a white-and-blue jersey with the number ten. Soccer was far down on the list of favored sports in Ayers, and just seeing the legendary Argentinian player's jersey in the US felt like culture shock.

"Come on," Zahra said, barely blinking at the scene before her. "The halal grocer is this way."

Bianca and Leila traded surprised looks. Their dad had tried keeping halal when he moved to the US, but he said it had been too hard in Ayers. Now they were going to a whole store devoted to halal food? Bianca was about to ask Zahra a follow-up question, but her head throbbed as she tried to block out the questing djinn.

Answer us, little one.

Where do you come from?

We've never seen you before.

Did Cyrus send you?

Bianca shook her head. *I need to get out of here.*

They wove through the crowds, Leila and Bianca following Zahra like lost ducklings. Bianca gritted her teeth and tried not to flinch at how Zahra confidently crossed the street, sure that cars would yield to her. They walked over subway grates emitting warm steam that helped Bianca feel both cozy and gross through her thin pajama fabric. She was glad she ran warm these days, or this freezing New York weather would have had her shivering uncontrollably.

Finally, Zahra stopped in front of a small store with a

maroon awning. Bianca read the Arabicized script slowly, seeing the word for *halal*. Her reading and writing in Persian was rusty, but she could still sound out words from the alphabet. *Does it even matter now?* she wondered. *If I don't travel or go far away for college, will all these languages have been for nothing?*

College, she remembered with a pang. She hadn't applied anywhere near Ayers. She'd been so sure she would thrive out of state though she couldn't even afford a tour and had barely seen other campuses. Now that she was in the same place as NYU and Barnard, she knew deep down that they wouldn't be a good fit. She missed home too much already.

"Bianca, come on!" Leila prodded, holding open the store's front door. Bianca couldn't believe a grocery store was open on Christmas Day. In fact, she couldn't believe how many people were out and about acting as if today was like any other in the city. Christmas Day was a ghost town back home, where everyone celebrated it.

A small bell chimed above them, and they entered the cramped store. Bianca inhaled deeply. Scents of cardamom, fenugreek, dried lime, and pungent kashk all mixed together in an intoxicating smell.

"Salaam!" Zahra called out to the shop owner, a small, wrinkled man with Coke-bottle glasses, his eyes glued to bootleg Persian TV.

"Salaam," the man said, looking up at Zahra, Bianca, and Leila.

"Salaam, sob bekheir," Bianca said back.

The man nodded, and Bianca tried not to cry. It was the first time she'd ever had a casual interaction in Persian with someone who wasn't her father. *This day keeps getting more and more unbelievable.*

She wished she'd brought her wallet. The glimmering rows and rows of lavashak, Persian fruit leather, winked back at her in their plastic labels of pomegranate, sour plum, apricot, and barberry. Delicate cakes and pastries stared at her from a refrigerated glass case, looking almost like pistachio petit fours. Blocks of feta floated in rectangular tubs on the other side, along with different cuts of meat. Maybe when this was all over, Leila could teleport here with a grocery list.

"My mouth is already watering," Leila said next to her.

"Same," Bianca said, the back of her jaw prickling with the specific drool that only sour Persian foods could create. "Hey, Zahra, can you buy me a lavashak?" she asked, half joking.

"The evil eyes are back here" was all Zahra replied, stone-faced. She passed through the tight rows with ease, already knowing where to go. Zahra stopped in front of an aisle with tiny prayer rugs, tasbihs, evil eyes, and, randomly, henna hair dye. She began stuffing evil eyes into a small shopping basket, clearing out the whole display.

"Don't just stand there!" Zahra snapped. "Grab some!"

Bianca jumped to attention, Leila following her, and they all began packing the store's evil eyes into their baskets. Bianca flinched as Zahra reached for green-and-yellow packets of esfand from the Sadaf brand that Iranian American goods always came in. She knew the esfand would come in handy, but still. It smelled terrible, even if it didn't make her cough through the plastic.

"Okay, that should be enough," Zahra said.

Bianca tried not to laugh. "Ya think?" she replied. The entire wall of evil eyes was gone, now in the three baskets each of them held.

"I still want to try one of those fruit roll-up thingies," Leila added.

Zahra threw a pomegranate one into the basket for her, and Bianca watched as Leila's face went crimson. She tried not to smile.

When they went to check out, the cashier barely blinked. Before Bianca could even ask how they were going to pay for all this, Zahra passed over a heavy black credit card, the kind that was so fancy it didn't even have numbers on the front.

Bianca balked. *Just how much money does djinn hunting bring in?*

They exited the small store, weighed down with plastic shopping bags. "Okay, let's head back and make sure Mom and Dad are safe," Leila said anxiously. "We've got enough supplies to fight them."

"Whoa," Zahra said, stopping in the busy street. "You're not going anywhere until my dad gets here."

Bianca recoiled. "And who are you to stop us?" she asked, turning on Zahra. She didn't feel very imposing in her pajamas, but still. A crowd of people parted around them, folks grumbling about how they were blocking the sidewalk, but Bianca didn't care. They needed to get home. If Cyrus wasn't keeping his word, then they needed to check on their parents.

Zahra puffed her chest, sizing Bianca up. "Don't make me get out the esfand," she growled. Bianca glared back at her. Still, Zahra handed Leila her lavashak.

"I'm really worried about Mom and Dad," Leila pressed. "What if they're hurt? They would have called us by now, right?" She held up her phone, showing an empty home screen.

"We need to check on them," Bianca said. "Let's go." She gestured to a sheltered doorway where Leila could teleport them back home.

Leila reached for Bianca's hand, but before they could make contact, Zahra whipped out the iron sphere of incense. "I'm afraid I can't let you do that."

Bianca raised her eyebrows, stunned. "Are you seriously trying to stop us?" She eyed the incense warily. She knew the second Zahra lit it, she and her sister would be on the sidewalk coughing, helpless to do anything but whimper.

How had they been chatting chummily on her couch half an hour ago only to now be held hostage? Bianca wasn't just scared; she was disappointed. Here was someone she'd hoped could be an ally, but Zahra was still in that gray area between friend and foe.

"I'll light this esfand if I have to," Zahra growled. Her long black hair whipped in the cold December wind, making her look even more menacing.

"You're not going to make *us* do *anything*," Bianca spat. She knew she should try to be nicer to her sister's crush, but anyone who threatened them was going to get the full dose of Bianca Mazanderani.

Zahra lit the incense. In that moment, Bianca made up her mind.

She reached for Zahra. Zahra gasped as her eyes instantly went blue. Pedestrians now gave them a wide berth, not caring enough to ask what was happening but still wary. It was almost disturbing to Bianca, how anonymous she felt here. If this had happened in Ayers, at least a dozen people would have already asked what was going on.

Zahra fell to her knees as Bianca's will took over. Bianca could sense Zahra's fight against her, could feel Zahra's will struggle to break free, but it was no use. *We're leaving*, she spoke into Zahra's mind. *Whether you like it or not*. Slowly, a dumb grin spread across Zahra's face. She nodded.

"Come on, Leila," Bianca said, holding out her other hand. "Let's blow this popsicle stand."

Leila's face was pale as she looked between Zahra and her sister. "What do we do about her?"

"I guess she's our hostage now."

"Bianca! We can't just kidnap someone!"

"Her dad was going to come over here to deal with us. And I don't think it was going to be very nice," Bianca pointed out.

Leila bit her lip and looked at Zahra, who was now staring at a limestone gargoyle in the alcove. Leila sighed and grabbed Bianca's free hand, opened the building's door, and entered the vestibule. Bianca watched her sister scan the ceiling for cameras.

"Don't hurt her," Leila finally said.

Bianca grinned. "I won't. Well, not too badly."

Leila sighed, and Bianca closed her eyes, repulsed by the feeling of the flames crawling up her legs. She did not enjoy teleporting, she decided.

But when she opened her eyes in Ayers, everything was on fire.

LEILA

Leila's blood hummed. New York was *amazing.* The crush of people, the feel of buildings overhead, the sights and the sounds. Nobody cared what she looked like, that she was Persian and Argentinian and wearing a dirt-covered sweater and crushing on the wrong person. *I'm going back as soon as I can,* she promised herself. *And I'm gonna eat lavashak every day.*

Her head swam with everything Zahra had told them. How djinn had been tricking humans into deals for centuries, how her family came to be djinn hunters, and how djinn could be taking over Ayers this very second. Still, it was hard not to watch Zahra's rough hands as they expertly shopped in the halal store. Was there anything sexier than a competent woman?

It was strange to finally let herself have these thoughts instead of shoving them down deep inside.

I like Zahra.

I like girls.

It was a relief to admit it to herself. Having a crush on Nandani had been excruciating, all unrequited glances and long-distance pining her first year of high school. But Zahra was flesh and blood and right in front of her. And was she imagining it, or did Zahra hold Leila's looks longer too?

Leila thought back to Foster. She *had* really liked him. She had been truly attracted to him. Did this mean she was bi? Or pan? Or, or, or . . .

Slow down, Leila, she had to remind herself. *One step at a time. You don't have to figure it all out right now.*

Instead of taking them directly back to The Grove, Leila had picked the ruined shell of the Elmhursts' barn. It was fitting, in a way, to retreat to the place where this whole strange saga began. There, behind the burnt planks and hollowed-out walls of the barn, Leila and Bianca could spy on The Grove in the distance.

It was completely aflame.

The Grove, which housed some of Ayers's oldest trees, was now an inferno. All the beautiful hickory and oak trees looked like pyres now. This was the place where the last American chestnut in Ayers had died out, where countless teens had made core memories, and where Leila often went on long walks behind their house to keep her head from spinning. Now it was practically gone.

"No," Leila gasped. "No!"

There, through the burning trunks, were the outlines of unnatural flames dancing among the trees. It was barely noon, and they could still see the silhouette of the giant over the tree line, its form blacking out the sun. Leila worried for their home and about the smoke pouring their way. Would her parents still be safe inside their house?

Leila reached out with her hands, hoping that whatever power gave her the ability to create fire could help her quench it too.

Nothing.

Zahra groaned at their feet.

"Crap," Bianca said. "I let go of her."

Leila sighed. "Let her be. She has nowhere to go, anyway."

It was Christmas Day in a small town. The Elmhursts were in Richmond with their son, and they were the only residents here for miles. Leila doubted the fire department was going to come unless they called them directly.

Bianca pointed at something in the distance. "Look. It's spreading."

Leila followed Bianca's gaze to the back road, where blue and green flames lined it like a fiery trail. "They're on the move," Leila said grimly.

"That road leads to downtown Ayers," Bianca noted. "We just have to hope that everyone is at home for Christmas."

At their feet, Zahra groaned again. "It doesn't matter," she said, gasping for breath. "They'll find everyone."

"Thanks for the positive reinforcement!" Bianca snapped.

"Well, maybe if you hadn't possessed me, my family could be here to tell us what to do!" Zahra shot back.

"Why? So they can take us out too?" Bianca replied.

Zahra said nothing. Leila swallowed hard. Bianca had been right: the two of them were just djinn enemies for this ancient family.

"Come on," Leila said, flustered by all this new information. "Let's go make sure Mom and Dad are okay, at least."

"Yeah," Bianca agreed, aggressively saying it to Zahra's face for some reason.

"What? I'm great with parents!" Zahra said.

"Shut up and walk or I'll make you," Bianca barked.

Zahra just shrugged. "Shouldn't Leila just flame us in there? In case the djinn see us?"

"Good idea," Leila said, trying to restore the peace between Zahra and Bianca. Leila reached out for their hands, and this time Zahra took hers without complaining. Leila tried not to think about how gross and clammy her hand must feel to Zahra.

Leila concentrated on their living room and exhaled as the flames took over their bodies, like an old friend welcoming her again.

She opened her eyes. Instead of being inside the house, they were just outside the line of esfand Bianca had poured earlier.

"Whoops," Bianca said, careful to keep her feet away from the dark brown lines in the dry grass. She stepped over them, shivered, and headed to the front door. Leila did the same, wincing. It felt like being dunked in ice water for a split second.

Zahra looked at the esfand lines and the evil eye above the front door. "You know esfand works better if you light it, right? That'll barely affect an ifrit."

"Shut up. It was still incredibly unpleasant," Bianca growled, her face red. Leila made a mental note, though. That's probably why they could step over it so easily but coughed like crazy the second it was lit.

Leila opened the front door. What would her parents say? Would her dad feel even worse about everything he'd admitted? The Grove's blaze practically lit up the back of the house it was so huge. What if it spread to their house?

But when she stepped through, the house was empty. There was no movement in the kitchen, no creaking from their parents' room. She couldn't even hear her father's sobs— she had figured her parents would probably be holed up in their bedroom in serious conversation as their dad explained his doomed bargain to their mom.

What was stranger was that all the lights were off, even the Christmas lights, which made no sense. The grandfather clock in the entryway was eerily silent.

"Mamá?" Bianca shouted. "Baba?"

Something was very, very wrong. Leila didn't bother taking off her boots, that's how serious this all felt. She stormed into the living room, the floorboards creaking. There, sitting on the good furniture, was Cyrus. Leila froze. Zahra gasped.

Bianca stomped in behind them, saw Cyrus, and said, "Get off my couch."

"Hello, bachehah."

Cyrus looked relaxed, even though Leila had shot fireballs at him earlier today. In fact, he looked downright at
home with his crossed legs and a steaming cup of chai that he
sipped from their dad's favorite estekan glass. Just seeing his
lips touch the beloved tea set her father had carted from Iran
made her hands itch with rage-fueled flame.

"Where are our parents?" Bianca demanded. Leila was
still having trouble reconciling the monster with her home.
This was her haven, the place she'd known all her life. It didn't
make sense that Cyrus would be here.

"It was smart," Cyrus began, "for your dad to move here.
I can see why he did it. This place is so small, there are so few
people from the old world here . . . Yes, I can see why he chose
this village. He must have been the only believer."

Leila breathed hard. Their dad had told them they
moved here because this was the only university to give their
mom a scholarship for her graduate degrees. Had that been
a lie too?

"Where are our parents?" Bianca repeated through gritted teeth.

"Oh, them?" he drawled. "They're safe. For now." He said
the last part with a menacing smile, his teeth glittering.

Leila didn't trust that smile for one second. "Bring them
back."

She could feel her hands start to heat up. Even without
looking she knew flames were licking at her fingers. How dare

this demon enter their home? How dare he take her parents away?

"No," Cyrus said, his pleasant expression turning to stone. "A deal is a deal. Your father's protection is not promised until we have his offspring."

"But you already changed us!" Bianca shouted from next to Leila. "Look!" She gestured to the flames licking Leila's body, to her own bright-blue eyes.

"No," Cyrus growled. "Flesh for fate. We cannot live long in this world without controlling a human. Your soul is still intact. You still have free will. The deal is not final."

Leila closed her eyes, wishing this nightmare would end.

"And if we say no?" Bianca asked.

Cyrus stood up. He seemed taller than before, his complexion healthier and less sallow than that time he had introduced Leila to the desert. "If you say no, then we keep your parents in our prison, and we take your town, as is our due for an unmet bargain. You are not the only beings we can inhabit here. Just the only ones we have permission to."

Leila felt her throat tighten. It was an impossible situation. Give up their lives so their family and their town could live or keep their souls and be selfish.

Leila still had so much she wanted to do, so much of the world she wanted to see after that brief taste of freedom in New York City. Now, just when she knew she wanted more, her world was closing in on her.

Zahra cleared her throat. "Or we could fight you in honest battle. Let us decide our destinies for ourselves."

Cyrus laughed. "Honest battle? There are three of you, and an entire city of us. I brought only a sliver of our army to your home today. To agree would be cowardly!" He chuckled, as if this were the funniest thing he'd heard all day.

"Then what do you have to lose?" Zahra asked.

Cyrus's eyes narrowed. "Essme toh chieh?" He sniffed the air in front of Zahra, sticking out his tongue like a snake, the way he had with Steve.

Zahra said nothing, glowering at Cyrus. Leila was both impressed and horrified by her bravado, though she didn't understand what Cyrus had just asked her. How could Zahra think they even stood a chance against Cyrus's mighty army? There was no way the three of them could make a dent. Even Leila's fireballs had only bought them time; Cyrus was whole and unharmed despite taking one to the face earlier.

"Esfandiari," Cyrus finally snarled. "I should have known you'd get involved."

Leila shared a wide-eyed look with Bianca. Zahra's bloodline must have been powerful if Cyrus recognized it.

"So what, demon?" Zahra spat. "Worried we'll beat you?"

Cyrus looked between Zahra, Leila, and Bianca. Leila hated the feel of his eyes appraising her, could still remember the feeling of him possessing her. His handsome face disgusted her. She knew she would do almost anything to not feel the weight of his will again.

"Very well," Cyrus said. "Tomorrow, at sunset, we will battle." He held his fingers to his forehead, waiting for Zahra to do the same.

"Not so fast," Zahra said. "If you and your army lose, you leave this town and return to where you came from. If we lose, you may claim the twins, and nothing more."

At this Cyrus sneered. "You think we'll stop at just two souls after transporting our entire legion here? These girls have shown us our new home, our new solution to the problem of the djinn plane. That is no deal!"

Leila could see Zahra grind her jaw.

"Fine," Bianca said. "We lose, you take all of us. The whole town. Deal?"

"Bianca, wait!" Leila cried.

It was too much. Who were they to wager an innocent community on their father's promise?

Zahra gently put a hand on Leila's shoulder. "It's all we've got."

Leila sobbed. It wasn't fair. It wasn't right. The place that she loved so much was held in the balance of an impossible bargain. Even the warm touch of Zahra's hand on her shoulder did nothing to comfort her.

Zahra put her fingers to her forehead. Cyrus did the same. The two lowered their hands at the same time. "The deal is done," Zahra whispered.

"The deal is done. My army will see you tomorrow at sunset," Cyrus said. He gave a low bow, and with a swish of his cloak, he evaporated into a sinister green flame. Leila coughed at the sulfurous stench his fire left behind.

"Okay, we're gonna need a lot of fire hoses. Maybe the fire department will let us borrow their truck, if we explain that we have to battle a djinn army tomorrow," Bianca said, pacing around their lacquered coffee table. The estekan Cyrus had drunk from sat there like a stain.

Zahra looked out the front window, confirming that the djinn and giant had indeed left The Grove and taken all the fire along with them. "A fire truck? For what? There's no fire to put out," Zahra asked, baffled.

"To win tomorrow's battle, duh!" Bianca shouted.

"Water doesn't affect djinn flame," Zahra replied in her own *duh* voice. "Besides, my dad will be here soon. He can help us strategize."

Leila's heart stuttered. What would Zahra's dad do to them?

"Your dad?" Bianca cried, voicing Leila's fear. "So he can smoke us out?"

Zahra rolled her eyes. "Let's just call a truce, okay? You're clearly not walking around possessing people, except for me. Though if we get through this alive, we may need to set some ground rules . . ." Here her eyes wandered to Leila's hands, as if imagining fire coming out of them. Leila hid them in her pockets.

"We have help too," Bianca said. "My friends June and Steve."

"And Shivani," Leila added. She knew Shivani would help if she asked, though she would owe her for life.

Bianca rolled her eyes. "Yeah, and her. We're not completely alone here."

Zahra nodded. "Okay, that's good. We can teach them what to do, how to help." She looked at her phone. "Our plane will be landing in half an hour at some place called APR. We'd better get a move on."

"Appalachian Regional?" Leila asked. "But it's really small. I don't even know if there's anyone working there. The tower's been empty for years."

"Doesn't matter," Zahra said grimly. "My dad's jet will be landing there either way. Let's go. I left my car in that forest." She opened the front door, shouldering the backpack she'd used for their supply run.

Private plane? Fancy, Bianca mouthed at Leila, eyebrows high.

"Hold up; we can take our car. It's not a BMW, but it'll get us there," Bianca said, overly gracious.

It was Zahra's turn to roll her eyes from the back seat. "Just drive."

BIANCA

Bianca had never seen a private jet before. At least, not in person. She navigated the car across the weedy, overgrown dirt road that led to the dilapidated airstrip on the other side of town, still in disbelief that Zahra's family had a jet in the first place.

The whole thing felt like a charade to her. No way would anyone land on this pockmarked stretch of asphalt. There were still runway lights on either side, but bushes and saplings had encroached at either end of the clearing, giving aircraft way less space to operate. She parked the car and stood against her door with her arms folded as if to say *not a chance.*

Zahra and Leila quietly stood next to her, eyes squinting at the evening sky. Nobody felt like talking about their desperate deal with Cyrus. Nobody wanted to acknowledge just how miserable and hopeless the situation truly was. If Zahra was feeling confident about their odds once her family joined, she said nothing. Still, Bianca noticed how she kept stealing glances at Leila, with Leila doing the same. The two kept missing each other. It was honestly pathetic.

Bianca wondered if a better sister would ask Leila about her attraction to Zahra, but Bianca didn't see the point. First, they had to save their town. Then, she could wait for Leila to tell her in her own time.

Still, Foster didn't stand a chance next to Zahra's olive skin, perfect eyebrows, and gorgeously thick hair. She looked like a warrior goddess with a penchant for black leather. *See ya, sucker*, she wanted to shout at Foster. *You never stood a chance!*

Zahra's phone pinged. She pulled up a flight tracker and scrolled through. "They should be landing soon," she said.

How? Bianca wanted to ask. But she gritted her teeth and said nothing, staring so hard at the sky she willed the plane to reveal itself.

And then, suddenly, it did. They heard it before they saw it: the faint noise of a jet engine that slowly became louder and louder. In the distance Bianca saw red lights flash in the sky and heard the metallic clang of landing gear opening. She watched, slack-jawed, as a pristine Learjet landed on the tarmac, the bumpy airstrip giving the wheels a run for their money as it slowed down.

The plane had nowhere to taxi to. Bianca watched as it reversed to the center of the landing strip to be level with the car. The engines powered off and the airplane door opened.

"Baba," Zahra exhaled, her shoulders lowering from her ears.

A tall man with Zahra's cleft chin exited the plane. He wore a white suit and paisley blue tie, the outfit lit up by the red runway lights. In his hand was a briefcase that looked older than himself. He was like the cover of a *GQ* issue on "success at all ages," Bianca thought.

Behind him was a woman who had similar features to Zahra: the same proud nose, the same high cheekbones. *She must be her sister.* She was followed by a man who looked like Zahra's father, albeit less clean-cut, with tattoos like Zahra's and an all-black outfit. On his wrist were iron bands that looked as thick as handcuffs. Bianca winced.

Zahra's father frowned as he walked down the stairs to the asphalt, looking around the airstrip as he assessed its condition. *Yes*, Bianca wanted to shout. *It IS a miracle you landed at all!*

He walked up to his daughter and kissed her on the cheek. "Dokhtaram, khubi?"

"I'm okay." Zahra held her father's hand from where it cupped her cheek, and Bianca almost looked away, the moment too tender to be public. This whole ordeal had been incredibly hard on Bianca and Leila; she had never thought how it must have affected Zahra too.

Her father turned to the twins. "Salaam. My name is Ehsan." He put his hand on his chest and ducked his head. His voice, Bianca noticed, was deep and weathered, more regal-sounding than anything Cyrus could pull off.

"God, where are we even?" the young woman with Zahra's features asked, followed by the loud snap of bubble gum.

"Tara," Zahra sighed.

"Why would djinn come here? They don't even have a real airport. We had to use the Roanoke tower. I hate slam-dunk landings."

"This is my sister, the pilot," Zahra explained, turning to Bianca and Leila. Bianca assessed Tara: She wore denim overalls, Chucks, a bright pink sweater, and pilot's headphones. Her long black hair went down to her waist, and she had enough neon-blue eyeliner to stand out even against the dark airstrip. If Zahra was night, Tara was day.

"And my uncle, Mohsen," Zahra said, gesturing to the other member of her family. He was, if possible, even more tattooed than Zahra, with evil eye tattoos on his face and inscriptions on his palms. He gave the girls a curt nod before turning back to the airplane to unload cases and cases of steel luggage that looked straight out of a designer catalog.

Bianca winced, detecting what was inside. "Iron?" she asked Ehsan.

The older man seemed surprised. "You can sense it?"

Bianca nodded, her eyes glued to the luggage. Just how much iron was in there? She shivered. It must have been a lot for her to feel it fifty feet away.

"Does it hurt you?" Ehsan asked, eyes intent.

Bianca knew she needed to reply carefully here. For all Ehsan knew, Bianca was another malicious djinn who operated the same way as Cyrus and his subjects.

She turned to Leila, who also seemed to be considering the question. It didn't hurt, exactly, but it didn't feel great, either. How to explain that it's like when you're taking a bath and your back hits the cold porcelain? Or that feeling you get when you skip a stair? Iron was like one big flinch: once she embraced it, like her ring, she could forget about it. But did she dare tell that to Ehsan?

"It's okay," was all Bianca said. Anything to make this man think she was less djinn-like would work in her favor.

He said nothing, just giving her an appraising look before helping his brother unload the rest of the cargo. Zahra joined them, and Bianca and Leila silently watched the family unpack the tools that were supposed to help them.

"So," Zahra began. "We made a deal with Cyrus."

"Cyrus!" Ehsan's eyebrows nearly flew off his forehead. "The prince himself?"

Zahra nodded. Bianca noted how surprised Ehsan looked, how the strong hands that had gripped his luggage now shook a bit. *He's scared of Cyrus*, she realized.

"Tomorrow at sunset, we fight him and his army. If we win, they'll leave us alone. If we lose, he takes over the twins and the town."

Ehsan grabbed a tasbih in his pocket, thumbing the worry beads anxiously. "*That's* the deal you struck?"

"He brought giants, Baba. And si'lat, palis, ghuls, all of them," Zahra explained, almost defensively. "He already has their parents." Here, she gestured to Bianca and Leila.

Bianca stiffened. "We have names, you know."

Ehsan, who had been standing there, his expression

dazed, seemed to remember the twins. Bianca didn't blame him; it was a lot of information to take in. Still, she hated being talked about as if she weren't there.

"Whatever deal your relative bargained for, I hope it was worth it," Ehsan finally said.

Behind Ehsan, Tara and Mohsen talked low and urgently. The news of Cyrus being involved seemed to change everything. Gone was Tara's disdainful attitude. She was all business now as she talked to her uncle and began double-checking her luggage while she popped bright pink bubble gum.

"I still can't believe they have a jet," Leila finally said softly beside Bianca.

"I can't believe they landed it," she replied.

Then Bianca saw something that made her fists clench as it came off the plane. Crates and crates of esfand, followed by iron maces that could be swirled in the air like lassos. The spiky metal balls had holes inside that helped them whistle through the air, and, of course, give off wafts of incense.

Bianca's stomach roiled. There was no way she could hide the effects of esfand on her in front of Zahra's family. Even though the esfand was unlit, this much of it hurt to be near. Leila grabbed her hand, her palm sweaty as it affected her the same way.

"Zahra, you take the keys, okay? There's not enough room for all of us, anyway," Leila said. She grabbed the keys from Bianca's hands and tossed them to a surprised Zahra. "Just meet us at home."

"Wha—" Bianca began. But before she could finish, Leila had covered the two of them in flames. Ehsan, Tara, and Mohsen stared, their expressions filled with awe, as the sisters caught fire. Bianca blinked, and she was back at their front door. She stepped over the line of incense.

"God," Leila said, letting go of Bianca's hand and then flopping onto the couch. "I thought I was going to throw up, there was so much incense."

"Thanks for getting us out of there," Bianca replied, steadying herself. She went to the kitchen and poured them both glasses of water.

Leila finished hers in one gulp. "You'd better call June and Steve. I'll call Shivani."

Bianca sank onto the couch next to her. "Let me just sit here for a moment and process this messed-up day." She stared at the grandfather clock that had finally restarted. *Ticktock, ticktock.* The house felt even emptier than before.

"I can't believe it's only been a day," Leila said.

Bianca sighed. "First we learn that our father betrayed us. Then we almost got killed by a djinn army that, let me get this right, has a freaking *giant.* Then you teleported us to New York. We came back and found out Cyrus kidnapped our parents and that they're hanging out in God-knows-where, which means we had to make a ridiculous deal that there's no way we can win. *Then* we met Zahra's superrich djinn-fighting family? There is not enough therapy in the world for this mess." She exhaled, completely spent.

Bianca felt Leila sag next to her, the weight of all the odds settling on top of them. No matter what, though, it was nice to have a partner in all this. It felt deeply satisfying to be on the same side as her sister.

"Yeah," Leila croaked. "It's a lot." She rested her head on Bianca's shoulder.

Bianca smiled, knowing Leila couldn't see it. "At least Zahra is hot," Bianca added, unable to help herself.

"Bianca!" Leila cried, reaching for a pillow to cover her own face.

"What?" Bianca laughed. "I mean, she is."

Leila moaned from behind her pillow. "Is it that obvious?" She lowered the pillow and Bianca met Leila's eyes, Leila's flecks of gold and amber so different from Bianca's blue ones now.

Bianca patted Leila's knee. "Don't worry, she's into you too."

Leila bit her lip, trying hard not to smile. She opened her mouth as if to say something, then closed it again.

"Okay?" Bianca said. It was a reassuring okay. The kind of okay you ask someone to clarify: *We're good, right?*

"Okay," Leila replied. She finally let a small smile break out, and Bianca's heart melted just a tiny bit. She prayed that whatever happened, Leila would get to live her life the way *she* wanted when all this was done.

The nice moment was broken by the crunch of gravel in the driveway. Zahra's family was already here.

Leila lifted her head, sighing with exhaustion. "Come on. I'll put the kettle on and call Shivani."

Bianca nodded, getting out her phone. June might be mad at her for interrupting Christmas evening, but desperate times and all that.

June picked up on the first ring. "Bianca? You okay? I've been meaning to call you . . . Something's been off all day here—"

"June," Bianca interrupted. "Something's happened. I need you to come over. Wear your necklace."

She could hear June gulp through the phone, the sound of Christmas music muted in the background.

"Is it . . . ?" she whispered.

"Yes," Bianca replied. There was no way June could ask if this was about djinn in front of her family without getting doused in holy water. Actually, did holy water work? Bianca made a mental note to ask.

"I'll be right there."

Bianca hung up and debated calling Steve. Were they in phone-call territory yet? He *had* thrown a rock at her window, but making a call felt even more intimate somehow. She settled for a text message.

Steve, there's djinn stuff happening. Come over ASAP.

He instantly replied. **OMW.**

The perfect response. Bianca tried to ignore the blooming

feeling of warmth in her chest, but she couldn't deny it: she liked Steve Rosenberg. She pocketed the phone just as Zahra, Tara, Mohsen, and Ehsan all tentatively opened the front door.

"Hello?" Zahra called out.

Bianca waved them in and watched approvingly as they slipped off their shoes.

Just then, Leila emerged from the kitchen with a tray of black tea, cardamom, sugar cubes, and estekan. "Come in," she said, leading them to the formal living room. "Shivani is on her way," she added to Bianca.

"Thank you," Ehsan rumbled, leading his family through.

Bianca felt strange hosting guests on their own. Even though she didn't fully trust the Esfandiaris, she hoped she was doing her parents right by offering tea and welcoming them inside. Persian hospitality went deep, and something as uncomfortable as inviting in a family who might want to kill you was still eclipsed by good manners and chai.

"So," Ehsan said, sitting down across from Leila. He steepled his hands together, his forehead creased in deep thought. "Your father made a bargain. Just like our ancestor did, many years ago."

Leila said nothing, so Bianca piped up. "Yep. He doomed our souls to eternal damnation, et cetera."

"Well, I don't think he planned on having children, to be fair," Leila added.

Ehsan sighed. "He wasn't the only young man to make a

deal to leave. Theocratic rule in Iran was becoming very hard on people. Many other men made the same bargain for Germany, Sweden, and Australia to dodge the draft. Try not to judge your father too harshly," he said, directing the last part to Bianca.

Bianca tried hard not to roll her eyes. She didn't want to be disrespectful, but still, it was easy for him to say. *His* soul hadn't been bartered.

Tara, however, had no problem speaking up. "Just let the poor girl drink her chai without a lecture, Baba," she said. She looked at Bianca pityingly, and even though Bianca liked her whole cute-but-deadly vibe, she could have done without that sympathetic look.

Mohsen said nothing, just slurped his chai loudly.

Zahra clapped her hands together, glossing over the awkward moment. "We need a plan. I was thinking we could try to surround them. Cyrus doesn't know how many of us there are—we have the element of surprise on our side."

Knock knock, went the front door.

"June and Steve are here already?" Bianca sprang off the couch, all too happy for an excuse to leave this tense conversation. There at the door stood Steve, June, and Shivani, all three of them smiling, all of them with glowing eyes.

"Hello, Bianca," they said in unison.

God, that was weird. June, she noticed, hadn't worn the evil eye necklace like she'd asked her to. Bianca looked up over the doorframe where she'd hung an evil eye before. *It's gone!* Bianca realized with a start. *Did Cyrus take all our wards away?*

"Aren't you going to let us in?" Shivani asked, her grin looking far more threatening than normal.

Suddenly, Zahra was behind her in the doorway. "Bianca, run!"

"What?" Bianca asked. Why would she run from her friends? But then Shivani's hands lunged for Bianca's throat, and she stepped back just in time to avoid being choked by her acrylics.

She watched in horror as June's easygoing smile was replaced by a snarling, twisted grimace. June windmilled her arms toward Bianca as Zahra tried to fend the others off. Mohsen, Tara, and Ehsan were already there, swinging amulets and smoking esfand in their faces.

No, Bianca wanted to scream, her throat choking from the esfand. *No, Cyrus can't have gotten my friends already. We had a deal!*

Then Leila was beside her, helping her stand. But it was no use—her sister was coughing just as much as Bianca was. They watched, helpless, as the Esfandiaris mercilessly fought their friends.

"Be careful!" Leila cried out, but they didn't hear her plea. Steve, June, and Shivani barely seemed present in the bodies that fought them. They looked completely unrecognizable with their sneering faces and red eyes. The djinn had sucked all recognition out of her friends, and Bianca had no idea who to root for.

"You!" Ehsan snapped, turning on Leila and Bianca. "I

knew this was a trap! All djinn are bad djinn. I told her. I told her!"

"Baba, nah!" Zahra cried. Ehsan stalked closer to Leila and Bianca, swinging the mace full of esfand, unable to see the difference between their possessed friends and the twins. Bianca's feet were rooted to the floor in fear. She could barely breathe, much less move.

No, no, no! she wanted to scream. *You've got it all wrong!*

It was all too much. Starting Christmas day on four hours of sleep. Realizing her own father betrayed them. Seeing a djinn army encroach on her town. Visiting New York and realizing it wasn't everything it was cracked up to be. Then her parents' kidnapping, and now this, her best friend and the guy who took her out for pie last night trying to kill her. Now the only backup they had, this strange family who had promised to help, had turned on them too.

Mohsen and Tara joined Ehsan as they bore down on Leila and Bianca. Bianca curled into a ball, ready to let their weird sense of justice take over. She closed her eyes, sobbing.

Suddenly she felt Leila's hand close over her wrist, clutching it tightly.

And then everything went quiet.

LEILA

It was too much. Seeing Shivani try to choke her sister was terrifying, but seeing Zahra's family go from drinking her tea to attacking her was the final straw. Yes, Zahra was dazzling and gorgeous and the spicy, musk-scented perfume she wore was intoxicating, but her family was trying to kill her. She grabbed Bianca's hand without thinking and suddenly the smoke and the screaming disappeared. She had teleported the two of them out of Ayers without even realizing it.

"Where are we?" Bianca asked, squinting in the dark. The air was saltier here, cooler but not as cold as Ayers. It felt humid and calm after the chaos of their house.

"I . . . I don't know," Leila admitted. She felt sand beneath her feet, heard the breaking sound of ocean waves, but those were her only clues. It was too dark to see anything else beyond the lights of the boardwalk behind them.

"Wait!" Bianca shouted. "We came here when we were little, remember? To the Outer Banks?"

Leila turned to look at the dunes behind them, the

seagrass swaying in the mild air. The Outer Banks were a full ten hours from their house. She remembered digging for sand crabs and playing in the tide pools with Bianca when they were younger.

Maybe that's why her subconscious had taken them there: it was the last place she could remember feeling as close to Bianca as she did now.

"Yeah." Leila breathed in the salty night air. She lowered herself onto the cool sand, which felt good after the heat of their home. Bianca sat down next to her, and the two watched the waves roll in with what little moonlight was left.

"We're really on our own now," Bianca said hollowly.

It was true. They had no family, no friends. Shivani, June, and Steve were still at the house, and Leila had no idea how to help them. Cyrus had already started possessing the town, and they didn't even have their parents to talk to about it all. She cursed herself for not specifying that Cyrus had to wait until the battle to begin possessing people. He fought dirty, and now Leila had no idea how many other people in Ayers were suffering.

"It's just the two of us," Leila agreed, turning to Bianca.

Bianca's electric blue eyes shone in the dark. She squeezed Leila's hand, and Leila squeezed back. They sat there for a while in the silence, listening to the roar of the ocean. Leila felt a bone-deep weariness overtake her, the kind where her body begged for sleep while her brain whirred with a thousand thoughts a minute. It wasn't healthy, this pace they'd had to sustain all day. Her teeth chattered from exhaustion, not cold.

She couldn't fight Cyrus like this tomorrow. She needed help. "Bianca?" she finally asked.

"Yeah?" her sister replied.

"Could you help me go to sleep? Just for a little bit? I'm so tired." Leila was hoarse, her normally clear voice husky and spent.

"Like . . . you want me to take over?" Bianca asked, sounding hesitant.

"Yeah," Leila replied. She hoped Bianca wouldn't turn her down. She needed to rest so badly she wanted to cry. She couldn't remember the last time she felt this wiped.

"You sure?"

Leila nodded, eyes pleading.

Bianca sighed and put a hand on Leila's shoulder. Leila sagged with relief as she felt the cool blue static pass through her. She didn't fight it this time; she welcomed it with open arms. Her shoulder buzzed and crackled from the point of contact, then a slow warmth spread through the rest of her body. A wonderful calm feeling passed over her, and she waited for Bianca to issue a command that she'd be glad to follow.

Sleep, Bianca ordered into her. *Go to sleep.* Leila closed her eyes, blissed out with obedience, and fell into a deep slumber.

"Goodnight, Leila," Bianca whispered.

Leila woke up the next morning to a sunrise that looked straight out of a desktop wallpaper. She sat up and hugged her knees in the growing light.

Bianca lay next to her, her hair splayed out in the sand, her mouth open as she snored. Leila felt clear-headed, the effects of the esfand long gone.

There was no way they could win, no way they could come out victorious and save their town, not with these odds. Leila looked at her sleeping sister and felt guilty, so incredibly horrible, for bringing her into this mess. *It's just a fraction of how guilty Dad must feel, though*, Leila reminded herself.

What would have happened if she had just let Foster scream and yell in that field? She could have let him faint on his own, wake up, and head home by himself. Then maybe Cyrus wouldn't have found them and started this whole chain reaction. Maybe Cyrus would have let them live their small lives in peace.

But then she would have still been that pale version of herself. She'd have still been dating Foster, wondering if something was missing. She would still be that girl who never wanted to leave home, whose life plan was to never venture more than ten miles from Ayers.

And now, as she looked at the ocean, she could see the world was so much bigger than that. The thought of staying in Ayers felt claustrophobic. She couldn't picture living there, couldn't imagine staying home for college. Just when the odds were stacked against her, when certain doom was basically guaranteed, she wanted *more* from life.

She thought of Zahra, living alone in her own apartment in New York City. Of the people who strode back and forth on the busy sidewalk with such purpose. What if Leila became one of those people? What if she lived in a city like that, holding a cup of coffee as she headed to class? She didn't have to study agricultural science. She could take new classes, try everything out. Maybe she could even take a textile design course and learn more about sewing and garment making.

It was a completely new fantasy.

A seagull squawked loudly and Bianca stirred. Just then, a jogger crested the dunes, frowning at the two sand-covered girls who had clearly spent the night there.

"Morning," Leila croaked. The woman said nothing, shaking her head as she jogged past, muttering something about "vagrants."

"Bianca," Leila whispered, shaking her gently. She hated to wake her early before their big day.

"Ngghhh," Bianca replied. She slowly opened her eyes, blinking out sand. "What."

"We'd better get moving. People are starting to wake up."

Bianca dragged herself into a cross-legged position and yawned, stretching her arms above her head as her back gave a satisfying *pop!* "All right," she said. "Where to?"

Leila shrugged. "I don't know. Somewhere with coffee?"

Bianca brushed sand out of her hair, wincing as it scattered over her. "Okay, well, you could probably teleport us to the fanciest coffee shop in the world if you wanted."

Leila looked back at the ocean. Bianca was right. She'd teleported them across the world to Australia, and hundreds of miles to the Outer Banks. Where else could she take them?

"And preferably somewhere warm?" Bianca shivered, still wearing her pajamas.

Leila got out her phone, sighing at the low battery. She hadn't thought to bring a charging cable or a toothbrush or anything else she needed right now. The only other thing she had was the wallet she'd tucked into her back pocket for the drive to the airport last night.

Teleporting home was out of the question. She wouldn't be surprised if the Esfandiaris had turned their house into an HQ of sorts before they tried to battle the djinn themselves. Even just teleporting to her bathroom for some mouthwash seemed risky—she'd likely end up landing outside the esfand line.

She instead googled a coffee shop nearby that was open the day after Christmas. "How do we get there, though? It's almost daylight. We might get seen."

Bianca scrunched her nose in thought. "Lemme see," she said, holding her hand out for Leila's phone. She watched as Bianca turned on Street View, scrolling around until she found an empty parking lot with a dumpster.

"There," she said triumphantly, pointing at the screen.

"You can port us behind that dumpster. There aren't any other shops there, so the parking lot should be empty. And if we do get spotted, worst case you instantly take us somewhere else really fast."

Leila exhaled, apprehensive. This all seemed so risky. It was luck that had teleported them here unseen in the first place. Would they get lucky again?

Her stomach rumbled. She hadn't eaten dinner last night, and she could feel her body demanding fuel. She stared hard at the Street View picture and imagined teleporting her and Bianca there, the same way she had when they'd gone to Zahra's apartment.

"Better do it quick; there's another jogger coming around behind that dune," Bianca warned, grabbing Leila's wrist.

The flames took over them both. Instead of closing her eyes this time, Leila watched as a cocoon of fire surrounded them and deposited them right next to the dumpster from the photo. She was learning to teleport faster now.

The lot was abandoned. Leila remembered to breathe. She had teleported them to the exact same place she had envisioned them standing in. She was getting better at this.

"Merry Christmas to us, baby," Bianca chuckled. She peered around the corner of the dumpster and motioned to a diner lit up with an old-school OPEN sign.

The bell rang cheerily as they entered, and Leila hungrily eyed the plates of eggs and waffles in front of them.

"Sit anywhere ya want," a voice with a southern drawl

hollered from the other end. It was different from the hill accent they had in Ayers, and it made Leila feel like the plain diner was just a tiny bit more exotic.

Leila smoothed down her messy hair as Bianca beelined for a booth in the back corner. She sank down into the vinyl seat, trying not to flinch as she felt sand skitter down to the floor.

A server materialized next to them, barely batting an eye over the girls' rough appearance. "What-can-I-getcha?" he asked.

"Coffee," Leila croaked. "And can you please charge my phone?"

"Same," Bianca said, eyeing the menu. "And a plate of bacon and eggs. With a side of pancakes."

"And food?" the server asked Leila. He held out his hand for her smartphone. Leila's mouth watered at the thought of bacon, something they never ate.

"Same," she repeated. She couldn't remember the last time she'd eaten pork.

The server nodded and whisked Leila's phone away to the front counter, where Leila saw him plug it in to the outlet on the Formica countertop. He quickly came back with two steaming mugs of coffee. Leila almost melted into hers she was so grateful. In this moment, she could completely understand how wars could be won and lost over hot meals and food.

Bianca loaded her coffee with cream and sugar while Leila gulped hers down black. The two sat there in silence for a while, enjoying the warm booth as they looked at the empty main street of a beach town in winter.

The server returned with heaping plates of pancakes, bacon, and eggs. "Plate's hot," he warned. He refilled their cups before Leila needed to ask, then swept away to the other end of the diner.

Leila took a big bite of eggs. They weren't as good as the way her dad cooked them, but right now, they tasted like the best thing she'd ever eaten. She inhaled the rest of them with ketchup and hot sauce before turning to her bacon.

"I honestly haven't eaten pork in years," Leila admitted.

Bianca took a bite of bacon and brandished a piece. "Are we even Muslim, though?"

Leila frowned. Were they? "Well, we just celebrated Christmas, and the week before that was Shab-e Yalda, which is a Zoroastrian holiday, technically."

"I dunno how to pray." It was Bianca's turn to fess up now. "Like, on the little rug. I have no idea where Mecca is right now."

Leila chewed. She knew people in Ayers who considered themselves Christian who never went to church, who probably didn't even know all the prayers. Was there a Muslim equivalent?

"Well, djinn are Muslim, right?" Leila asked. She whispered the "Muslim" part, not sure if this was the type of town that treated the word *Muslim* the same as *Taliban* and *sharia law*.

"Yeah, but they're not the only ones who believe in

them . . . ," Bianca began, looking out the window thoughtfully. "Zoroastrians believe in djinn too, and that religion is way older than Islam. I wouldn't be surprised if djinn are older than Zoroastrianism, even."

Leila took a big chomp of her bacon. "Monsters are always older than gods, I guess." She felt guilty over how much she enjoyed the salty, crispy texture.

She watched Bianca top her pancakes up with butter, maple syrup, and a packet of sugar. "What?" she asked when she caught Leila staring.

"Nothing."

"Anyway, if we're gonna win this fight, we gotta do it together," Bianca said, mouth full. "And that means honing our powers."

Leila stopped, a piece of bacon halfway to her mouth. "What do you mean?"

Bianca wiped syrup off her face. "Well, you just figured out you could teleport, right? Does that mean you can teleport five feet away when Cyrus tries to punch you? Can you strobe in and out so you can't be hit? How big are your fireballs? How far can you launch them? We know the basics, but what about combat?"

A man in a trucker hat who had just sat down at a table nearby frowned at Bianca.

"Because that would be ten points damage . . . and then we could win their wizard card?" Bianca asked quickly.

Leila raised an eyebrow, but the man looked away.

"I didn't even think about all that," Leila admitted.

"And what about me?" Bianca added. "What can my character do? Could I possess you if someone's in your blind spot and save you? Or what if I touched a . . . bad guy who was holding on to another bad guy? Does that mean I could control both of them? Then we'd win the game for sure."

Leila's eyes went wide. Bianca's imagination stretched so much further than Leila's. It sounded like they actually had a shot.

"But how would we figure all this out?" Leila asked.

"We'll just have to try it," Bianca said decisively, stabbing a piece of bacon with her fork. She seemed to have no problem eating it.

"Just how often do you eat bacon?" Leila asked.

Bianca shrugged. "I dunno. Like once a week? June's mom makes a mean BLT."

Leila gasped.

"What?"

"Nothing . . . I just . . . well . . ." It felt like Bianca had this whole other life Leila barely knew anything about. "I'm just glad we're eating breakfast together, that's all."

Bianca held up her mug and clinked it with Leila's. "Cheers, Sis."

"You've got whipped cream on your nose," Leila pointed out.

"And the moment of sisterly bonding is gone," Bianca sighed.

Leila giggled. Bianca started to too. Pretty soon the two were cackling at their booth, the other diners giving them strange looks, but Leila didn't care. She took another bite.

BIANCA

*B*ianca's *stomach finally started* to feel full, her raging appetite satiated. She stirred her third coffee, thinking. This could be their last breakfast together. After today, they could be controlled by a djinn prince who over-accessorized.

"Is there anything on your bucket list? You know, before we eventually die in a fiery inferno tonight?" Bianca was curious what Leila had always imagined herself doing. Bianca already knew what had been on hers. Eat sushi in Japan, go to a concert at a real stadium, and, of course, live in New York City. Her list was laughably outdated now.

After their trip to Australia, the idea of living anywhere else was now painful. Her friends, her family, everything she had ever known was in Ayers, and she was starting to realize that wasn't a bad thing. Still, a part of her felt ashamed for changing her mind. Bianca had been famously anti-Ayers. Everyone at school knew she couldn't wait to leave. She had always projected a cosmopolitan front, and now it felt like a sham. She felt like Steve Rosenberg, pretending to be someone he wasn't all for the show of it. They had a lot more in common than she'd realized.

The truth was, she had always imagined herself as an urban bruja, but maybe she was just a cottage witch at heart. *Cottage witch*, she thought to herself. *Yeah.*

Leila crumpled up her napkin. "I thought I knew what I wanted, but I have no idea," she admitted. "Everything feels so different now."

Bianca nudged her with her black boots. "Okay, but like . . . what about seeing the Eiffel Tower? Or going sky-diving or something?"

Leila met Bianca's eyes, and a new kind of fire blazed in them. One that wasn't golden or red, like the djinn they'd been fighting: it was a fierceness she'd had there all along. "I want to do *everything*," Leila said. "I want to travel the world. I want to have an apartment somewhere with a balcony. I wanna live somewhere where I don't speak the language. I want it *all*."

Bianca gave a low whistle.

"What?" Leila asked. She seemed defensive, as if sharing her deepest, darkest desires made her an easier target.

"Nothing," Bianca said. "That's an awesome list."

"Really?" Leila asked, surprised. "You think so?"

Bianca smiled. "Leila, with your powers, you can pretty much do all those things."

Leila chewed her lip. "All we gotta do is defeat a giant djinn army."

Bianca nodded, heart sagging. "All we gotta do is defeat a giant djinn army," she agreed.

"What about you?" Leila asked.

She settled for the simplest item on the list.

"Well, I've always wanted to see a concert. Like, in a big stadium."

"Who?" Leila asked. "Some cool indie band?"

Bianca blushed. "Taylor Swift." It felt painful voicing her hopes and dreams out loud. She gave Leila credit for saying hers first.

"You're a Swiftie?" Leila asked, eyes wide.

Bianca bristled. "What? She writes great songs!"

Leila held up her hands. "No judgment here. I just didn't think we had the same taste in music, that's all. Taylor Swift doesn't wear much black."

"She contains multitudes," Bianca replied sagely.

Leila nodded, her face thoughtful. "I'm glad I learned this about you."

Bianca rolled her eyes. "Okay, okay, let's not get all touchy-feely."

Just then, their server approached with their check. "Whenever you're ready," he said.

Leila paid the bill and stood up. "Come on," she said grimly. "We've got some wizards to destroy. And I wanna practice some moves before sunset."

The trucker at the table next to them looked over.

"Let's destroy some wizards," Bianca replied. Leila grabbed

her phone from the charger and the two exited the cozy diner, unsure when they'd ever get a moment like this again.

Please don't let this be the last breakfast we share, Bianca prayed.

Bianca had always wanted to be a part of a training montage. Getting swole on the beach, lifting tree trunks, having a wise teacher nod approvingly. Unfortunately for her, the gymnasium of Ayers High, Virginia, would have to do for her transformation.

Leila had teleported them somewhere Cyrus wouldn't think of, and a place that would be useless to the Esfandiaris: their own high school.

"This is so creepy," Bianca said as she looked around the empty gym in the fading sunlight. The day after Christmas was guaranteed to be a ghost town, and the dim emergency lighting gave everything a faint, eerie glow. "Man," she said, kicking a loose piece of flooring. "This is way less epic than I thought it would be."

Leila sighed. "Try again, Bee."

For the past couple of hours, Bianca had been trying to possess Leila and use her teleportation and fire powers. If she could make Leila sit and stand, why couldn't she launch a fireball through her? It was no use. Bianca was ready to throw in the towel and leave the flashier powers up to her sister.

She sighed and reached for Leila's hand. Leila didn't put up a struggle as Bianca tried to take over the part of Leila's brain that let her catch fire. "Come on," Bianca said, gritting her teeth. She could see her reflection in the windows of the gym, and it looked like she was trying to get over some serious constipation.

A puff of smoke erupted from Leila's palm. Bianca shook her head.

"I can't do it," she said. "It's just not there."

"You'll figure it out," Leila said, rubbing Bianca's back. "Maybe you just need a break."

Bianca nodded, sitting down on a bleacher. "This is exhausting."

"I'll go," Leila offered. "I wanted to try that strobing trick you mentioned."

Bianca watched as Leila concentrated hard, staring at a point on the other side of the gym underneath all the sports pennants. Veins started to pop out of her forehead as small flames flickered all over her body. Then, Leila evaporated. A second later, she was back. She went back and forth like this for a while, until the gaps between her disappearances became shorter and shorter. She had done it: she was strobing, just like Bianca had suggested.

Bianca wanted to feel happy for her sister but instead felt like an even bigger failure for not being able to push her powers further too.

"Whoa," Leila said, her form going solid. It looked

like she was twinkling, the flames barely able to alight the faster she teleported. "I did it! I teleported between here and the language arts hallway. It probably looks like I'm strobing there too."

"You did it," Bianca agreed, trying not to sound bitter. After all, any win for Leila was a win for their family, their town, and for themselves.

Leila sat down next to Bianca. "Wanna try?"

"Huh?" Bianca asked.

Leila took Bianca's hand. "Come on."

Bianca exhaled. This was a low point. Just a low point. They could only go up from here. "Okay."

And then Leila disappeared, leading Bianca along. They reappeared for a split second by a random bank of lockers. Then, as quickly as Bianca got her bearings, they teleported back to the gym. Over and over, they alternated between the two locations, Bianca's vision spinning until she learned to spike her sight between the swim team pennant and locker 403. Faster and faster they went, the two going in and out of either location so fast Bianca wondered if this trick made them practically bulletproof.

Finally, Leila stopped, breathing heavily as she took a sip from the water fountain. "Pretty cool, right?"

Bianca grinned. It had worked. She did feel better. "Pretty cool," she agreed.

Leila stood up again but stumbled over a loose sneaker lace. Bianca instinctively reached out to grab her.

"Be careful," Bianca said. But when Leila stood back up, her eyes were bright blue.

"Bianca?" she asked, still conscious despite Bianca's possession. "Did you break my fall?"

Bianca gasped. "No. You did!" She let go of Leila's hand, horrified she had possessed her without even realizing it.

"I was in there, though. I had control. You just . . . nudged me in the right direction," Leila said, a slow smile creeping on her face.

"What?" Bianca said, not liking where this was going.

"We can work with this," Leila replied, a smug look on her face.

Bianca groaned. "Oh no."

They trained hard into early afternoon. Leila's accuracy with teleporting was getting better now, and all Bianca had to do was throw a basketball as far as she could only for Leila to catch it seconds later. Not only that, but Leila learned she could grow her fireballs to the size of a car, though it took her a while to recharge her flames after such a large blast. The football field would survive.

Bianca's power had been trickier to train, since her only test subject was Leila. But after possessing her over a dozen times, Bianca finally learned that she didn't even need to touch her sister anymore to take control. *You there?* Bianca could ask.

Right here, Leila would reply. They'd done it. They'd achieved twin telepathy, albeit by very unconventional means. But if she could do it, that meant Cyrus could too. Bianca shivered at the thought of him controlling her own town with only a whisper of a thought. Like a puppeteer with dozens of marionettes, he could completely take over Ayers.

By three P.M., they were exhausted. Leila teleported to a sandwich shop and got them both huge foot-long subs, chips, and giant sodas. Bianca gulped hers down, ending in a large belch.

"Bianca!" Leila chided her.

"What? There's no one here to care."

Leila said nothing. Because Bianca was right. They drained their sodas in minutes, Bianca wishing she'd asked for more food. Something about using her powers made her extra hungry.

"The sun will set soon," Leila reminded her.

"Ugh," Bianca groaned. For a moment she'd forgotten that sunset came earlier in winter. She was sweating so much from training that she'd barely felt the cold. "So now we wait."

"Now we wait," Leila repeated grimly.

LEILA

Leila couldn't believe that it had all led up to this. Three weeks ago she was trying to figure out the perfect way to wrap her wet hair so she could wake up with nice curls for school. Now, she was about to throw herself on the front lines of a supernatural war. Life was truly strange.

"There's something I wanted to ask you," Leila said. Her mouth suddenly went dry, and she wasn't sure if Bianca would say yes. But the alternative was too much to bear.

"Shoot," Bianca said from her spot on the bleachers. She'd scrounged some clothes from the lost and found and was finally out of her reindeer pajamas. She looked just as nervous as Leila, her face pale, her normally confident stance now crumpled and hunched.

Leila wet her lips, then let the words tumble out. "If . . . if Cyrus takes me, I want you to end me," she said. "I don't want him to win."

Bianca gasped, horrified. "Like, kill you?"

"Please," Leila croaked. "You don't know how bad it is.

Having someone inside your head, controlling everything you do. It wouldn't be living. There'd be nothing left to kill at that point. He'd have my powers, though. He'd have everything."

Bianca looked at her sister, eyes wide. For once, Bianca Mazanderani was speechless.

Leila crouched on the seat next to her, clutching Bianca's hands. She no longer felt a spark when Bianca touched her, just the warmth of something melting into her skin, like it was already part of her too.

"Please," she begged. "I need this."

Bianca shook her head, her expression hollow. "I . . . I . . ."

"Bianca," Leila pressed.

"Okay," Bianca said, her voice shaky. "I—I will. I'll do it."

"Thank you," Leila breathed, resting against her. "Thank you." There, she'd covered all her loose ends. Cyrus wouldn't be able to control her, no matter what happened. It felt like a small weight had been lifted off her, a tiny dumbbell in a pile of anchors. But she'd take it.

"We could still surrender," Bianca said in a small voice. "We could still just let them take us completely. Save the town, our friends, Mom and Dad. I could make it so you wouldn't feel it."

"No, Bianca. We'd be puppets on his string. Even if I couldn't feel it, you *could*. We can't give in." She shivered, the thought too unbearable to visualize.

Bianca nodded, as if this had been a test and Leila had

passed. "We'd better leave," she said, reaching for Leila's hand. "You wanna go over the plan again?"

Leila exhaled. Their "plan" was more of a loose series of movements and tricks up their sleeves, with ways to use their powers in tandem. It was all they had. "I remember it."

Bianca was silent for a moment. Then: "I love you, Leila."

"Love you too, Bee," Leila said, her chest filling with warmth. She reached for Bianca and gave her a hug. Bianca squeezed her back, and Leila couldn't remember the last time they'd done this. "Here we go," Leila said, not moving.

"Here we go," Bianca repeated.

And then, still embracing, the two teleported to the site of the battle.

The Grove was deathly quiet. Leila hadn't known what to expect, but it definitely wasn't this abandoned, haunted feeling. Everything was so still that their breathing was loud, the sound echoing against the now-burnt trees. Leila blinked into the murky dusk and scanned for any flickers of fire or djinn.

Nothing.

"Leila?" a voice that wasn't Bianca's whispered. Leila snapped her head toward the noise that came from one of the trees' top branches. There, perched in the crook of an old oak tree, was Zahra, her body glinting with iron armor. The metal creaked and groaned as she tried to find purchase on a bouncy limb.

"Zahra?" Leila whispered back. Even covered head to toe in cold iron, Zahra was luminous, like a Persian Joan of Arc.

Still, they hadn't counted on meeting up with the Esfandiaris before the battle. Leila felt vulnerable standing twenty feet below her now, and all she wanted to do was run. Bianca tugged on Leila's sweater, as if to say the same thing.

"No, wait," Zahra said. "Please, we're on the same side. I'm sorry, I really am."

Leila scanned the rest of the trees. "Where's your family?" She knew that it wasn't Zahra she had to look out for but her father, Ehsan.

"They're coming," Zahra grimaced.

"Leila," Bianca warned. "The djinn aren't here, and her family hates us. We'd better go find Cyrus somewhere else."

Leila nodded. "Good idea."

But then something shifted in the forest. A thin tendril of fog, low to the ground, began creeping along in the waning light.

Leila and Bianca watched, mesmerized, as the fog rolled in. Was this a weather phenomenon? Or something more sinister?

"RUN!" Zahra screamed from the tree. She jumped down, her armor clanging. She roughly pushed Leila and Bianca forward. "That fog makes you blind! It's a djinn that makes you forget! Go, go, go!" she shouted.

Leila ran, making sure Bianca was alongside her. They pumped their arms and legs away from the mist that was quickly gaining on them like a strong gust of wind. She took in a ragged breath, a stitch forming in her side, but it didn't matter. The battle had begun, and it had started with another one of Cyrus's dirty tricks. Blinding them would have made the battle over in seconds.

Leila hated to admit it, but they were lucky Zahra had been there.

"Leila!" Bianca shouted as another djinn appeared. But before Leila could see what it was, Bianca was there, in her mind, jerking her to the left, forcing Leila's feet to move sideways instead of straight ahead. Just in time, a shot of fire grazed the spot where Leila had stood, leaving a crater in the pine-needle floor. Zahra yelped from the other side of Bianca. It had been a close call.

They made it out of the woods to the other side of The Grove, opposite from Leila and Bianca's house. This side had nothing but empty fields and dry, knee-high grass. Leila didn't like being so exposed, and she knew they had to keep moving.

She snuck a glance behind them and stumbled: There, less than a hundred yards away, was a si'lat, its neck crooked, its skin looking like it was two sizes too small for the demon beneath. And worst of all, it looked exactly like their father.

"Leilaaaa," it moaned. Its teeth were sharp, its eyes wicked with a red gleam.

"You're not our real dad!" Bianca screamed.

Leila faltered. Seeing a djinn impersonate her father was disturbing, and a reminder of just what their stakes were. If they lost, this is what the whole town would look like. This is the fate they'd be subjecting everyone to, only it wouldn't be a shape-shifter impersonating people. It would be djinn truly possessing their human bodies and minds.

In that moment the si'lat grinned, its pointed teeth gleaming in the dusk. It morphed back into a demon, its nails more like claws. "Jusssst wait," the thing hissed across the clearing. "I'll get your father ssssoon."

The second it turned back into its natural form, Leila summoned flames. She prodded the heat to stay in her hands and grow, and before she knew it, she'd launched a giant ball of fire at the si'lat. It screamed as it dissolved, its ashes scattering everywhere. Leila felt like one of those siege engines she'd read about in history class, like a Medieval trebuchet.

"Nice one," Zahra said from next to her. Leila blushed but didn't answer, simply scanning the tree line for more djinn. Then she felt it: the ground began to shake, the cold dirt and long grass buckling beneath her like someone was double bouncing her on a trampoline.

"Uh-oh," Bianca said darkly next to her. A flock of birds erupted from the forest, the sounds of their cawing and squawking ominous. The giant's face reared over the treetops, its red, charred flesh making straight for their trio.

Zahra gasped. She fumbled for her phone and made a call. "Now, now now now!" she shouted into the receiver.

Leila took this opportunity to size Zahra up. She wore a thin iron breastplate, along with iron gauntlets covering her arms and legs. Around her neck were several evil eye necklaces, and her eyes were rimmed with kohl. She was luminous. She was like no one she had met before. Leila took a mental photograph, so that no matter what happened, she'd always have that image to remember Zahra by, even if her family tried to destroy Leila's again.

Bianca's head suddenly jerked upward, as if listening for something. Then Leila heard it too. The low drone of a plane buzzing overhead.

"Finally," Zahra breathed.

Leila watched, awestruck, as the Esfandiaris' private plane flew overhead, straight for the giant towering over the forest trees.

"Here," Zahra said. "I brought these just in case." She pulled two gas masks from the backpack she wore, the huge kind that Leila had seen graffiti artists use.

"Why do we need—" Bianca began, and then they smelled it. The plane wasn't just buzzing overhead; it was crop-dusting the field with esfand.

Leila began to cough, the smell searing through her lungs. She snatched a mask from Zahra and shoved it on, not caring how ridiculous she looked. She inhaled deeply, her breath tasting like rubber and plastic, but it was an improvement over esfand. Still, the mask limited her vision. She watched Bianca shove hers on and give the same relaxed inhale.

"Naaaaaaaah!" The giant boomed.

The plane had reached the forest, and the giant faltered, the esfand confusing it as it started stumbling, clutching tree limbs for purchase. The ground beneath them shook as the giant finally fell with a loud crash.

"See? I told you my family would handle it," Zahra said smugly.

Bianca rolled her eyes through the gas mask, her bright blue eyes still visible in the last rays of light. "Gee, thanks," Bianca said.

"Seriously, you guys can go," Zahra said. "We've got it covered."

"This is *our* town," Leila growled.

"Yeah, and *our* parents," Bianca snapped.

Zahra bit her lip. "My family still doesn't understand you," she said. "I just don't want anyone to get hurt."

And then they heard him, the low, dry chuckle that sent the hairs on the back of Leila's neck standing. Cyrus had appeared at the other side of the clearing.

"Well, well, well," he said.

BIANCA

She hated Cyrus. She hated his stupid face and his stupid clothes and the way he acted as if he had already won. She wanted to wipe the smirk right off his skull as he stood at the edge of the forest, chuckling at them. *What's so funny?* she wanted to scream. *My fist in your face?*

The plane droned overhead, esfand smoke falling like fog.

"Interesting." Cyrus frowned, staring up at the incense that was now falling on his shoulders. The other djinn seemed to be affected, their figures cowering, their flames flickering. A ghul howled in rage, then evaporated into an oil slick. Cyrus, however, stood untouched.

"Shouldn't it kill him?" Bianca whispered to Zahra.

Zahra didn't say anything, her face pale. "I thought it would . . . ," she began, confused.

"Mareed," Cyrus intoned. A blue flame appeared next to him, morphing into a giant djinn with an iron collar around its neck. It bowed low before Cyrus, revealing huge muscles, its body covered in scars.

"I wish for you to bring me a storm, and I wish for more protection from the esfand," Cyrus said casually, as if this was possible.

"Your wish is my command," the mareed said in a deep voice.

Bianca watched, rapt, as the mareed bowed once more and disappeared in a puff of blue flame. Was Cyrus making wishes off other djinn?

And then they heard it: a low rumble of thunder.

"Oh my god," Zahra breathed. "They're gonna bring the plane down."

"Seriously?" Bianca cried, looking back at Cyrus's smug face. Sure enough, she felt a fat plop of rain hit her gas mask, the water blocking her vision.

Zahra got out her phone. "Land! Land!" she yelled into the receiver. "He's trapped a mareed! It's going to bring a huge storm!"

Trapped! That was why all the djinn here had iron collars. They weren't Cyrus's soldiers. They were his servants, held against their will, bound to do his bidding.

Leila grimly looked at the graying clouds, and Bianca watched as she summoned her flames in the steady rain. The flames definitely weren't as big as before.

The three of them stood in the deluge, trying to see Cyrus through the gloom.

"Djinn!" Cyrus shouted across the field. "Assemble!"

The three held their breath. Zahra tightened her grip on

a mace full of esfand, now useless in the storm. Lights began to flicker across the field, and Bianca gasped as far more djinn than they'd first seen at The Grove danced in flames across from them.

"There's got to be almost a thousand," Leila said weakly from next to her.

"And he's controlling all of them," Bianca added grimly.

"He's summoning every single djinn in the world," Zahra said, amazed. "What's so special about this place?"

Bianca bristled. She felt more protective of Ayers than she had before. This was a vibrant community, a shelter in the beautiful mountains, and a place that helped shape Virginia into what it was. She hated to admit it, but nothing made her appreciate Ayers more than having someone try to take it from her. Cyrus would be lucky to call this place home.

Plus, they technically weren't *all* the djinn in the world. Bianca remembered the feeling of her mind brushing up against the djinn in New York City, the ones who seemed free of Cyrus's command. She wondered if Zahra knew as much about djinn as she thought she did.

"What do we do?" Bianca asked. "There's too many of them!" Just trying to keep up with every new burst of flame made her dizzy. And there was Cyrus, smirking in front of them all in the pouring rain.

"We fight," Zahra said grimly, brandishing her mace.

"We've got no other choice, Bee," Leila said from beside her.

Bianca planted her feet firmer in the dirt, which was

slowly turning to mud. They were right; fighting was their last option. At least she and Leila had practiced, so they weren't completely off guard. Bianca pulled her gas mask off, the filter useless now that the rain tamped the esfand down. Leila did the same, and Bianca tried not to flinch as icy rainwater poured into the borrowed gym clothes she wore. She really wished she'd had time to put on jeans and a sweater.

Here we go, Bianca thought to herself.

Just then they heard an engine behind them. They turned around: it was Zahra's white BMW, driving onto the field at breakneck speed—the Esfandiaris had already returned.

Bianca wasn't sure how to feel about them now. Clearly, they were on the same side, but would they try to take her and Leila out again?

"Don't worry about my family," Zahra said quickly. "We need to fight Cyrus first."

"That doesn't exactly comfort me, but okay," Bianca replied. What Zahra had said was basically the equivalent of *We'll deal with you later.* If they made it out alive, of course.

Bianca tried not to scowl as she saw Ehsan, Mohsen, and Tara join their lineup, all of them squaring off against Cyrus, the Esfandiaris' past attempt at fighting the twins forgotten.

"'Sup," Tara said flatly. She wore iron armor like Zahra, but it was painted with green and red evil eyes, giving it a colorful graffiti effect. Her bright yellow jumpsuit helped her stand out in the rain.

Bianca said nothing. Leila shivered next to her, and

Bianca reached for her hand and clasped it tight. No matter what happened, they were in this together.

Both sides stood across from each other in an empty meadow the size of a football field. There were so many djinn now that they outnumbered the trees in the forest.

"Let's do this," Mohsen growled, the first time Bianca had heard Zahra's uncle speak.

From the other end of the meadow came a glint of copper from Cyrus as he held up the scimitar he wore on his belt. "CHARGE!" he shouted.

The battle had truly begun.

The distant flickers of light surged forward, and Bianca watched, fascinated, as every flame morphed into a different kind of djinn that she'd read about online. Monsters and demons of all shapes seemed to be in attendance; some were half-human and half-crocodile, or half-human, half-dog. Others were just wisps of gas or smoke in the shape of humans. Some djinn were terrifying, their arms and legs bent at odd angles, their tongues lashing, and some looked small and harmless until they bared their teeth. Yet still they came, like a rising tide of nightmares.

"Come on!" Leila shouted, grabbing Bianca's hand and plunging forward. Her boots had a tough time navigating the now-wet field, the grass underneath churning into mud. It was hard to believe that this was what their supernatural fight had turned into: an old-school battle on open land. How fitting for a place that had seen similar battles before.

Mohsen ran ahead, clutching two scimitars that looked like they were made of iron. He was the first to make contact in the middle of the field, slashing two djinn as he whirled his blades into the crowd. The demons screamed as they disappeared into puffs of smoke. Ehsan wasn't far behind, wearing the same armor as his brother and Zahra, the older man slicing and stabbing with an iron spear like a seasoned swordsman.

Tara, however, had a different fighting style that consisted of no swords but a long chain with two iron daggers on each end. She twirled it around her, taking out djinn as she nimbly danced around them. Just a prick from the iron dagger was enough to eviscerate a snarling, seething monster before Tara yanked it back.

"Bianca!" Leila shouted. Bianca turned around just in time to see the giant mareed who had summoned the rain standing over her, his fists raised. But Leila was there in an instant, teleporting to Bianca's side and blinking her out of there just as quickly. Bianca watched from twenty feet away as the mareed's fists came down on the spot she had been seconds before.

"Thanks," she gasped.

"No problem," said Leila. But before Bianca could catch her breath, a slithery si'lat was already there, wearing Leila's face and shooting flames at close range. Leila didn't have time to grow a fireball, so Bianca did the next best thing: she grabbed the si'lat by its slimy skin, trying hard not to think about how it looked exactly like Leila, and took control.

It was easy to take over the djinn's mind. What was difficult was realizing that she wasn't the *only* one controlling it. There, in the murky back of the si'lat's consciousness, was another power, another force: Cyrus.

Kill, kill, kill the humans! His will echoed inside the djinn. It was like a steady drumbeat that thumped throughout the djinn's existence. *Kill, kill, kill!*

That's how Cyrus is controlling them, Bianca realized. *He isn't just using an iron collar; he's possessing each and every one.*

Bianca thought back to the iron collar on the huge mareed. Iron, possession, esfand—there were many ways to bend djinn to your will, and Cyrus was using them all.

In that moment she felt *sorry* for these pathetic djinn, forced to fight a battle they had no say in.

Go back to where you came from, Bianca ordered, overpowering Cyrus's command inside the si'lat. Cyrus's orders were weak, his control spread too thin. It was easy to overtake the prince's will inside this poor demon.

Bianca watched as the djinn's eyes turned blue from her order. It exhaled slow and deep, its twisted face relaxing before turning into a flame and winking out of this plane. She hoped it was enough to keep that djinn from reappearing. In that split second before the si'lat had gone, it had looked relieved, like it hadn't wanted to be here at all. *Let's hope I never see you again.*

Bianca shifted her focus to the horde of djinn that the Esfandiaris were currently decimating, all of their enemies vanishing into puffs of smoke and oil.

"Why didn't you finish it?" Leila said from next to Bianca, where she'd watched the whole exchange.

"Because Cyrus was possessing it. He's possessing all of them."

Leila gave a sad shake of her head. "I felt something was off with them. But how can he control so many?"

"I don't know, but I think if we get to Cyrus, we can finish this once and for all." Instead of dealing with each puppet, Bianca wanted to take out the puppet master himself.

Leila gave a grim nod. "Let's get him."

Bianca looked up to the hill where she'd last seen Cyrus by the trees, but he was nowhere in sight. Next to them, the Esfandiaris were like human blurs, slicing and dicing djinn left and right. But just then, a sneaky, oily ghul had snuck up on Mohsen's feet.

"Ahhh!" he yelled as the slimy ghul encased his right leg in ooze. Instantly, Mohsen's face went pale, his body freezing up.

"No!" Tara screamed. Leila teleported her and Bianca over to Mohsen in a flash, and Bianca plunged her hands into the ghul's slimy body.

Stop, she commanded it. *Leave us alone.* But it was too

late; the ghul enjoyed sucking on Mohsen's flesh too much, its consciousness filled with ecstasy. Bianca felt, rather than saw, Leila's fireballs end its life, her connection to the ghul suddenly cut.

"Thank you," Mohsen gasped. He was looking at the twins differently now. He seemed surprised and grateful. It was the look of someone recalculating, and Bianca hoped it meant that saving his life proved the twins weren't evil, that they were on the same side.

Before the twins could regroup, more flames rained down on them as attacking djinn approached. The Esfandiaris had their iron armor, but Leila and Bianca were completely exposed.

"Strobe!" Bianca shouted, ducking as a giant ball of flame sailed dangerously close to their heads. Leila's arm shot out and she grabbed Bianca's sleeve. In an instant, they were back in the gymnasium of Ayers High. Bianca had a split second to register the EXIT sign over the doorway before they were instantly back in the field, a djinn howling as its shot missed them. Then it was back to the gym, back to the meadow, back to the gym—

"Coo–!" Tara's voice shouted. But the twins were already gone, Bianca's head swimming from all the teleporting. There wasn't even enough time for the flames to die around Leila with each teleportation, so the two constantly swam in a sea of fire as the sisters sneakily approached the djinn horde, each strobe bringing them closer and closer.

In the gym, Leila took a break from teleporting and turned to Bianca. "There's a djinn that looks like a dog about to tear into Zahra. If I get you close enough, can you take it out?"

Bianca nodded, grateful to catch her breath and give her inner ear a break. But before she could fully reorient herself, Leila gripped her hand and teleported them a foot away from the approaching dog/human djinn, or heen, with snarling teeth and red eyes, its human hands at odds with its snout.

"Bianca! Now!"

She was ready. The thing's drooling face snapped close to hers, but before it could sink its teeth into her, she snatched it by the scruff of the neck.

ENOUGH, she intoned silently, forcing it to capitulate. With a whimper, the djinn's eyes turned blue. *LEAVE US*, Bianca ordered. In a flash, the djinn was gone.

"Nice," Leila said.

"I know, right?" Bianca made as if to brush her shoulders, but something a hundred yards away in the gloom made her stop in her tracks. There, close to the tree line, she recognized someone. "Shivani? Steve? June!"

There were their friends, their shirts ragged and torn, wearing the same outfits they'd worn last night when they'd tried to jump Bianca and Leila. But it wasn't really them. Their eyes glowed bright red, and their faces snarled.

"Leila!" Bianca cried, pointing out their friends. "We've got to help them!"

"Oh my god," Leila gasped. "You go. I'll cover you!"

There wasn't much distance to clear to get to her friends; the second they'd seen her, they'd made a beeline for her, their gaits off, their body language completely different. Instead of sashaying like she owned the place, Shivani was hunched and limping. Steve's eyes were completely unrecognizable, the gentleness and humor gone. And June, poor June, was a sneering, cackling monster, her face twisted and cruel. Bianca grabbed June's arm first as Leila stood nearby, ready to throw fireballs at anyone who tried to interrupt or, worse, if their friends didn't cooperate.

The instant Bianca grabbed June's hand, she felt June's torture and pain of being under Cyrus's control. While Leila had described possession as a throbbing background noise, this possession was all screams and confusion, June's mind begging for release. Leila hadn't been joking: Cyrus's possession wasn't anything like Bianca's. It was constant mental torture. Bianca summoned blue sparks at their point of connection while trying hard to keep June's other hand from clawing her face. June's face was covered in dirt, her thin hair sticking out at odd angles. It hurt to see her friend like this.

"Stop. Trying. To. Kill. Me!" Bianca gasped, struggling to assert her will over June's. It was harder than the ghul's. Harder than Leila's willing participation. Beads of sweat broke out on Bianca's forehead, mixing with the slick raindrops from before. Finally, the blue sparks sank into June's skin.

Stop, Bianca commanded. *This isn't you. You are June McCullough.*

"Gah!" Leila cried.

Bianca whipped her head up. She had barely noticed how Leila was trying to hold back Steve and Shivani, the two of them trying their hardest to pluck Bianca's eyes out. Leila's hands glowed red as she corralled them in a lasso of fire, the two friends snarling in their makeshift holding circle.

June lunged for Bianca.

"It's not working!" Bianca cried. Her best friend, her confidante, was gone. Suddenly everything felt so hopeless, so woefully unwinnable. *I can't do this without my best friend.* Bianca wanted to sob and scream and run away, and every time she looked up from her possessed bestie, she was greeted by scenes of Zahra and Tara fighting a war of inches as they tried to gain ground, of Mohsen and Ehsan whirling esfand and iron. *I'm not strong like them*, Bianca realized. *I can't do it.*

"Try again, Bianca!" Leila urged her, her hands gripping Steve and Shivani in place. "Remind her who she is!"

Bianca took a deep breath and looked into her friend's red eyes, the flames dancing across her irises. *I have to try*, Bianca reminded herself. *I owe it to June.*

Bianca clutched June's arms again, and this time, June-but-not-June screamed, steam rising from their point of contact. Bianca summoned another crackle of blue sparks and felt her head throb with concentration as she forced each bead of light into June's skin. June shrieked again, arching her back unnaturally, her scream unlike anything Bianca had ever heard. She knew she didn't have much time.

You are June McCullough, Bianca began again. *Your favorite cake is dulce de leche. Your secret favorite sport is figure skating because you love the costumes, even though we don't have a team. You love Liam Fitzpatrick and when you graduate you really want to major in statistics, which I know because I looked at your application when you went to use the bathroom during study break, even though everyone thinks you want to major in sports therapy. Your favorite color is yellow, your favorite sibling is your elder brother August, and your best friend is Bianca Mazanderani.*

It was like talking to a bucking bronco, Bianca's voice soft and gentle as she tried to calm the skittish animal. *Bianca Mazanderani is your best friend, and she loves you so much, she doesn't know if she can leave you and everyone here behind.*

She hadn't realized it was the truth until she'd spoken it into her friend's mind. She couldn't leave Ayers. Despite all her complaining and bemoaning, she *loved it here.* Bianca blinked, the realization weighing down on her, making her want to fight for this town even more. June's body went slack.

"Bianca?" June croaked.

Bianca looked at her friend. Her pale blue eyes had returned, her rosy cheeks cold in the December air. Bianca hugged her.

"June," Bianca breathed. "I was so worried!"

June looked around her in disbelief, the battle raging on. "What happened? Where am I?"

"Bianca!" Leila cried. Shivani and Steve struggled to break free of the lasso of flame she'd roped around them. "Help, please!"

"Soon!" Bianca shouted to June as she ran to Leila. "I'll answer everything, I promise! Go stand by that white car!"

She didn't have time to make sure June made it safely out of the scrum. Bianca was already holding Shivani with one arm and Steve with the other. They screamed as Bianca made contact, her confidence in her new power building. It was easier to force her spark into their skin this time, easier to overpower their wills with her own.

Stop, she intoned in their minds, like a clear, crisp-sounding bell. *You are Shivani Shah and Steve Rosenberg. Stop.* Their minds were just as tortured as June's, but Bianca's power was no match for Cyrus's weak claim on them.

She repeated this a few more times until she felt their muscles relax, their snarling, spitting faces relaxing into shock.

"Whoa," Steve said, blinking the red from his eyes. Bianca's heart swelled as she watched the warm hazel color return.

Meanwhile, Shivani's reunion with her consciousness was a bit more dramatic. "WHAT IS HAPPENING!" she shrieked. "WHAT AM I EVEN WEARING?"

"Go wait by that car!" Leila cried, pointing to where June was huddled by the white BMW. "Now!"

"I'm not leaving you, you dummy," Shivani balked. "That dude made me sleep without doing my skincare regimen! I will never forgive him!" She pointed an accusatory finger at Cyrus, who now stood at the edge of the meadow, watching the whole thing.

"Then go to the car and grab iron and incense!" Bianca cried back. "Go!"

"DUCK!" Zahra suddenly cried, snapping them out of their friendly reunion. They ducked without thinking, just as a huge burst of flame sailed over the group's head.

Bianca looked at who'd thrown it. It was another giant, not as big as the first, with Cyrus now riding its shoulders.

"Oh dear," Ehsan said. Bianca would have used stronger words than *oh dear*, but yes, this was a very big problem.

Leila shouted, "I can get us up to the giant's shoulders, and you can take him out, Bee."

Bianca took a deep breath. Here it was, her showdown with Cyrus. It was her will against his. Did she really have what it took to overpower a djinn prince? But then Bianca remembered how vulnerable Cyrus had to be while he controlled so many others. His focus was split into a thousand pieces. Bianca still didn't know much about her power, but she knew it took a lot of concentration.

She nodded. "Let's go."

"Wait!" Steve grabbed her hand. He gave her a tight hug, his arms wrapping around her soaked clothes. "Be careful, okay?" His skin looked gray, his clothes in tatters, but in that moment, Bianca thought he was the most handsome boy she'd ever seen.

"I will," she agreed.

Steve let go of Bianca, his expression concerned.

Please, Bianca prayed. *Please let me see him again soon.* Leila reached for her hand, and Bianca closed her eyes. When she opened them, she almost screamed.

They were more than thirty feet off the ground, on the giant's shoulder. Cyrus gave an undignified yelp the second he spotted them, his whole body flinching with surprise.

"Hi." Bianca smirked, trying to cover up the fact that she was trembling. *Here goes nothing,* she thought, taking a big inhale. Then she jumped across the bouncing giant's neck and tackled Cyrus on the other shoulder. He shouted, but it didn't matter. Bianca had already made contact. She clutched his arm through his decorated military-style jacket and pushed her blue spark into him, a crackle of static surging through them both. She had been right: he was so distracted that it was easy to force her spark into him.

She penetrated Cyrus's mind, but it was so fractured and torn apart that she had trouble knowing where to start. There were thousands of lines leading from his will, all connected to the djinn he was controlling in the field. Instead of the amorphous blob of minds she'd tried to control before, Cyrus's mind was a spiderweb, and finding the center felt impossible.

"Get . . . out . . . of . . . there!" he shouted, trying to push Bianca off him. In a flash, Leila was next to her. She braced Bianca against Cyrus, Bianca holding on to him for dear life.

Bianca gritted her teeth. She struggled to pierce Cyrus's spirit, watching his face for his eyes to turn blue. *Stop this war!* she screamed into his mind. She saw a blue flicker appear over his coal-black eyes and felt his will give in just a little bit.

Finally, Bianca thought. But she'd celebrated too soon. Suddenly Cyrus's eyes turned back to black, like coffee overtaking cream, and Bianca felt her hold loosen.

NEVER! Cyrus screamed into her brain.

Bianca recoiled, losing her grip on him. "Whoa, whoa!" she said, trying to hold on to the giant's galloping body. She lost her footing, her body arcing painfully into the air. But then Leila grabbed her hand, helping her back up from what would have been a fatal fall.

"Fool!" Cyrus seethed. "You thought you could overtake me? The prince of djinn? How do you think the royal family got its throne? We're the strongest of our line, the best at possession. How do you think I overtook my own parents? You are nothing but an ant to be quashed under my boot!"

And then he grabbed Bianca by her shirt, lifting her up into the air. Her whole body went into a panic—her neck ached from where her shirt collar cut into her. Her feet kicked in midair, desperate for purchase. *He's going to throw me off*, Bianca realized. But then he did something even worse.

Hello, a voice inside her mind said. Dimly, she heard Leila scream "NO!" but it felt so far away now. *Hello*, Bianca replied calmly.

Stop fighting, the voice commanded. It didn't sound like Cyrus. It sounded gentler, more caring. It was nothing like the screaming commands she'd heard inside June.

"STOP!" Leila begged. But Leila's voice sounded like it was in another room. So, so far away.

Bianca felt a cool calm take over. She felt good. No, better than good. She was the most relaxed she'd ever been. Bianca felt her body go limp, her whirling brain finally, blissfully quiet.

This wasn't so bad.

There, the soothing voice said. *Nice and easy now. I need you to do something for me, hoharam.* Sister. The voice thought of her as a sister. That was nice, wasn't it?

Anything, Bianca thought, her body so pliable she felt like she could fold into a pretzel, her muscles more relaxed than they'd ever felt in her life. Were her shoulders always this far away from her ears? Who knew the muscles in her jaw could detach so low?

See that girl over there? the deep voice asked.

Bianca nodded, her vision suddenly clearing up. There was Leila, looking at her like she'd just eaten a bug, her face horrified.

I need you to push her for me.

Bianca exhaled. That sounded like a reasonable request. She could do that. She could push Leila easily from here.

Anything to feel this peaceful again.

Then Bianca did the unthinkable.

She pushed Leila off the giant, sending her tumbling below.

LEILA

One moment she had been bolstering her sister on top of a giant, and the next she was free-falling thirty feet to the ground.

She had no room to process what was happening as the ground came up quickly beneath her. Adrenaline made it almost impossible for her to think, her head pounding as the wind whipped past her.

And then she remembered she could teleport.

Milliseconds before hitting the ground, Leila disappeared from Ayers. Her flames tickled the dirt—that's how close a call it had been. She picked the first place she could think of: the beach where they'd woken up earlier that day. She still wasn't sure how her velocity changed whenever she teleported, so she picked a spot ten feet above the waves, hoping she wouldn't hit them too hard.

She appeared above the ocean and slammed into the water, the built-up gravity from Ayers transferring to her dive. She plugged her nose as she cut into the icy cold surface, hitting it hard.

She went far, far into the waves, almost hitting the ocean bed below from the velocity of falling off the giant. It was a struggle to swim up for oxygen, and she practically choked for breath. She knew if she teleported from the bottom of the water to the beach, she'd have issues depressurizing. So, she swam up slowly, reaching the surface and sucking in as much air as she could through her coughs and splutters.

She paddled to the shore, flailing in her sweater and jeans. Every part of her body ached, her muscles screaming in protest. She would not be doing that ever again if she could help it.

By the time she crawled up onto the cold sand, she was exhausted. A child with a jacket and a glow stick who she hadn't noticed before stared at her with wide eyes. Thank goodness it was winter, or more people would have seen her.

"Hi," Leila croaked.

"Mooooom!" the child cried, running back up to the dunes.

Leila lay like that, gasping for breath, her chest heaving.

Bianca had pushed her off the giant. No, not Bianca, *Cyrus*. He was controlling her now. Bianca hadn't been strong enough to overtake him, and now she was a part of his horde, too.

What do I do? Leila lay in the sand, waiting for a brilliant answer to appear, but nothing came. Her heart broke, wondering if Bianca felt the same pain Leila had from Cyrus.

"This wasn't supposed to happen!" Leila suddenly shouted, hitting her fist into the sand. She didn't care if anyone heard her. Their hours of training and preparation were for nothing now. They hadn't anticipated Cyrus taking over Bianca, only Leila. They had no plan for this.

She shivered, her skin clammy and covered in sticky sand. This was an absolute low.

There was nothing to do but teleport back with her tail between her legs and figure out how to save Bianca's life.

She had failed, both as a big sister and as this new, supernatural being who was supposed to have all this power. Leila closed her eyes and gritted her teeth, urging the flames to overtake her. Slowly, achingly slowly, the flames heated up her icy skin. She dreamed of Ayers, praying that nothing worse had happened in the five minutes she'd been gone.

When she opened her eyes, she was relieved to see the meadow less chaotic now. She had teleported back by the Esfandiaris' car, bracing for a raging battle, but all she could see was Zahra and her family in an emptying field. Mohsen and Ehsan picked off straggling djinn in the high grass.

"Zahra!" Leila shouted. Zahra stood back with Tara, keeping watch for any new djinn. Cyrus was nowhere to be found.

"Leila!" Zahra said, her grim face relaxing into something that looked like hope. Leila tried not to let her heart belly flop at that sweet, tender look, but she couldn't help it. Everything had gone wrong today, and it was nice to relish this moment.

"Where did you go?" she asked. "When Bianca pushed you . . . I thought . . . we all figured . . ."

"I teleported into water," Leila answered. Thankfully, her flames had dried most of her clothes by now.

Zahra's eyebrows rose. "That was smart. I wouldn't have thought of that."

Leila smiled, glad the darkness hid her skin's flush. "Where'd all the djinn go?" she asked, quickly changing the subject. "Have you seen Bianca?"

Zahra shook her head. "We're down to the stragglers now, but we haven't seen Bianca or Cyrus."

And just like that, Leila's warming heart sank back into icy cold. Her sister was missing, and she was still controlled by Cyrus.

Then she heard it.

"Leila jan." She didn't need to turn around to know whose voice that was.

There stood her father, not more than twenty feet from her and Zahra. Next to him was her mother, the two of them standing eerily still.

"Dad?" Leila called out, rushing toward him. But then she stopped.

Her dad's brown eyes were red. Same with her mother's normally blue ones.

They weren't her parents right now. They were under Cyrus's control.

"NO!" Leila shouted. "This wasn't part of the deal! You haven't won!"

Her father's face twisted into a sneer, and then, with horrifying speed, he began sprinting toward her.

Zahra waved her esfand mace, the iron chain clinking.

"No!" Leila shouted. "You'll hurt them!" But her parents were gaining speed, her mother's face manic with desire, her eyes practically glowing. *What do I do? What do I do?*

But Zahra decided for her, wafting esfand into her parents' path. The two buckled over, choking, and Leila's heart twisted as she retched. Seconds ago, they had been about to take her out. Was this a more humane way of dealing with them?

Ehsan approached, his face grave.

"I don't understand," Leila began. She couldn't help it now; tears were streaming down her face, her body and soul so tortured over this turn of events that she had no idea how to cope without her sister, without her parents.

Ehsan looked at her sorrowfully. "Your father still hasn't paid the price for his wish. Cyrus has your sister, but you're still free. Cyrus can do whatever he wants to your family. Their safety is not guaranteed."

Leila sank into the charred field at a complete loss. Her parents hacked and writhed feet away from her, and she watched as Tara solemnly placed iron cuffs around their hands. They stilled.

A cackle came from the edge of the forest only fifty feet from their group. There stood Cyrus, surveying the scene, his face triumphant. By his side was Bianca, her face empty, her eyes bright red.

"Bianca!" Leila screamed. She made as if to teleport to her side, but Cyrus held up a hand. "Not so fast, little Mazanderani."

Leila heard the crunching of twigs and soft footsteps. Tara cocked her head, looking for the noise.

"Oh no," Mohsen groaned. There, at the edge of the forest, stood the residents of Ayers, all in a long, silent line. They looked like a grim funeral procession. And every single one of them had red eyes.

Leila's heart lurched. *He didn't. He couldn't. They'd promised!*

"This was not our agreement!" Zahra shouted. "The winner keeps the town!"

Cyrus grinned, his pointed teeth gleaming. "Oh, Esfandiari," he spat. "Can't you see I've already won?"

Leila was stunned. She had no idea how they were going to get out of this one. There was no way she could hurt her parents, her sister, her town. At the edge of the gloom stood Shivani and June, their faces slack, once again possessed. She spied Foster with his father, the two in ugly Christmas sweaters as if they'd been yanked straight from a holiday party. Teachers and classmates, store owners and parents—she saw them all, their spirits gone, their souls empty vessels for Cyrus to control as they silently stood beneath the trees.

"No, no, no," she moaned.

Zahra looked at her, not sure what to do. "Baba?" she asked, turning to her dad.

Ehsan and Mohsen shared a grim look, readying themselves to fight. Tara took one glance at their posture and assumed the same fighting stance.

It was clear to Leila then: these djinn hunters didn't care who they hurt, so long as they won.

Her feelings toward this town had become so complicated since she'd gotten this power. Ayers had been everything to her: her past, present, and future. But now it had shrunk to only a small part of herself. She still had so many places left to see, so many things she wanted to do. The thought of marrying Foster and starting a family straight after high school was laughable now, a distant dream she could barely understand.

In front of her stood something new and exciting whose twists and turns weren't yet visible. There was nothing stopping her from running, from teleporting to some remote part of the world and starting over.

But she owed it to her town, to her people. It was her family's fault this was happening, and even if her old dream was gone, she had affection for the place it started.

And suddenly, Leila knew what she had to do.

She made for her parents by the white BMW, her knees trembling.

"Leila? What are you—" Zahra began.

She ignored her, focusing on her mom and dad, whose snarling faces were at odds with the love and care they usually beamed at her.

In that moment, she understood her father. He, like Leila, had been so sure of his path. He was going to leave Iran, see the world, and never look back. He'd never be tied down to a family, never struggle the way his fellow citizens did under a new, tyrannical government that he'd been born under. He was going to be different.

And then he'd met Alma, and his world had changed.

Just like Leila's had.

"This ends now!" Leila shouted across the field. Cyrus looked at her, confused. Leila reached for her father's hands, his grasping claws still shackled in the iron manacles Tara had placed there.

"Te quiero, Mamá," Leila whispered to her mother's feral face. Leila could see tears leaking out of her mother's eyes, as if the real Alma was breaking through despite the possession. Leila's heart broke into even more pieces.

Across the field, understanding cracked over Cyrus's face. "No, no, you can't—!"

But Leila ignored him. She turned to her dad and gripped her father's palm in hers, the familiar warmth gone. She looked across the field to Bianca, to her twin, who stood silently next to Cyrus. She felt the iron on her father's hands that tried to block her escape, but she pushed through.

"See you soon," she whispered to her mom.

And then Leila and her father teleported in a burst of flame.

IRAN,
PRESENT DAY

The Caucasus Mountains towered over them, the snow-capped peaks standing out against the blue sky. Leila blinked in the bright sunlight, her eyes taking time to adjust after the darkness of Ayers at night. Her father crouched on the ground next to her, his red eyes slowly turning back to dark brown.

"Leila jan?" he asked. "Kojasteem?" But his choice of language had answered for him. Somewhere deep down, Khosrow knew where they were. They were back in Iran, where this had all started.

Leila hadn't had time to look at a picture of Tehran, the capital city, before making her decision. It seemed like they were somewhere else in the country, far from any metropolis.

Across from the mountain valley she spied a village along with a small creek that ran alongside its dirt road. The trees here still had green on them, despite the crisp mountain air. She took in a deep breath, clearing her head. She could hear her father do the same.

"Here," she said. She bent down and grabbed the iron manacles on his wrists, wincing at the cold metal as she used her extra strength to snap them off. She let them drop with a thump in the dirt.

He massaged his hands, then suddenly hugged Leila close. "I thought I'd lost you forever," he croaked.

Leila hugged him back. Today had been terrifying, with Leila unsure what Cyrus would do to her parents. She felt so relieved to have her father back. That made this decision even harder.

He pulled away, his gaze catching on something in the distance. "This is the village where I was born."

Leila's eyes went wide. She had no idea how she'd brought him here, to this exact place. She hadn't even known he'd been born in a village, figuring he had lived his whole life in the capital of Tehran. "Where are we?"

"Near the sea of Mazanderan. That's where we get our last name from. The Caspian Sea, in English."

She'd never known he was born here. There were so many things she didn't know about him, and now she wondered if she ever would. She stared hard into the distance, drinking in the lush valley and the mountains. It didn't seem like a bad place to grow up.

Her heart lurched, knowing what she had to do.

"Dad," Leila began. "I have to leave you here."

There was no other way. Cyrus's deal had been to help her father leave Iran in exchange for his firstborn. But if her father stayed, there was no deal. Cyrus would lose the terms of the agreement and be forced to leave.

It wasn't a perfect solution. But it was the only one they had right now.

Her father turned to her, his eyes baleful. Cyrus wasn't possessing him anymore, the distance too great to control, but his eyes still looked tortured.

"When I was young, I swore to myself I would never have children," he began. "That was the price of freedom for me: to never have a family of my own. You must understand, I went from being able to go to concerts, to hanging out with my friends in Iran, to absolute lockdown. That was how fast everything changed. I couldn't voice my opinion. I couldn't even start college because they wanted to draft me. So I paid the price, and I made my peace with it."

Leila swallowed all the questions she wanted to ask, about Iran before the revolution, about what it was like to see your government fall, about how he had thought to contact a djinn in the first place.

"And then . . . well, I met your mom," his voice broke, and Leila had to bite her lip to keep her sobs in. "She was like no one else I had ever met before. She was smart, and strong, and she had just left a country that was as weak as mine at the time. She wasn't from Iran, but we had so much in common.

She said she didn't want children, that she wanted to focus on her career, and I knew we were a good match."

Leila couldn't help it; tears started to silently track down her face. She'd never known this about her parents.

"And then, Alma got pregnant. I was afraid, yes, like a new father should be. But deep down, I was terrified because of my bargain. I told Alma I didn't want to raise our family in a city, and she agreed to go to a small college in Virginia, even though there weren't as many opportunities. I lied to her," he said, his voice cracking. "I lied to my wife and never told her the truth. I picked Ayers because there was no one like me there, and still, they found us."

He was crying now, and Leila was too.

"It's okay, Dad," Leila choked. She hugged her father, getting snot all over his shirt, and clutched him fiercely. She had wondered why they had picked Ayers. She had never known that her parents hadn't planned on children. She felt like she had the last pieces of the puzzle, and instead of feeling satisfied, the revelation made her ache even more.

"It's okay, baba jan," her father said, rubbing her back as she heaved another sob. "Now you know."

They stood in silence for a while, the two embracing. Leila's throat felt tight from crying, her body spent from fighting djinn. A part of her just wanted to stay here and never leave, to never go back to Ayers and face the raging battle that was destroying her town. But she knew she couldn't do that.

"I'll be back as soon as I can, okay?" Leila finally said, breaking the sniffly silence. "Do you still have family here?"

She hadn't asked, *Do* we *have family here?* because this place felt so different, so new, that she still couldn't fathom how she was part of this country too.

"Go," her dad said, urging her on. "Go get Bianca and Alma. I'll be fine."

In that moment her dad looked so small. His shirt was torn, his house slippers still on. Cyrus had taken him by surprise, and now all he had were the clothes on his back.

Still, he was safe, and that was a miracle right now.

"I love you, Baba," Leila whispered.

"Love you too, jiggar."

Leila willed the flames of her body to surge outward. Her father's eyebrows rose, his whole face stunned as he again witnessed her teleportation. But before Leila could see his full reaction, she was back on the battlefield, back to Ayers.

BIANCA

The thing about being possessed is that it feels wonderful and horrible, thought Bianca hazily. She stood next to Cyrus as she watched all her friends, classmates, and community members shamble zombie-like to the Esfandiaris. It was as if she was floating over herself, mildly interested in what happened next, and not worried about the potential slaughter of her entire town, her mother included. She and Cyrus stood on the singed forest floor, toward the back of the horde. He gripped Bianca's shoulder, and from their connection point she could feel calm pumping into her body. She never wanted it to stop.

There was Zahra winding up her esfand mace in the oncoming tide of bodies. Tara spun her daggers like a dervish. Ehsan and Mohsen looked like old, weathered knights who didn't want to have to take out the bad guys but would, when pressed. And there was Bianca, with her proverbial popcorn, without a care in the world.

Suddenly, Cyrus buckled, falling to his knees. He gave a soft grunt as he sank to the dirt, his chest heaving. Bianca felt a twinge inside her, as if one of the puppet strings that controlled her had snapped.

"No," Cyrus screamed. "No!"

Bianca wasn't imagining it. Cold panic started to flood her body, her heart rate skyrocketing. All feelings of calm evaporated.

She blinked. She moved her hands and her feet and looked at Cyrus, who was now writhing on the ground in pain. All around him, other djinn had stopped as well, and they looked at their leader impassively, without concern.

And then, all the strings holding Bianca back broke. She felt the fog of her mind finally clear. She took a deep breath of her own free will. It felt incredible.

She realized, then, how gross she felt from Cyrus's possession. She had a raging headache and her mouth felt unnaturally dry. It was like she had been in stasis, in a sticky cocoon she'd been happy to hide in. Now that she'd emerged, the fresh air was uncomfortable and wonderful, and she never wanted to feel possessed like that again.

It made her respect her power more, to know how horrible it felt to be out of control of your own body and mind. She vowed then that she would use her power only when she needed to.

Bianca had no idea why Cyrus was suddenly incapacitated, but she didn't care. She considered stomping on him for good measure, but he was in so much agony that she instead ran to her mamá, who was on the outside of the circle of dazed Ayers folk, still frozen, as if waiting for orders. Her dad must be somewhere close.

She looked around the clearing, past everyone waking up from their mental prison. Where was Leila? Why wasn't she here next to her? Instead, she saw June with Steve and Shivani, their faces slack. Bianca knew what she had to do.

"June?" Bianca asked. Instead of snarling and trying to claw her face off, June mutely turned to Bianca, eyes empty. Bianca reached for June's hand, sinking a blue spark into her skin.

Wake up, she ordered.

June instantly came to, the effects of Cyrus's possession wearing off quicker than the last time.

"Bianca?" June asked. "Is that really you?"

Bianca smiled. "It is. Now, I need your help. See your family over there? I need you to wake them up."

Dazed, June scanned the crowd of people all waiting by the forest edge and spied her parents and siblings. "Oh my god," she said. She jogged toward them, giving Bianca a quick backward glance.

Bianca turned to Steve and Shivani. She grabbed their hands, her spark barely needing to sink in before they both gasped for air.

"Bianca!" Steve cried. "You did it!"

"Where's Leila?" Shivani demanded, eyes narrowing.

Bianca took a deep breath, the pain of not knowing where Leila was catching up to her. "I'm not sure, but I need you guys to help me wake up the rest of the town, okay? Just remind them of who they are."

Steve gave a tight nod, setting off toward his parents on the other side of the clearing. Shivani took one look at her singed clothes, her tangled hair, and the dirt caked under her nails. "Do I have to?"

Bianca gave her a hard stare.

"You are definitely the meaner twin," Shivani huffed.

"That's kind of like a thank-you, but different," Bianca sighed.

She watched as June, Steve, and Shivani woke up their families, who in turn began waking up other residents of Ayers. Just then the Esfandiaris passed Bianca, a grim look on their faces as they made their way toward Cyrus. The prince was still crumpled at the back of the group. Bianca gave them a wide gap. She'd let them deal with the djinn prince, and hopefully, they wouldn't deal with Bianca and Leila, either.

Just then, she spotted her mother in a group of Ayers College students a dozen yards away. "Mamá!" Bianca cried. Her mother was trembling, her arms starting to shiver, her face still blank. Bianca hugged her close, pouring blue static into her. Alma gasped, her slack body now gripping her daughter's.

"Bianca!" she cried. "What happened? What's going on?"

"I'm so glad you're safe," Bianca said, nuzzling her mom

instead of answering her questions. Bianca melted into her hug, smelling her mom's signature moisturizer. She hadn't been sure she'd ever see her again.

"Where's your father?" Alma asked into Bianca's singed hair, still holding her close.

Bianca pulled away from her mom. "I thought he was with you."

Alma shook her head, the warm moment over. Alma whipped her head around the clearing, frantically looking for her husband. "And where's Leila?" she asked.

Bianca suddenly went cold. All the memories of what she had done while possessed came rushing back. She had pushed Leila off the giant. She had harmed her own sister, and she was relieved there was no body. Had she teleported? Her heart wrenched at the thought of them making it this far only to have her sister and father not celebrate this moment too. *Please be okay*, Bianca prayed. *Please!*

Several people from town now crowded around Shivani, Steve, and June. It didn't take much to free them, just a couple words and a soft reminder. And then those people turned to their loved ones and did the same. Slowly, slowly, Ayers was returning to itself.

A burst of flame ignited at the edge of the clearing, and the townsfolk screamed, anticipating another attack. But it was only Leila.

And she was alone. Still, Bianca almost collapsed with relief.

Leila slowly made her way to Bianca and Alma. "Leila!" Foster called to her. "Leila! What's going on?"

Leila ignored him, an ashen look on her face as she made her way to her mother and sister, the crowds of people parting as she walked through.

"Leila!" Alma cried, hugging her close. Leila hugged her mother tightly, and Bianca thought her twin's eyes looked wet.

"Leila," Bianca said in a low voice. "Where's Baba?"

Bianca wasn't imagining it. Tears began to stream down Leila's face as she slowly turned to Bianca.

"I sent him home," Leila said. "Back to Iran."

Alma gasped. "He's in Iran? Why? How?"

But Leila didn't answer; she just looked at Bianca as if waiting for her approval.

Why would Leila send Baba back? Bianca thought frantically. And then she realized why. The original deal was for the djinn to help their father get out of Iran. But if he was back there, the deal was void. No wonder Cyrus had started writhing in pain out of nowhere. He was overleveraged, the terms of his deal suddenly pulled out from under him.

She looked back at Leila, who still seemed about to flinch at her sister's wrath, and instead said, "You figured it out. You stopped the war."

Leila looked relieved. "He's safe. For now."

Bianca nodded. That was the most they could ask for these days.

A shriek filled the air. It was the sound of Cyrus being clamped with an iron neck brace by Ehsan and Mohsen. He thrashed and kicked, desperately trying to wrench the collar off, but it was no use. It looked at odds with his glittering military dress and shined shoes. Now he was just another prisoner, like the army of djinn he'd created.

"Stop," Ehsan intoned. Cyrus did.

The second the iron was clamped around Cyrus's neck, curious lights began to fill the field. Si'lat and mareed, heen and ghul, all began to grow brighter as their thin iron collars fell from their necks. The djinn that had been fighting were becoming clear of Cyrus's possession. Many of them simply popped out of existence, turning into flames before leaving for the djinn plane. Others howled and gnashed their teeth in sorrow, reeling from the loss of their comrades. Soon, the field began to empty of all creatures except humans, iron littered at their feet.

The war was over.

It felt strange, being the one in charge of the town's rehabilitation. After the possession wore off, townspeople began to ask questions and mumble things in Bianca's general direction, as if she was the one with all the answers.

No humans had died. Nobody had gotten hurt (at least, not too badly). Still, she felt an ache for her family. Things were going to be different now, with their father living in Iran. Even with Leila's power of teleportation, she would never see him bustle around in the kitchen. She'd never hear him whistle as he worked on cars in the back lot or taste his chai in her own house.

Bianca had always been the one planning on leaving Ayers, and now her father had beaten her to it.

Since Leila was busy teleporting Alma to Iran so she could talk to their dad, it was up to Bianca to think quickly on her feet and explain why the entire town was in the woods, in the dark, the day after Christmas.

"Zahra!" Bianca hissed. "Quick—do you have a memory eraser thingy?"

Zahra snorted, her arms singed, her face covered in dirt. "No."

"I still haven't made my mind up about you," Bianca said, eyes narrowing. Before Zahra could give her some pithy comeback, Bianca ran over to June, Steve, and Shivani, who all stood huddled under an old oak tree, exhausted from waking everyone.

"Are you guys okay?" Bianca asked. It warmed her heart to see her friends again, but their ripped clothes, muddy shoes, and haunted expressions were painful to take in.

June was the first to respond, her teeth chattering. "I'm okay, but I still haven't seen Liam yet."

"Is anyone going to explain to me what the hell is going on?" Shivani demanded, hands on her hips. Bianca winced.

Leila must not have told Shivani anything, and now it was left up to her.

"Do you know what djinn are?" Bianca asked.

"Like, in *Aladdin*?" Shivani asked suspiciously.

"Um, sort of . . . ," Bianca replied, distracted by all the people coming to. At this point if someone began brandishing a pitchfork, Bianca would have understood.

"A bunch of djinn took over the town," June explained.

"Yeah, and one is an evil prince with really great eyebrows," Steve added.

Bianca shot him a look. "I need you all to help me come up with a better story than a djinn prince with good eyebrows though, okay? Or they'll run my family out of town!"

June, hair askew, held up a muddy hand. "I got this." She squinted into the night, the only lights coming from the BMW's high beams, and seemed to recognize someone. She ran off to the other end of the clearing.

Foster's dad, Mr. Hutchins, was making a beeline for them. Bianca gulped. He did not look happy. How could she explain what happened without the whole town hating her family? Did people remember what had even happened to them, or were they as blissed-out as she had been during Cyrus's possession? Maybe they just blacked out, like Foster had that first time. But then, how to explain them waking up next to The Grove?

Mr. Hutchins approached Bianca in a ridiculous Santa sweater, a thunderous look on his face. He had the same broad physique as Foster, and the same blue eyes and blond hair. But before Mr. Hutchins could interrogate her, the last person she ever thought would save her skin spoke up: June's mother, Mrs. McCullough. She had found a dead tree stump and was now yelling from atop it in the glow of the BMW's headlights.

"This is what you all get for being sinners on Christmas!" she screamed. "The devil has come into our town because we have not been faithful to our lord!" Next to her, June was nodding smugly, as if to say, *Yeah! You sinners suck!*

A chorus of agreements came forth. Mr. Hutchins stopped in his tracks, turning away from Bianca to Mrs. McCullough.

"Today was a warning! A reminder! To be good Christians, especially on this holiest of days!" The townsfolk cheered louder. "Let this be a lesson to you all!" she screamed. "And Merry Christmas!" Mrs. McCullough spat.

The crowd murmured, and Bianca watched as folks nodded, seeming to believe every word. They stood there as if waiting for something else.

"Well, don't just stand there!" June cried from next to her mother. "This is a week of worship! Get back to your homes."

At this, the crowd began to disperse, thoroughly chastened by June and her mom. Bianca gave a huge sigh of relief. That was not what she had expected as a cover-up, but she'd take it.

June hurried back to the group, and Bianca gave her a fierce hug. "Junebug, you're a genius," Bianca said.

June smiled. "I know."

"June!" Mrs. McCullough called out. "Where did you go?"

June winced. "I'd better go. Call me later?"

Bianca smiled. "You bet. Love you, Junie."

"You too, sinner," June snickered.

Bianca watched her friend go and kept back as towns-people coordinated how to get rides home. The rush of the battle was gone, and in its place, Bianca felt spent and weary.

Steve cleared his throat. Bianca had almost forgotten he was there. "So . . . ," he began.

"So . . . ," Bianca said. Now that their lives weren't in danger, she felt strangely shy around Steve.

"Oh my god," Shivani groaned from next to them. Bianca jumped. She'd also forgotten Shivani was there. "Just make out already! I'm gonna go find Leila." With that, she stomped off, leaving Bianca and Steve to stew in awkward silence.

Bianca swallowed. What could she even say to Steve to show how she felt? *Sorry you got possessed by an evil djinn because of me, thanks for the pie, let's date!* She settled for something simpler.

"Maybe when this is all over, we could grab a normal dinner? At a normal time?" Bianca asked him.

Steve smiled, his face at odds with the broken twigs and mud smeared across his forehead. "I'd like that." Then: "Can I kiss you now?"

Bianca froze. "Yes?" she said, her brain finally catching up with her body.

Steve swooped her up into his warm arms and gave her a

firm, leg-meltingly good kiss. If there had been an audience, she was sure they would have cheered.

He placed her back on her feet, and Bianca was too stunned to say anything.

"I promised myself that if we made it out alive . . . ," Steve said into the silence, by way of explanation. But that was all he could get out before it was Bianca's turn to smash her face into his.

She grabbed his shirt, his chest warm beneath her hands, and tried not to melt as he wrapped her in his arms. *He tastes like blackberries*, Bianca realized. She kissed him even harder.

"Okay, guys, that's enough now," Zahra called out behind them, annoyed.

"Did you hear something?" Steve asked, nuzzling Bianca's neck.

"Nope," she replied. "Not a blessed thing."

LEILA,
ONE MONTH LATER

It had taken a long time to get their dad settled in Iran. As soon as the bank opened after the Christmas holidays, Leila withdrew a bunch of money and stuffed it into a suitcase with their father's clothes, toothbrush, books, and anything else he might need. Her dad had luckily reconnected with the Mazanderani clan in the village, and they'd generously offered to let him stay there until he and Alma could figure out a longer-term solution. Thankfully the town was quiet enough that nobody had asked any questions about the random relative coming to stay in the countryside for a few weeks.

Bianca and their mother clutched Leila's arms, and she teleported them back to Iran.

It had taken their mother a long time to understand what had happened, and what kind of deal her husband had made. Leila and Bianca had gone on a lot of "walks" in Iran to give their parents private time. As they enjoyed the lush hills and clear winter weather, they could hear the sound of their parents' raised voices in the valley, the two arguing. There were times when her mother had asked Leila to drop her off to see their father alone, and other times her father had asked for their mother to come, with Alma refusing. It had taken weeks for them to finally rebuild their trust in each other, and it had been a couple of days since they'd gotten to see their father this time.

"Baba!" Bianca cried, hugging him close. He didn't look too different, but he seemed more at peace now. His manner was calmer, his movements slower. Gone was the nervous energy and constant need to be puttering around. He was a man whose skeletons had escaped the closet, and Leila was glad he had nothing left to hide.

Alma held him close, with a small suitcase of her own. She was going to stay with him until he got situated in a little apartment above the local bakery, which a relative's friend's cousin said was up for rent. Leila would come back and transport her mother home in time for spring semester at the college.

It wasn't perfect, but it was a start.

"I'm sorry you had to deal with my mistakes," their father finally said, over chai and sabzi khordan. They'd arranged a blanket under a spindly tree, and the family enjoyed their makeshift picnic, eating lavash, feta, walnuts, and handfuls of fresh herbs.

Leila closed her eyes, relishing the calm. Being here safe and sound with her family was a gift she never thought she'd receive again. "We know, Baba," Leila said.

Bianca squeezed her shoulder and gave her a smile. It wasn't telepathy, but Leila knew her sister felt the same way.

"So," their dad began, taking a sip of chai. "Is the town back to normal?"

Leila and Bianca shared a look. *Normal* was a strong word. The clearing outside The Grove was burnt to a crisp, and The Grove itself would take years, if not generations, to get back to its original growth. But the people of Ayers had recovered quickly, chalking it up to a test of faith.

"Yeah," Leila finally replied. "As normal as it'll ever get."

She shared a smile with her sister. Bianca grinned.

"Does this mean we can start smuggling Persian rugs and pistachios back to Ayers now?" Bianca asked. "We could make some serious money."

"Bianca!" her mother chided.

Their father shook his head. "Absolutely not."

"Worth a shot," Bianca sighed. She lay back on the blanket, staring up at the clouds. Leila joined her, followed by their mother and father.

"So, this is how it's going to be for a while, nenas," their mother said solemnly.

"This isn't so bad," Leila replied.

"Yeah, this is actually pretty cool," Bianca added, taking a bite of walnut.

"Thank you," their dad said, squeezing their hands on either side of him. "For everything."

The Mazanderanis lay like that for a long time, soaking in the blue sky and puffy clouds.

It wasn't normal, but for now, that was okay.

We're safe, Leila reminded herself. *And that's all that matters.*

AYERS, ONE YEAR LATER

Hey, Bianca thought as she lay down in her big, queen-size bed that night. She loved her new apartment. It was in the heart of downtown, had a garage for her new truck, and still had a view of the Blue Ridge Mountains. Best of all, Steve wasn't too far, over at Ayers College, and it was easy to meet him on campus for lunch between his classes.

Hey, Leila said back, somewhere in New York City. It had taken a while for Bianca to figure out how to talk to Leila with her powers. All Leila had to do was keep a small spark of Bianca inside her, and they could keep their connection open indefinitely, no matter the distance.

I gotta go to Istanbul. Can I get a lift? Bianca asked.

Ugh, Leila groaned. *I already did my skincare.*

So let me drive! Bianca insisted.

Fine, Leila relented.

It had been a shock to her parents to learn that Leila,

not Bianca, was the one who was going to leave Ayers. While Bianca appreciated temporarily globe-trotting, she felt unmoored when she had to leave the rolling hills and cicada songs of home for too long. Meanwhile, Leila lived on campus at her dorm in New York City, in one of the few singles the university had.

Her twin was the city mouse now, getting her morning coffee from a hip café and riding the train all over Manhattan. In a twist of events that stunned even Bianca and Leila, the two had been offered jobs by the Esfandiaris, tasked with hunting down djinn around the world.

The only stipulation was that the twins could only use their powers against other djinn, not on defenseless humans.

Bianca concentrated on her connection to Leila, their bond unbreakable. She felt Leila's mind, could see the ceiling of her room in Greenwich Village that she had covered in glow-in-the-dark stars so Bianca could have something to focus on.

Bianca had finally mastered the ability to possess Leila and wield her teleportation powers. It came in handy for moments like this. She took over Leila's mind, and in a flash, Leila was next to Bianca in her apartment in Ayers, a face mask on, her pajama set buttoned up to the neck.

"Go on," Leila yawned. "I'm about to pass out. We had to chase someone in Brooklyn who keeps trying to make another deal with a djinn."

Bianca grimaced. Leila's new job with the Esfandiaris

meant she was only brought in as backup whenever they had tricky dealings with djinn, giving her time to focus on her studies. Bianca, however, worked full-time. Her powers made her able to sense djinn in nearby towns, an important skill in this line of work.

Her new role was to free people who were being unjustly possessed, and Ayers was a calming HQ for a very draining day job. She was lucky Leila had agreed to be her transport, otherwise Bianca would have had to live in the city with her. Bianca didn't mind traveling now, as long as she had Ayers to get back to.

"Thanks," Bianca said. She closed her hand around Leila's, staring at the picture on her phone of a bustling neighborhood in Istanbul where evil eyes abounded. Unfortunately, those didn't help whatever was affecting the poor five-year-old whose parents had been complaining of evil spirits possessing her. That, or the kid was just being a kid, no djinn necessary. Either way, it was midmorning there, and Bianca would get to the bottom of it.

Instantly, they were outside the Turkish apartment building in a narrow alley where they couldn't be spotted.

"See ya, Bee." Leila yawned again, her pajamas at odds with the dusty sunlight of their new surroundings.

"Thanks, Leila. Mind if you take me to Dad's later?" Bianca asked, giving her a hug.

"Sure," Leila mumbled sleepily. "But I'm meeting Zahra for brunch, so not *too* late."

"Brunch date." Bianca waggled her eyebrows seductively. "How cosmopolitan."

"Shut up," Leila laughed.

"Love you," Bianca said.

"Love you too." Leila winked at Bianca. Then her body erupted into flames, and she disappeared.

Bianca gazed up at the apartment building, relishing the feeling of being in a new country, of having a purpose, of feeling centered but also able to explore.

She opened the door to the building.

She had a job to do.

Acknowledgments

When I entered this book into the New Visions Award contest, I figured it was already doomed. After more than forty rejections on the full manuscript (even one from my current agent!), I submitted the book for the contest, printed it out, then put it in a shoebox never to be seen again. "Well, that was fun," I thought, glad that I'd finished my National Novel Writing Month book. For six months, I didn't think about it again.

The day I received a call from a New York 212 number, my life was changed. Apparently I had won the contest, and my book would be published! The publisher had been trying to contact me over email, but I had figured it was a scam. After all, who would want to publish my book after so many rejections? Stacy Whitman, my editor and the publisher of Tu Books, did. For that I will be forever grateful.

I had assumed that I would have to close the door on the writing portion of my life. But instead, Tu Books and the New Visions Award gave me the courage to give it a real go. I got an agent (the one who had kindly rejected me), and have since published two books, making this book my third but not last. To that I credit Stacy Whitman, Tu Books, and Lee and Low for seeing something in me that literally no one else did. I will always be indebted to her. Thank you, thank you, thank you, Stacy!

To my agent, Jim McCarthy: Phew, we did it. You are proof that kindness is still so important in this industry. Thank you and everyone else at Dystel, Goderich and Bourret for helping me see this book through!

To Axie Oh: I would have never known about this competition if it weren't for your book *Rebel Seoul*. Your novel blew my mind wide open, and your kindness and encouragement made all the difference. I am so lucky to call you my friend.

Thank you to author friends Yamile Saied Mendez, Kristine Perez, Amina Mae Safi, and Romy Goldberg for helping keep me sane. Thank you, Shouka Rohanizadeh, for being an amazing beta reader, and a special thank-you to Crystal Maldonado for the blurb and for helping me bolster my confidence with this novel. I could not have done it without you all.

Thank you to Isabelle Carbonell and Noelle Melody, Kate Heidinger, and Berit Coleman, for being my earliest readers. Thank you to Hillary Wilson for the gorgeous cover, and designer Sheila Smallwood for putting it all together. Many thanks to managing editor Melissa Kavonic, copyeditor Oona Patrick, proofreader Liz Byer, and marketing team Jenny Choy, Shaughnessy Miller, Jennifer Khawam, and Sacha Chadwick.

Most important, thank you to my family. To my parents for instilling a huge love of reading in me, to my sister and her partner for inspiring me with their amazing creativity, and to my in-laws for always being so supportive of my work and my dreams.

But most of all, thank you to my husband and children. I'm writing this acknowledgments page with one of you still inside me, waiting to come any day now, as my other baby sleeps next door. How beautiful, how wonderful, to wake up in the cold light of morning and write my own stories before you wake and write your own. I could never do this without you. I love you all so much.